P9-CDG-161

p.d

SILVER PITCHERS

"WHY, ROSE! YOU LOOK QUITE GLORIFIED."

Romance of a Summer Day. *Page* 159

Silver Pitchers
and
Independence

By

Louisa M. Alcott

Author of "Little Women," "An Old-Fashioned Girl," "Little Men."

GROSSET & DUNLAP
PUBLISHERS NEW YORK

CONTENTS

SILVER PITCHERS

CHAPTER I

HOW IT BEGAN

"WE can do nothing about it except show our displeasure in some proper manner," said Portia, in her most dignified tone.

"*I* should like to cut them all dead for a year to come; and I 'm not sure that I won't!" cried Pauline, fiercely.

"We *ought* to make it impossible for such a thing to happen again, and I think we *might,*" added Priscilla, so decidedly that the others looked at her in surprise.

The three friends sat by the fire "talking things over," as girls love to do. Pretty creatures, all of them, as they nestled together on the lounge in dressing-gowns and slippers, with unbound hair, eyes still bright with excitement, and tongues that still wagged briskly.

Usually the chat was of dresses, compliments, and all the little adventures that befall gay girls at a merry-making. But to-night something of uncommon interest absorbed the three, and kept them talking earnestly long after they should have been asleep.

Handsome Portia looked out from her blonde locks with a disgusted expression, as she sipped the chocolate thoughtful mamma had left inside the fender. Rosy-faced Pauline sat staring indignantly at the fire; while in gentle Priscilla's soft eyes the shadow of a real sorrow seemed to mingle with the light of a strong determination.

Yes, something had happened at this Thanksgiving festival which much offended the three friends, and demanded grave consideration on their part; for the "Sweet P's," as Portia, Pris, and Polly were called, were the belles of the town. One ruled by right of beauty and position, one by the power of a character so sweet and strong that its influence was widely felt, and one by the wit and winsomeness of a high yet generous spirit.

It had been an unusually pleasant evening, for after the quilting bee in the afternoon good Squire Allen had given a bountiful supper, and all the young folks of the town had joined in the old-fashioned games, which made the roof ring with hearty merriment.

All would have gone well if some one had not privately introduced something stronger than the cider provided by the Squire, — a mysterious and potent something, which caused several of the young men to betray that they were decidedly the worse for their libations.

That was serious enough; but the crowning iniquity was the putting of brandy into the coffee, which it was considered decorous for the young girls to prefer instead of cider.

Who the reprobates were remained a dead secret, for the young men laughed off the dreadful deed as a joke and the Squire apologized in the handsomest manner.

But the girls felt much aggrieved and would not be appeased, though the elders indulgently said, "Young men will be young men," even while they shook their heads over the pranks played and the nonsense spoken under the influence of the wine that had been so slyly drank.

Now what should be done about it? The "Sweet P's" knew that their mates would look to them for guidance at this crisis, for they were the leaders in all things. So they must decide on some line of conduct for all to adopt, as the best way of showing their disapproval of such practical jokes.

When Pris spoke, the others looked at her with surprise; for there was a new expression in her face, and both asked wonderingly, "How?"

"There are several ways, and we must decide which is the best. One is to refuse invitations to the sociable next week."

"But I 've just got a lovely new dress expressly for it!" cried Portia, tragically.

"Then we might decline providing any supper," began Pris.

"That would n't prevent the boys from providing it, and I never could get through the night without a morsel of something!" exclaimed Polly, who loved to see devoted beings bending before her, with offerings of ice, or struggling manfully to steer a glass of lemonade through a tumultuous sea of silk and broadcloth, feeling well repaid by a word or smile from her when they landed safely.

"True, and it *would* be rather rude and resentful; for I am sure they will be models of deportment next time," and gentle Pris showed signs of relenting, though that foolish joke had cost her more than either of the others.

For a moment all sat gazing thoughtfully at the fire, trying to devise some awful retribution for the sinners, no part of which should fall upon themselves. Suddenly Polly clapped her hands, crying with a triumphant air, —

"I 've got it, girls! I 've got it!"

"What? How? Tell us quick!"

"We *will* refuse to go to the first sociable, and that will make a tremendous impression, for half the nice girls will follow our lead, and the boys will be in despair. Every one will ask why we are not there; and what can those poor wretches say but the truth? Won't that be a bitter pill for my lords and gentlemen?"

"It will certainly be one to us," said Portia,

thinking of the "heavenly blue dress" with a pang.

"Wait a bit; our turn will come at the next sociable. To this we can go with escorts of our own choosing, or none at all, for they are free and easy affairs, you know. So we need be under no obligation to any of those sinners, and can trample upon them as much as we please."

"But how about the games, the walks home, and all the pleasant little services the young men of our set like to offer and we to receive?" asked Portia, who had grown up with these "boys," as Polly called them, and found it hard to turn her back on the playmates who had now become friends or lovers.

"Bless me! I forgot that the feud might last more than one evening. Give me an idea, Pris," and Polly's triumph ended suddenly.

"I will," answered Pris, soberly; "for at this informal sociable we can institute a new order of things. It will make a talk, but I think we have a right to do it, and I'm sure it will have a good effect, if we only hold out, and don't mind being laughed at. Let us refuse to associate with the young men whom we know to be what is called 'gay,' and accept as friends those of whose good habits we are sure. If they complain, as of course they will, we can say their own misconduct made it necessary and there we have them."

"But, Pris, who ever heard of such an idea?

People will say all sorts of things about us!" said Portia, rather startled at the proposition.

"Let them! I say it's a grand plan, and I'll stand by you, Pris, through thick and thin!" cried Polly, who enjoyed the revolutionary spirit of the thing.

"We can but try it, and give the young men a lesson; for, girls, matters are coming to a pass, when it is our *duty* to do something. I cannot think it is right for us to sit silent and see these fine fellows getting into bad habits because no one dares or cares to speak out, though we gossip and complain in private."

"Do you want us to begin a crusade?" asked Portia, uneasily.

"Yes, in the only way we girls can do it. We can't preach and pray in streets and bar-rooms, but we may at home, and in our own little world show that we want to use our influence for good. I know that you two can do any thing you choose with the young people in this town, and it is just that set who most need the sort of help you can give, if you will."

"*You* have more influence than both of us put together; so don't be modest, Pris, but tell us what to do and I'll do it, even if I'm hooted at," cried warm-hearted Polly, won at once.

"You must do as you think right; but *I* have made up my mind to protest against wine-drinking in every way I can. I know it will cost me much, for I have nothing to depend upon but the good opinion of my friends; nevertheless, I shall do what seems my duty, and I may be able to save some other girl from the heart-aches I have known."

"You won't lose our good opinion, you dear little saint! Just tell us how to begin and we will follow our leader," cried both Portia and Polly, fired with emulation by their friend's quiet resolution.

Pris looked from one to the other, and, seeing real love and confidence in their faces, was moved to deepen the impression she had made, by telling them the sad secret of her life. Pressing her hands tightly together, and drooping her head, she answered in words that were the more pathetic for their brevity, —

"Dear girls, don't think me rash or sentimental, for I *know* what I am trying to do, and you will understand my earnestness better when I tell you that a terrible experience taught me to dread this appetite more than death. It killed my father, broke mother's heart, and left me all alone."

As she paused, poor Pris hid her face and shrank away, as if by this confession she had forfeited her place in the respect of her mates. But the girlish hearts only clung the closer to her, and proved the sincerity of their affection by sympathetic tears and tender words, as Portia and Polly held her fast, making a prettier group than the marble nymphs on the mantelpiece; for the Christian graces quite outdid the heathen ones.

Polly spoke first, and spoke cheerfully, feeling, with the instinct of a fine nature, that Priscilla's grief was too sacred to be talked about, and that they could best show their appreciation of her confidence by proving themselves ready to save others from a sorrow like hers.

"Let us be a little society of three, and do what we can. I shall begin at home, and watch over brother Ned; for lately he has been growing away from me, somehow, and I'm afraid he is beginning to be 'gay.' I shall get teased unmercifully; but I won't mind if I keep him safe."

"I have no one at home to watch over but papa, and he is in no danger, of course; so I shall show Charley Lord that I am not pleased with him," said Portia, little dreaming where her work was to be done.

"And you will set about reforming that delightful scapegrace, Phil Butler?" added Polly, peeping archly into the still drooping face of Pris.

"I have lost my right to do it, for I told him to-night that love and respect must go together in my heart," and Pris wiped her wet eyes with a hand that no longer wore a ring.

Portia and Polly looked at one another in dismay, for by this act Pris proved how thoroughly in earnest she was.

Neither had any words of comfort for so great

a trouble, and sat silently caressing her, till Pris looked up, with her own serene smile again, and said, as if to change the current of their thoughts, —

"We must have a badge for the members of our new society, so let us each wear one of these tiny silver pitchers. I 've lost the mate to mine, but Portia has a pair just like them. You can divide, then we are all provided for."

Portia ran to her jewel-case, caught up a pair of delicate filigree ear-rings, hastily divided a narrow velvet ribbon into three parts, attached to each a silver pitcher, and, as the friends smilingly put on these badges, they pledged their loyalty to the new league by a silent good night kiss.

CHAPTER II

A DECLARATION OF INDEPENDENCE

GREAT was the astonishment of their "set" when it was known that the "Sweet P's" had refused all invitations to the opening sociable.

The young men were in despair, the gossips talked themselves hoarse discussing the affair, and the girls exulted; for, as Polly predicted, the effect of their first step was "tremendous."

When the evening came, however, by one accord they met in Portia's room, to support each other through that trying period. They affected to be quite firm and cheerful; but one after the other broke down, and sadly confessed that the sacrifice to principle was harder than they expected. What added to their anguish was the fact that the Judge's house stood just opposite the town-hall, and every attempt to keep away from certain windows proved a dead failure.

"It is *so* trying to see those girls go in with their dresses bundled up, and not even know what they wear," mourned Portia, watching shrouded figures trip up the steps that led to the paradise from which she had exiled herself.

"They must be having a capital time, for every one seems to have gone. I wonder who Phil took," sighed Pris, when at length the carriages ceased to roll.

"Girls! I wish to be true to my vow, but if you don't hold me I shall certainly rush over there and join in the fun, for that music is too much for me," cried Polly, desperately, as the singing began.

It was an endless evening to the three pretty pioneers, though they went early to bed, and heroically tried to sleep with that distracting music in their ears. Slumber came at last, but as the clocks were striking twelve a little ghost emerged from Portia's room, and gliding to the hall window vanished among the heavy damask curtains.

Presently another little ghost appeared from the same quarter, and stealing softly to the same window was about to vanish in the same capacious draperies, when a stifled cry was heard, and Portia, the second sprite, exclaimed in an astonished whisper, —

"Why, Pris, are you here, too? I saw Polly creep away from me, and came to take her back. How dare you go wandering about and startling me out of my wits in this way?"

"I was only looking to see if it was all over,"

quavered Pris, meekly, emerging from the right-hand curtain.

"So was I!" laughed Polly, bouncing out from the left-hand one.

There was a sound of soft merriment in that shadowy hall for a moment, and then the spirits took a look at the world outside, for the moon was shining brightly. Yes, the fun was evidently over, for the lamps were being extinguished, and several young men stood on the steps exchanging last words. One wore a cloak theatrically thrown over the shoulder, and Polly knew him at once.

"That 's Ned! I *must* hear what they are saying. Keep quiet and I 'll listen," she whispered, rolling herself in the dark folds of the curtain and opening the window a crack, so that a frosty breeze could blow freely into her left ear.

"You 'll get your death," murmured Portia, shivering in her quilted wrapper.

"O, never mind!" cried Pris, who recognized the tallest man in the group, and was wild to catch a word from "poor Phil."

"They think they 've done a fine thing; but, bless their little hearts, we 'll show that we can do without them by not asking them to the next sociable, or taking notice of them if they go. That will bring them round without fail," said one masculine voice, with a jolly laugh.

"Many thanks for letting us know your plots,

Mr. Lord. Now we can arrange a nice little surprise for *you,*" and Portia made a scornful courtesy in the dark.

"Faith! I don't blame the girls much, for that was a confoundedly ungentlemanly trick of yours, and I 'll thank you not to lay any of the blame of it on me; I 've got as much as I can carry without that," said the tall figure, stalking away alone.

"I 'm *so* glad to know that Phil had nothing to do with it!" breathed Pris, gratefully.

"Come on, Charley! I must get home as soon as possible, or Polly will be down on me, for she has taken a new tack lately, and holds forth on the error of my ways like a granny."

"Won't I give Ned an extra lecture for that speech, the rascal!" and Polly shook a small fist at him as her brother passed under the window, blissfully unconscious of the avenging angels up aloft.

"'Tis well; let us away and take sweet counsel how we may annihilate them," added Polly, melodramatically, as the three ghosts vanished from the glimpses of the moon.

Every one turned out to the sociables, for they were town affairs, and early hours, simple suppers, and games of all sorts, made it possible for old and young to enjoy them together.

On the night of the second one there was a goodly gathering, for the public rebuke administered to the young men had made a stir, and everybody was curious to see what the consequences would be when the parties met.

There was a sensation, therefore, when a whisper went around that the "Sweet P's" had come, and a general smile of wonder and amusement appeared when the girls entered, Portia on the arm of her father, Polly gallantly escorted by her twelve-year-old brother Will, and Pris beside Belinda Chamberlain, whose five feet seven made her a capital cavalier.

"Outwitted!" laughed Charley Lord, taking the joke at once as he saw Portia's gray-headed squire.

"I *knew* Polly was plotting mischief, she has been so quiet lately," muttered Ned, eying his little brother with lofty scorn.

Phil said nothing, but he gave a sigh of relief on seeing that Pris had chosen an escort of whom it was impossible to be jealous.

The Judge seldom honored these gatherings, but Portia ruled papa, and when she explained the peculiar state of things, he had heroically left his easy chair to cast himself into the breach.

Master Will was in high feather at his sudden promotion, and bore himself gallantly, though almost as much absorbed by his wristbands as Mr. Toots; for Polly had got him up regardless of expense, with a gay tie, new gloves, and, O, crowning splendor! a red carnation in his button-hole.

Buxom Belinda was delighted with the chance to play cavalier, and so get her fair share of all the fun going, for usually she stood in a corner smiling at an unappreciative world, like a patient sunflower.

The faces of the young men were a study as the games began, and the three girls joined in them with the partners they had chosen.

"The Judge is evidently on his mettle, but he can't stand that sort of thing long, even to please Portia; and then her Majesty will have to give in, or condescend to some one out of our set," thought Charley Lord, longing already to be taken into favor again.

"Polly will have to come and ask me to lead, if she wants to sing her favorite songs; for I 'll be hanged if I do it till she has humbled herself by asking," said Ned, feeling sure that his sister would soon relent.

"If it was any one but Belinda, I don't think I could stand it," exclaimed Phil, as he watched his lost sweetheart with wistful eyes; for, though he submitted to the sentence which he knew he deserved, he could not relinquish so much excellence without deep regret.

But the young men underrated the spirit of the girls, and overrated their own strength. The "Sweet P's" went on enjoying themselves, apparently quite indifferent to the neglect of their once devoted friends. But to the outcasts it was perfectly maddening to see stately Portia promenading with stout Major Quackenboss, who put his best foot foremost with the air of a conquering hero; also to behold sweet Pris playing games with her little pupils in a way that filled their small souls with rapture. But the most aggravating spectacle of all was captivating Polly, chatting gayly with young Farmer Brown, who was evidently losing both head and heart in the light of her smiles.

"It 's no use, boys; I *must* have one turn with Portia, and you may hang me for a traitor immediately afterward," cried Charley at last, recklessly casting both pride and promise to the winds.

"O, very well; if you are going to give in, we may as well all eat humble pie 'together,'" and Ned imitated his weak-minded friend, glad of an excuse to claim the leadership of the little choir who led off the weekly "sing."

Phil dared not follow their example as far as Pris was concerned, but made his most elegant bow to Belinda, and begged to have the honor of seeing her home. His chagrin may be imagined when the lofty wall-flower replied, with a significant emphasis that made his face burn, —

"No, thank you. I need a very *steady* escort, for I should n't take a fall into a snow-bank as lightly as Pris did not long ago."

Charley met with a like fate at Portia's hands, for she outraged established etiquette by coldly declining his meek invitation to promenade, and two minutes later graciously accepting that of an unfashionable young man, who was known to belong to a temperance lodge.

But Ned's repulse was the most crushing of all, for in reply to his condescending hint, —

" I suppose people won't be satisfied unless we give them our favorites, hey, Polly? " he received a verbal box on the ear in the sharp answer, —

" We don't want *you,* for I intend to lead myself, and introduce a new set of songs which won't be at all to your taste."

Then, to his utter amazement and confusion, Miss Polly began to sing one of the good old temperance songs, the burden whereof was, —

" O, that will be joyful, joyful, joyful,
O, that will be joyful,
When young men drink no more ! "

It was taken up all over the hall, and the chorus rang out with an energy that caused sundry young men to turn red and dodge behind any capacious back they could find, for every one understood Polly's motive, and looked approvingly upon her as she stood singing, with an occasional quiver in the voice that usually was as clear and sweet as a blackbird's.

This unexpected manœuvre on the part of the fair enemy produced direful perplexity and dismay in the opposing camp, whither the discomfited trio fled with tidings of their defeat. None of them dared try again in that quarter, but endeavored to console themselves by flirting wildly with such girls as still remained available, for, sad to relate, many of the most eligible took courage and followed the example of the "Sweet P's." This fact cast added gloom over the hapless gentlemen of the offending set, and caused them to fear that a social revolution would follow what they had considered merely a girlish freak.

"Shouldn't wonder if they got up a praying-band after this," groaned Ned, preparing himself for the strongest measures.

"Portia had better lead off, then, for the first time I indulged too freely in the 'rosy' was at her father's house," added Charley, laying all the blame of his expulsion from Eden upon Eve, like a true Adam.

"Look here, boys, we ought to thank, not blame them, for they want to help us, I 'm sure, and some of us need help, God knows!" sighed Phil, with a look and tone that made his comrades forget their pique in sudden self-reproach; for not one of them could deny his words, or help feeling that the prayers of such innocent souls would avail much.

CHAPTER III

WHAT PORTIA DID

"I KNOW your head aches, mamma, so lie here and rest while I sit in my little chair and amuse you till papa comes in."

As Portia bent to arrange the sofa-cushions comfortably, the tiny silver pitcher hanging at her neck swung forward and caught her mother's eye.

"Is it the latest fashion to wear odd ear-rings instead of lockets?" she asked, touching the delicate trinket with an amused smile.

"No, mamma, it is something better than a fashion; it is the badge of a temperance league that Pris, Polly, and I have lately made," answered Portia, wondering how her mother would take it.

"Dear little girls! God bless and help you in your good work!" was the quick reply, that both surprised and touched her by its fervency.

"Then you don't mind, or think us silly to try and do even a very little towards curing this great evil?" she asked, with a sweet seriousness that was new and most becoming to her.

"My child, I feel as if it was a special providence," began her mother, then checked herself and added more quietly, "Tell me all about this league, dear, unless it is a secret."

"I have no secrets from you, mother," and nestling into her low chair Portia told her story, ending with an earnestness that showed how much she had the new plan at heart.

"So you see Polly is trying to keep Ned safe, and Pris prays for Phil; not in vain, I think, for he has been very good lately, they tell me. But *I* have neither brother nor lover to help, and I cannot go out to find any one, because I am only a girl. Now what *can* I do, mamma, for I truly want to do my share?"

The mother lay silent for a moment, then, as if yielding to an irresistible impulse, drew her daughter nearer, and whispered with lips that trembled as they spoke, —

"You can help your father, dear."

"Mamma, what can you mean?" cried Portia, in a tone of indignant surprise.

"Listen patiently, child, or I shall regret that your confidence inspired me with courage to give you mine. Never think for one moment that I accuse my husband of anything like drunkenness. He has always taken his wine like a gentleman, and never more than was good for him till of late. For this there are many excuses; he is growing old, his life is less active than it was, many of the pleasures he once enjoyed fail now, and he has fallen into ways that harm his health."

"I know, mamma; he does n't care for company as he used to, or business, either, but seems quite contented to sit among his papers half the morning, and doze over the fire half the evening. I 've wondered at it, for he is not really old, and looks as hale and handsome as ever," said Portia, feeling that something hovered on her mother's lips which she found it hard to utter.

"You are right; it is *not* age alone that makes him so unlike his once cheerful, active self; it is — bend lower, dear, and never breathe to any one what I tell you now, only that you may help me save your father's life, perhaps."

Startled by the almost solemn earnestness of these words, Portia laid her head upon the pillow, and twilight wrapt the room in its soft gloom, as if to shut out all the world, while the mother told the daughter the danger that threatened him whom they both so loved and honored.

"Papa has fallen into the way of taking more wine after dinner than is good for him. He does not know how the habit is growing upon him, and is hurt if I hint at such a thing. But Dr. Hall warned me of the danger after papa's last ill turn, saying that at his age and with his temperament apoplexy would be sure to follow over-indulgence of this sort."

"O mamma, what can I do?" whispered

Portia, with a thrill, as the words of Pris returned to her with sudden force, "It killed my father, broke mother's heart, and left me all alone."

"Watch over him, dear, amuse him as you only can, and wean him from this unsuspected harm by all the innocent arts your daughterly love can devise. I have kept this to myself, because it is hard for a wife to see any fault in her husband; still harder for her to speak of it even to so good a child as mine. But my anxiety unfits me to do all I might, so I need help; and of whom can I ask it but of you? My darling, make a little league with mother, and let us watch and pray in secret for this dear man who is all in all to us."

What Portia answered, what comfort she gave, and what further confidences she received, may not be told, for this household covenant was too sacred for report. No visible badge was assumed, no audible vow taken, but in the wife's face, as it smiled on her husband that night, there was a tenderer light than ever, and the kiss that welcomed papa was the seal upon a purpose as strong as the daughter's love.

Usually the ladies left the Judge to read his paper and take his wine in the old-fashioned way, while they had coffee in the drawing-room. As they rose, Portia saw the shadow fall upon her mother's face, which she had often seen before, but never understood till now; for *this* was the dangerous hour, this the moment when the child must stand between temptation and her father, if she could.

That evening, very soon after the servant had cleared the table of all but the decanters, a fresh young voice singing blithely in the parlor made the Judge put down his glass to listen in pleased surprise.

Presently he stepped across the hall to set both doors open, saying, in a half-reproachful tone, —

" Sing away, my lark, and let papa hear you, for he seldom gets a chance now-a-days."

"Then he must stay and applaud me, else I shall think that speech only an empty compliment," answered Portia, as she beckoned with her most winsome smile.

The Judge never dreamed that his good angel spoke; but he saw his handsome girl beaming at him from the music stool, and strolled in, meaning to go back when the song ended.

But the blue charmer in the parlor proved more potent than the red one in the dining-room, and he sat on, placidly sipping the excellent coffee, artfully supplied by his wife, quite unconscious of the little plot to rob him of the harmful indulgence which too often made his evenings a blank, and his mornings a vain attempt to revive the spirits that once kept increasing years from seeming burdensome.

That was the beginning of Portia's home mission; and from that hour she devoted herself to it, thinking of no reward, for such "secret service" could receive neither public sympathy nor praise.

It was not an easy task, as she soon found, in spite of the stanch and skilful ally who planned the attacks she dutifully made upon the enemy threatening their domestic peace.

When music ceased to have charms, and the Judge declared he *must* get his "forty winks" after dinner, Portia boldly declared that she would stay and see that he had them comfortably. So papa laughed and submitted, took a brief nap, and woke in such good-humor that he made no complaint on finding the daughter replacing the decanter.

This answered for a while; and when its efficacy seemed about to fail, unexpected help appeared; for mamma's eyes began to trouble her, and Portia proposed that her father should entertain the invalid in the evening, while she served her through the day.

This plan worked capitally, for the Judge loved his good wife almost as much as she deserved, and devoted himself to her so faithfully that the effort proved a better stimulant than any his well-stocked cellar could supply.

Dr. Hall prescribed exercise and cheerful society for his new patient, and in seeing that these instructions were obeyed the Judge got the benefit of them, and found no time for solitary winebibbing.

"I do believe I 'm growing young again, for the old dulness is quite gone, and all this work and play does not seem to tire me a bit," he said, after an unusually lively evening with the congenial guests Portia took care to bring about him.

"But it must be very stupid for you, my dear, as we old folks have all the fun. Why don't you invite the young people here oftener?" he added, as his eye fell on Portia, gazing thoughtfully into the fire.

"I wish I dared tell you why," she answered wistfully.

"Afraid of your old papa?" and he looked both surprised and grieved.

"I won't be, for you are the kindest father that ever a girl had, and I know you 'll help me, as you always do, papa. I don't dare ask my young friends here because I 'm not willing to expose some of them to temptation," began Portia, bravely.

"What temptation? This?" asked her father, turning her half-averted face to the light, with a smile full of paternal pride.

"No, sir; a far more dangerous one than ever I can be."

"Then I should like to see it!" and the old gentleman looked about him for this rival of his lovely daughter.

"It is these," she said, pointing to the bottles and glasses on the sideboard.

The Judge understood her then, and knit his

brows, but before he could reply Portia went steadily on, though her cheeks burned, and her eyes were bent upon the fire again.

"Father, I belong to a society of three, and we have promised to do all we can for temperance. As yet I can only show bravely the faith that is in me; therefore I can never offer any friend of mine a drop of wine, and so I do not ask them here, where it would seem most uncourteous to refuse."

"I trust no gentleman ever had cause to reproach me for the hospitality I was taught to show my guests," began the Judge, in his most stately manner.

But he got no further, for a soft hand touched his lips, and Portia answered sorrowfully, —

"One man has, sir; Charley Lord says the first time he took too much was in this house, and it has grieved me to the heart, for it is true. O papa, never let any one have the right to say that again of us! Forgive me if I seem undutiful, but I *must* speak out, for I want my dear father to stand on my side, and set an example which will make me even fonder and prouder of him than I am now."

As Portia paused, half frightened at her own frankness, she put her arms about his neck, and hid her face on his breast, still pleading her cause with the silent eloquence so hard to resist.

The Judge made no reply for several minutes, and in that pause many thoughts passed through his mind, and a vague suspicion that had haunted him of late became a firm conviction. For suddenly he seemed to see his own weakness in its true light, to understand the meaning of the watchful love, the patient care that had so silently and helpfully surrounded him; and in Portia's appeal for younger men he read a tender warning to himself.

He was a proud man, but a very just one; and though a flush of anger swept across his face at first, he acknowledged the truth of the words that were so hard to speak.

With his hand laid fondly on the head that was half-hidden, lest a look should seem to reproach him, this brave old gentleman proved that he loved his neighbor better than himself, and honestly confessed his own shortcomings.

"No man shall ever say again that *I* tempted him."

Then as Portia lifted up a happy face, he looked straight into the grateful eyes that dimmed with sudden tears, and added tenderly, —

"My daughter, I am not too proud to own a fault, nor, please God, too old to mend it."

CHAPTER IV

WHAT POLLY DID

SINCE their mother's death, Polly had tried to fill her place, and take good care of the boys. But the poor little damsel had a hard time of it sometimes; for Ned, being a year or two older, thought it his duty to emancipate himself from petticoat government as rapidly as possible, and do as he pleased, regardless of her warnings or advice.

Yet at heart he was very fond of his pretty sister. At times he felt strongly tempted to confide his troubles and perplexities to her, for since the loss of his mother he often longed for a tender, helpful creature to cheer and strengthen him.

Unfortunately he had reached the age when boys consider it "the thing" to repress every sign of regard for their own women-folk, sisters especially; so Ned barricaded himself behind the manly superiority of his twenty years, and snubbed Polly.

Will had not yet developed this unpleasant trait, but his sister expected it, and often exclaimed, despairingly, to her bosom friends, —

"When *he* follows Ned's example, and begins to rampage, what *will* become of me?"

The father — a learned and busy man — was so occupied by the duties of his large parish, or so absorbed in the abstruse studies to which his brief leisure was devoted, that he had no time left for his children. Polly took good care of him and the house, and the boys seemed to be doing well, so he went his way in peace, quite unconscious that his eldest son needed all a father's care to keep him from the temptations to which a social nature, not evil propensities, exposed him.

Polly saw the danger, and spoke of it; but Mr. Snow only answered absently, —

"Tut, tut, my dear; you are over-anxious, and forget that young men all have a few wild oats to sow."

While Ned silenced her with that other familiar and harmful phrase, "I'm only seeing life a bit, so don't you fret, child," little dreaming that such "seeing life" too often ends in seeing death.

So Polly labored in vain, till something happened which taught them all a lesson. Ned went on a sleighing frolic with the comrades whom of all others his sister dreaded most.

"Do be careful and not come home as you did last time, for father will be in, and it would shock him dreadfully if I should n't be able to keep you quiet," she said anxiously.

"You little granny, I was n't tipsy, only cheerful, and that scared you out of your wits. I 've got my key, so don't sit up. I hate to have a woman glowering at me when I come in," was Ned's ungracious reply; for the memory of that occasion was not a pleasant one.

"If a woman had not been sitting up, you 'd have frozen on the door-mat, you ungrateful boy," cried Polly, angrily.

Ned began to whistle, and was going off without a word when Polly's loving heart got the better of her quick temper, and, catching up a splendid tippet she had made for him, she ran after her brother. She caught him just as he opened the front door, and, throwing both her arms and her gift about his neck, said, with a kiss that produced a sensation in the sleigh-full of gentlemen at the gate, —

"Ah, do be friends, for I can't bear to part so."

Now if no one had been by, Ned would have found that pleasant mingling of soft arms and worsted a genuine comforter; but masculine pride would not permit him to relent before witnesses, and the fear of being laughed at by "those fellows" made him put both sister and gift roughly aside, with a stern, —

"I won't be molly-coddled! Let me alone and shut that door!"

Polly did let him alone, with a look that

haunted him, and shut the door with a spirited bang, that much amused the gentlemen.

"I 'll never try to do anything for Ned again! It 's no use, and he may go to the bad for all I care!" said Polly to herself, after a good cry.

But she bitterly repented that speech a few hours later, when her brother was brought back, apparently dead, by such of the "cheerful" party as escaped unhurt from a dangerous upset.

There was no concealing this sad home-coming from her father, though poor Ned was quiet enough now, being stunned by the fall, which had wounded his head and broken his right arm.

It *was* a shock, both to the man and the minister; and, when the worst was over, he left Polly to watch her brother, with eyes full of penitential tears, and went away, to reproach himself in private for devoting to ancient Fathers the time and thought he should have given to modern sons.

Ned was very ill, and when, at last, he began to mend, his helplessness taught him to see and love the sweetest side of Polly's character; for she was in truth his right hand, and waited on him with a zeal that touched his heart.

Not one reproach did she utter, not even by a look did she recall past warnings, or exult in the present humiliation which proved how needful they had been. Everything was forgotten except the fact that she had the happy privilege of caring for him almost as tenderly as a mother.

Not quite, though, and the memory of her whose place it was impossible to fill seemed to draw them closer together; as if the silent voice repeated its last injunctions to both son and daughter, "Take care of the boys, dear;" "Be good to your sister, Ned."

"I 've been a regular brute to her, and the dear little soul is heaping coals of fire on my head by slaving over me like an angel," thought the remorseful invalid, one day, as he lay on the sofa, with a black patch adorning his brow, and his arm neatly done up in splints.

Polly thought he was asleep, and sat quietly rolling bandages till a head popped in at the door, and Will asked, in a sepulchral whisper, —

"I 've got the book Ned wanted. Can I come and give it to you?"

Polly nodded, and he tiptoed in to her side, with a face so full of good-will and spirits that it was as refreshing as a breath of fresh air in that sick room.

"Nice boy! he never forgets to do a kindness and be a comfort to his Polly," she said, leaning her tired head on his buttony jacket, as he stood beside her.

Will was n't ashamed to show affection for "his Polly," so he patted the pale cheeks with a hand as red as his mittens, and smiled down at her with his honest blue eyes full of the protecting affection it was so pleasant to receive.

"Yes, *I 'm* going to be a tiptop boy, and never

make you and father ashamed of me, as you were once of somebody we know. Now don't you laugh, and I 'll show you something; it 's the best I could do, and I wanted to prove that I mean what I say; truly, truly, wish I may die if I don't."

As he spoke, Will pulled out of his vest-pocket a little pewter cream-pot, tied to a shoe-string, and holding it up said, with a funny mixture of boyish dignity and defiance, —

"I bought it of Nelly Hunt, because her tea-set was half smashed up. Folks may laugh at my badge, but I don't care; and if you won't have me in your society I 'll set up all alone, for I 'm going into the temperance business, any way!"

Polly hugged him on the spot, and made his youthful countenance glow with honest pride by saying solemnly, —

"William G. Snow, I consider our league honored by the addition of so valuable a member; for a boy who can bear to be laughed at, and yet stick to his principles, is a treasure."

"The fellows *do* laugh at me, and call me 'Little Pitcher;' but I 'd rather be that than 'Champagne Charlie,' as Ned called Mr. Lord," said Will, stoutly.

"Bless the little pitchers!" cried Polly, enthusiastically surveying both the pewter pot and its wearer.

A great tear was lying on her cheek, checked

in its fall by the dimple that came as she looked at her brother's droll badge. Will caught it dexterously in the tiny cup, saying, with a stifled laugh, —

"Now you 've baptized it, Polly, and it 's as good as silver; for your tear shines in there like a great big diamond. Wonder how many it would take to fill it?"

"You 'll never make me cry enough to find out. Now go and get my little silver chain, for that dear pewter pot deserves a better one than an old shoe-string," said Polly, looking after him with a happy face, as the small youth gave one ecstatic skip and was off.

"I 'm afraid we 've waked you up," she added, as Ned stirred.

"I was only day-dreaming; but I mean this one shall come true," and Ned rose straight up, with an energy that surprised his sister.

"Come and have your lunch, for it 's time. Which will you take, Mrs. Neal's wine-jelly or my custard?" asked Polly, settling him in his big chair.

To her astonishment, Ned pitched the little mould of amber jelly into the fire, and tried to eat the custard with his left hand.

"My dear boy, have you lost your senses?" she ejaculated.

"No; I 've just found them," he answered, with a flash of the eye, that seemed to enlighten Polly without more words.

Taking her usual seat on the arm of the chair, she fed her big nursling in silence, till a sigh made her ask tenderly, —

"Is n't it right? I put in lots of sugar because you like it sweet."

"All the sugar in the world won't sweeten it to me, Polly; for there 's a bitter drop at the bottom of all my cups. Will said your tear shone like a diamond in his little pitcher, and well it might. But you can't cry happy tears over me, though I 've made you shed enough sad ones to fill the big punch-bowl."

Ned tried to laugh, but somehow the custard choked him; and Polly laid the poor, cropped head on her shoulder for a minute, saying softly, —

"Never mind, dear, I would n't think about the old troubles now."

She got no farther, for with a left-handed thump that made all the cups dance wildly on the table, Ned cried out, —

"But I *will* think about the old troubles, for I don't intend to have any new ones of that sort! Do you suppose I 'll see that snip of a boy standing up for what is right, and not have the pluck to do the same? Do you suppose I 'll make my own father ashamed of me more than once? Or let the dearest little girl in the world wear herself out over me, and I not try to thank her in the way she likes best? Polly, my dear, you can't be as proud of your elder brother as you are of the younger, but you shall never have cause to blush for him again; *never,* sir, *never!*"

Ned lifted his hand for another emphatic thump, but changed his mind, and embraced his sister as closely as one arm could do it.

"I ought to have a badge if I 'm going to belong to your select society; but I don't know any lady who will give me an ear-ring or a cream-pot," said Ned, when the conversation got round again to the cheerful side of the question.

"I 'll give you something better than either," answered Polly, as she transferred a plain locket from her watch-guard to the one lying on the table.

Ned knew that a beloved face and a lock of gray hair were inside; and when his sister added, with a look full of sweet significance, "For her sake, dear," he answered manfully, —

"I 'll try, Polly!"

CHAPTER V

WHAT PRIS DID

PRISCILLA, meantime, was racking her brain to discover how she could help Philip; for since she had broken off her engagement no one spoke of him to her, and she could only judge of how things were going with him by what she saw and heard as she went about her daily task.

Pris kept school, and the road which she must take twice a day led directly by the office where Phil was studying medicine with old Dr. Buffum. Formerly she always smiled and nodded as she passed, or stopped to chat a moment with the student, who usually chanced to be taking a whiff of fresh air at that instant. Little notes flew in and out, and often her homeward walk was cheered by a companion, who taught the pretty teacher lessons she found it very easy to learn.

A happy time! But it was all over now, and brief glimpses of a brown head bent above a desk near that window was the only solace poor Pris had. The head never turned as she went by, but she felt sure that Phil knew her step, and found that moment, as she did, the hardest of the day.

She longed to relent, but dared not yet. He longed to show that he repented, but found it difficult without a sign of encouragement. So they went their separate ways, seldom meeting, for Phil stuck to his books with dogged resolution, and Pris had no heart for society.

Of course the affair was discussed with all the exasperating freedom of a country town, some blaming Pris for undue severity, some praising her spirit, and some friends, — not gossips, — predicting that both would be the better for the trial, which would not separate them long. Of this latter class were Portia and Polly, who felt it their duty to lend a hand when matters reached a certain point.

"Pris, dear, may I tell you something that I think you 'd be glad to know?" began Polly, joining her friend one afternoon, as she went home weary and alone.

"*You* may tell me any thing," and Pris took her arm as if she felt the need of sympathy.

"You know Dr. Buffum let Phil help with Ned, so we have seen a good deal of him, and that is how I found out what I 've got to tell you."

"He spoke of me, then?" whispered Pris, eagerly.

"Not a word till Ned made him. My boy is fond of your boy, and they had confidences which seem to have done them both good. Of course Ned did n't tell me all about it, as *we* tell things (men never do, they are so proud and queer), but he said this, —

"'Look here, Polly, you must be very kind to Phil, and stand by him all you can, or he will go down. He is doing his best, and will hold on as long as he can, but a fellow *must* have comfort and encouragement of some sort, and if he don't get the right kind he 'll try the wrong.'"

"O Polly! you will stand by him?"

"I have; for I just took Phil in a weakish moment, and found out all I wanted to know. Ned is right and you are wrong, Pris, — not in giving back the ring, but in seeming to cast him off entirely. He does not deserve that, for he was not to blame half so much as you think. But he won't excuse himself, for he feels that you are unjust; yet he loves you dearly, and you could do any thing with him, if you chose."

"I do choose, Polly; but how *can* I marry a man whom I cannot trust?" began Pris, sadly.

"Now, my child, I 'm going to talk to you like a mother, for I 've had experience with boys, and I know how to manage them," interrupted Polly, with such a charmingly maternal air that Pris laughed in spite of her trouble. "Be quiet and listen to the words of wisdom," continued her friend, seriously.

"Since I 've taken care of Ned, I 've learned a great deal, for the poor lad was so sick and sorry he could n't shut his heart against me any more. So now I understand how to help and comfort him, for hearts are very much alike, Pris, and all need lots of love and patience to keep them good and happy. Ned told me his troubles, and I made up my mind that as *we* don't have so many temptations as boys, we should do all we can to help them, and make them the sort of men we can both love and trust."

"You are right, Polly. I 've often thought how wrong it is for us to sit safe and silent while we know things are going wrong, just because it is n't considered proper for us to speak out. Then when the harm is done we are expected to turn virtuously away from the poor soul we might perhaps have saved if we had dared. God does not do so to us, and we ought not to do so to those over whom we have so much power," said Pris, with a heart full of sad and tender memories.

"We won't!" cried Polly, firmly. "We began in play, but we will go on in earnest, and use our youth, our beauty, our influence for something nobler than merely pleasing men's eyes, or playing with their hearts. We 'll help them to be good, and brave, and true, and in doing this we shall become better women, and worthier to be loved, I know."

"Why, Polly, you are quite inspired!" and Pris stopped in the snowy road to look at her.

"It is n't all *my* wisdom. I 've talked with

father as well as Ned and Phil, and they have done me good. I 've discovered that confidence is better than compliments, and friendship much nicer than flirting; so I 'm going to turn over a new leaf, and use my good gifts for higher ends."

"Dear thing, what a comfort you are!" said Pris, pressing Polly's hands, and looking into her bright face with grateful eyes. "You have given me courage to do my duty, and I 'll follow your example as fast as I can. Don't come any farther, please: I 'd better be alone when I pass Phil's window, for I 'm going to nod and smile, as I used to in the happy time. Then he will see that I don't cast him off and leave him to 'go down' for want of help, but am still his friend until I dare be more."

"Now, Pris, that 's just lovely of you, and I know it will work wonders. Smile and nod away, dear, and try to do your part, as I 'm trying to do mine."

For an instant the little gray hat and the jaunty one with the scarlet feather were bent close together; but what went on under the brims, who can say? Then Polly trotted off as fast as she could go, and Pris turned into a certain street with a quicker step and a brighter color than she had known for weeks.

She was late, for she had lingered with Polly, and she feared that patient watcher at the window would be gone. No; the brown head was there, but it lay wearily on the arms folded over a big book, and the eyes that stared out at the wintry sky had something tragic in them.

Poor Phil did need encouragement, and was in the mood to take the worst sort if the best failed him, for life looked very dark just then, and solitude was growing unbearable.

Suddenly, between him and the ruddy sunset a face appeared, — the dearest and the loveliest in the world to him. Not half averted now, nor set straightforward, cold and quiet as a marble countenance, but bent towards him, with a smile on the lips, and a wistful look in the tender eyes that made his heart leap up with sudden hope. Then it vanished; and when he sprung to the window nothing could be seen but the wave of a well-known cloak, fluttering round the corner.

But Priscilla's first effort was a great success; for the magic of a kind look glorified the dingy office, and every bottle on the shelves might have been filled with the elixir of life, so radiant did Phil's face become. The almost uncontrollable desire to rush away and recklessly forget his loneliness in the first companionship that offered was gone now, for a happy hope peopled his solitude with helpful thoughts and resolutions; the tragic look left the eyes, that still saw a good angel instead of a tempting demon between them and the evening sky; and when Phil shut up the big book he had been vainly trying to study, he felt that he had discovered a new cure for one of the sharpest pains the heart can suffer.

Next morning Pris unconsciously started for school too soon, so when she passed that window the room was empty. Resolved that Phil should not share her disappointment, she lifted the sash and dropped a white azalea on his desk. She smiled as she did it, and then whisked away as if she had taken instead of left a treasure. But the smile remained with the flower, I think, and Phil found it there when he hurried in to discover this sweet good-morning waiting for him.

He put it in the wine-glass which he had sworn never should be filled again with any thing but water, and sitting down before it listened to the little sermon the flower preached; for the delicate white azalea was Pris to him, and the eloquence of a pure and tender heart flowed from it, working miracles. One of them was that when sunset came it shone on two faces at the window, and the little snow-birds heard two voices breaking a long silence.

"God bless you, Pris."

"God help you, Phil!"

That was all, but from that hour the girl felt her power for good, and used it faithfully; and from that hour the young man worked bravely to earn the respect and confidence without which no love is safe and happy.

"We are friends now," they said, when they were seen together again; and friends they remained, in spite of shrugs and smiles, ill-natured speeches, and more than one attempt to sow discord between them, for people did not understand the new order of things.

"I trust him," was the only answer Pris gave to all warnings and criticisms.

"I *will* be worthy of her," the vow that kept Phil steady in spite of the ridicule that is so hard to bear, and gave him courage to flee from the temptation he was not yet strong enough to meet face to face.

Portia and Polly stood by them stanchly; for having made her father's house a safe refuge, Portia offered Phil all the helpful influences of a happy home. Polly, with Ned to lend a hand, gave his comrade many a friendly lift; and when it was understood that the Judge, the minister, and the "Sweet P's" indorsed the young M. D., no one dared cast a stone at him.

All this took time, of course, but Phil got his reward at last, for one night a little thing happened which showed him his own progress, and made Pris feel that she might venture to wear the ring again.

At a party Phil was graciously invited to take wine with a lady, and refused. It was a very hard thing to do, for the lady was his hostess, a handsome woman, and the mother of a flock of little children, who all preferred the young doctor to the old one; and, greatest trial of all, several of his most dreaded comrades stood by to laugh at him, if he dared to let principle outweigh courtesy.

But he did it, though he grew pale with the effort to say steadily, —

"Will Mrs. Ward pardon me if I decline the honor? I am —"

There he stopped and turned scarlet, for a lie was on his lips, — a lie so much easier to tell than the honest truth that many would have forgiven its utterance at that minute.

His hostess naturally thought ill health was his excuse, and pitying his embarrassment, said, smiling, —

"Ah! you doctors don't prescribe wine for your own ailments as readily as for those of your patients."

But Phil, angry at his own weakness, spoke out frankly, with a look that said more than his words, —

"I cannot even accept the kind excuse you offer me, for I am not ill. It may be my duty to order wine sometimes for my patients, but it is also my duty to prescribe water for myself."

A dreadful little pause followed that speech; but Mrs. Ward understood now, and though she thought the scruple a foolish one, she accepted the apology like a well-bred woman, and, with a silent bow that ended the matter, turned to other guests, leaving poor Phil to his fate.

Not a pleasant one, but he bore it as well as he could, and when his mates left him stranded in a corner, he said, half aloud, with a long breath, as if the battle had been a hard one, —

"Yes, I suppose I *have* lost my best patient, but I 've kept my own respect, and that ought to satisfy me."

"Let me add mine, and wish you health and happiness, dear Phil," said a voice behind him, and turning quickly he saw Pris standing there with two goblets of water, and a smile full of love and pride.

"You know what that toast means for me?" he whispered, with sudden sunshine in his face, as he took the offered glass.

"Yes; and I drink it with all my heart," she answered, with her hand in his.

CHAPTER VI

HOW IT ENDED

THE leaven dropped by three girls in that little town worked so slowly that they hardly expected to do more than "raise their own patty-cakes," as Polly merrily expressed it. But no honest purpose is ever wasted, and by-and-by the fermentation began.

Several things helped it amazingly. The first of these was a temperance sermon, preached by Parson Snow, which produced a deep impression, because in doing this he had the courage, like Brutus, to condemn his own son. The brave sincerity, the tender earnestness of that sermon, touched the hearts of his people as no learned discourse had ever done, and bore fruit that well repaid him for the effort it cost.

It waked up the old people, set the young ones to thinking, and showed them all that they had a work to do. For those who were down felt that they might be lifted up again, those who were trifling ignorantly or recklessly with temptation saw their danger, and those who had longed to speak out now dared to do it because he led the way.

So, warned by the wolf in his own fold, this shepherd of souls tried to keep his flock from harm, and, in doing it, found that his Christianity was the stronger, wiser, and purer for his humanity.

Another thing was the fact that the Judge was the first to follow his pastor's example, and prove by deeds that he indorsed his words. It was hard for the hospitable old gentleman to banish wine from his table, and forego the pleasant customs which long usage and many associations endeared to him; but he made his sacrifice handsomely, and his daughter helped him.

She kept the side-board from looking bare by filling the silver tankards with flowers, offered water to his guests with a grace that made a cordial of it, and showed such love and honor for her father that he was a very proud and happy man.

What the Judge did was considered "all right" by his neighbors, for he was not only the best-born, but the richest man in town, and with a certain class these facts had great weight. Portia knew this, and counted on it when she said she wanted him on her side; so she exulted when others followed the new fashion, some from principle, but many simply because he set it.

At first the young reformers were disappointed

that every one was not as enthusiastic as themselves, and as ready to dare and do for the cause they had espoused. But wiser heads than those on their pretty shoulders curbed their impetuosity, and suggested various ways of gently insinuating the new idea, and making it so attractive that others would find it impossible to resist; for sunshine often wins when bluster makes us wrap our prejudices closer around us, like the traveller in the fable.

Portia baited *her* trap with Roman parties, — for she had been abroad, — and made them so delightful that no one complained when only cake and tea was served (that being the style in the Eternal City), but went and did likewise.

Artful Polly set up a comic newspaper, to amuse Ned, who was an invalid nearly all winter, and in it freed her mind on many subjects in such a witty way that the "Pollyanthus," as her brother named it, circulated through their set, merrily sowing good seed; for young folks will remember a joke longer than a sermon, and this editor made all hers tell.

Pris was not behindhand in her efforts, but worked in a different way, and got up a branch society among her little pupils, called "The Water Babies." That captivated the mothers at once, and even the fathers found it difficult to enjoy their wine with blue eyes watching them wistfully over the rims of silver mugs; while the few topers of the town hid themselves like night-birds flying from the sun, when, led by their gentle General, that little army of innocents marched through the streets with banners flying, blithe voices singing, rosy faces shining, and childish hearts full of the sweet delusion that *they* could save the world.

Of course the matrons discussed these events at the sewing-circle, and much talk went on of a more useful sort than the usual gossip about servants, sickness, dress, and scandal.

Mrs. Judge waxed eloquent upon the subject, and, being president, every one listened with due respect. Mrs. Ward seconded all her motions, for this lady had much surprised the town, not only by installing Phil as family physician, but by coming out strong for temperance. Somebody had told her all about the girls' labor of love, and she had felt ashamed to be outdone by them; so, like a conscientious woman, she decided to throw her influence into the right scale, take time by the forelock, and help to make the town a safer place for her five sons to grow up in than it was then.

These two leading ladies kept the ball rolling so briskly that others were soon converted and fell into rank, till a dozen or so were heartily in earnest. And then the job was half done; for in a great measure women make society what they choose to have it.

"We are told that home is our sphere, and advised to keep in it; so let us see that it is what it should be, and then we shall have proved our fitness for larger fields of labor, if we care to claim them," said Mrs. Judge, cutting out red flannel with charitable energy on one occasion.

"Most of us will find that quite as much as we can accomplish, I fancy," answered Mrs. Ward, thinking of her own riotous lads, who were probably pulling the house about their ears, while she made hoods for Mrs. Flanagan's bare-headed lasses.

"'Pears to me we hain't no call to interfere in other folks's affairs. This never was a drinkin' town, and things is kep' in fustrate order, so *I* don't see the use of sech a talk about temperance," remarked Miss Simmons, an acid spinster, whose principal earthly wealth consisted of a choice collection of cats.

"If your tabbies took to drinking, you *would* see the use, I 'm sure," laughed Polly, from the corner, which was a perfect posy-bed of girls.

"Thank goodness, *I 've* no men folks to pester myself about," began Miss Simmons, with asperity.

"Ah, but you should; for if you refuse to make them happy, you ought at least to see that they console themselves in ways which can work them no further woe," continued Polly, gravely, though her black eyes danced with fun.

"Well, that would n't be no more than fair, I'm free to confess; but, sakes alive, I could n't attend to 'em all!" said Miss Simmons, bridling with a simper that nearly upset the whole bevy of girls.

"Do make the effort, and help us poor things who have n't had your experience," added Pris, in her most persuasive voice.

"I declare I will! I 'll have Hiram Stebbins in to tea; and when he 's as good-natured as muffins and pie can make him, I 'll set to and see if I can't talk him out of his attachment to that brandy bottle," cried Miss Simmons, with a sudden yearning towards the early sweetheart, who had won, but never claimed her virgin affections.

"I think you 'll do it; and, if so, you will have accomplished what no one else could, and you shall have any prize you choose," cried Portia, smiling so hopefully that the faded old face grew almost young again, as Miss Simmons went home with something better to do than tend her tabbies.

"We 've bagged that bird," said Polly, with real satisfaction.

"That 's the way we set people to work," added Portia, smiling.

"She will do what we can't, for her heart is in it," said Pris, softly; and it was pleasant to see the blooming girls rejoice that poor old Hiram was in a fair way to be saved.

So the year went round, and Thanksgiving came again, with the home jollity that makes a festival throughout the land. The day would not be perfect if it did not finish with a frolic of some sort, and for reasons of their own the young gentlemen decided to have the first sociable of the year an unusually pleasant one.

"Everybody is going, and Ned says the supper is to be water-ice and ice-water," said Polly, taking a last look at herself in the long mirror, when the three friends were ready on that happy evening.

"I need n't sigh now over other girls' pretty dresses, as I did last year;" and Portia plumed herself like a swan, as she settled Charley's roses in her bosom.

"And I need n't wonder who Phil will take," added Pris, stopping, with her glove half on, to look at the little ring back again from its long banishment in somebody's waistcoat pocket.

Never had the hall looked so elegant and gay, for it was charmingly decorated; couches were provided for the elders, mirrors for the beauties, and music of the best sounded from behind a thicket of shrubs and flowers. Every one seemed in unusually good spirits; the girls looked their loveliest, and the young men were models of propriety; though a close observer might have detected a suspicious twinkle in the eyes of the most audacious, as if they plotted some new joke.

The girls saw it, were on the watch, and thought the secret was out when they discovered that the gentlemen of their set all wore tiny pitchers, hanging like orders from the knots of sweet-peas in their button-holes. But, bless their innocent hearts! that was only a ruse, and they were taken entirely by surprise when, just before supper, the band struck up,

"Drink to me only with thine eyes;"

and every one looked smilingly at the three girls who were standing together near the middle of the hall.

They looked about them in pretty confusion, but in a moment beheld a spectacle that made them forget themselves; for the Judge, in an impressive white waistcoat, marched into the circle gathered about them, made a splendid bow, and said, with a smile that put the gas to shame, —

"Young ladies! I am desired by the gentlemen now present to beg your acceptance of a slight token of their gratitude, respect, and penitence. As the first man who joined the society which has proved a blessing to our town, Mr. William Snow will now have the honor of presenting the gift."

Then appeared Mr. William Snow, looking as proud as a peacock; and well he might, for on the salver which he bore stood a stately silver pitcher. A graceful little Hebe danced upon the handle, three names shone along the fretted brim, and three white lilies rose from the slender vase, — fit emblems of the maiden founders of the league.

Arriving before them, Master Will nearly upset the equilibrium of his precious burden in attempting to make a bow equal to the Judge's; but recovered himself gallantly, and delivered the following remarkable poem, which the public was expected to believe an emanation of his own genius: —

"Hebe poured the nectar forth
  When gods of old were jolly,
But graces three *our* goblets fill,
  Fair Portia, Pris and Polly.
Their draughts make every man who tastes
  Happier, better, richer;
So here we vow ourselves henceforth
  Knights of the Silver Pitcher."

ANNA'S WHIM

"NOW just look at that!" cried a young lady, pausing suddenly in her restless march to and fro on one of the wide piazzas of a seaside hotel.

"At what?" asked her companion, lazily swinging in a hammock.

"The difference in those two greetings. It 's perfectly disgraceful!" was the petulant reply.

"I did n't see anything. Do tell me about it," said Clara, opening her drowsy eyes with sudden interest.

"Why, young Barlow was lounging up the walk, and met pretty Miss Ellery. Off went his hat; he gave her a fine bow, a gracious smile, and a worn-out compliment, and then dawdled on again. The next minute Joe King came along. Instantly Barlow woke up, laughed out like a pleased boy, gave him a hearty grip of the hand, a cordial 'How are you, old fellow? I 'm no end glad to see you!' and, linking arms, the two tramped off, quite beaming with satisfaction."

"But, child, King is Barlow's best friend; Kitty Ellery only an acquaintance. Besides, it would n't do to greet a woman like a man."

"Yes, it would, especially in this case; for Barlow adores Kate, and might, at least, treat her to something better than the nonsense he gives other girls. But, no, it 's proper to simper and compliment; and he 'll do it till his love gets the better of 'prunes and prisms,' and makes him sincere and earnest."

"This is a new whim of yours. You surely would n't like to have any man call out 'How are you, Anna?' slap you on the shoulder, and nearly shake your hand off, as Barlow did King's, just now," said Clara, laughing at her friend.

"Yes, I would," answered Anna, perversely, "if he really meant it to express affection or pleasure. A good grip of the hand and a plain, hearty word would please me infinitely better than all the servile bowing down and sweet nonsense I 've had lately. I 'm not a fool; then, why am I treated like one?" she continued, knitting her handsome brows and pacing to and fro like an angry leopardess. "Why don't men treat me like a reasonable being? — talk sense to me, give me their best ideas, tell me their plans and ambitions, let me enjoy the real man in them, and know what they honestly are? I don't want to be a goddess stuck up on a pedestal. I want to be a woman down among them, to help and be helped by our acquaintance."

"It would n't do, I fancy. They would n't like it, and would tell you to keep to your own sex."

"But my own sex don't interest or help me one bit. Women have no hope but to be married, and that is soon told; no ideas but dress and show, and I 'm tired to death of both; no ambition but to outshine their neighbors, and I despise that."

"Thank you, love," blandly murmured Clara.

"It is true, and you know it. There *are* sensible women; but not in my set. And I don't seem to find them. I 've tried the life set down for girls like me, and for three years I 've lived and enjoyed it. Now I 'm tired of it. I want something better, and I mean to have it. Men *will* follow, admire, flatter, and love me; for I please them and they enjoy my society. Very well. Then it 's fair that I should enjoy theirs. And I should if they would let me. It 's perfectly maddening to have flocks of brave, bright fellows round me, full of everything that is attractive, strong, and helpful, yet not be able to get at it, because society ordains twaddle between us, instead of sensible conversation and sincere manners."

"What shall we do about it, love?" asked Clara, enjoying her friend's tirade.

"*You* will submit to it, and get a mental dyspepsia, like all the other fashionable girls. I won't submit, if I can help it; even if I shock

Mrs. Grundy by my efforts to get plain bread and beef instead of confectionery."

Anna walked in silence for a moment, and then burst out again, more energetically than ever.

"Oh! I do wish I could find one sensible man, who would treat me as he treats his male friends, — even roughly, if he is honest and true; who would think me worthy of his confidence, ask my advice, let me give him whatever I have that is wise and excellent, and be my friend in all good faith."

"Ahem!" said Clara, with a significant laugh, that angered Anna.

"You need not try to abash me with your jeers. I know what I mean, and I stand by my guns, in spite of your 'hems.' I do *not* want lovers. I 've had dozens, and am tired of them. I will not marry till I know the man thoroughly; and how *can* I know him with this veil between us? They don't guess what I really am; and I want to prove to them and to myself that I possess brains and a heart, as well as 'heavenly eyes,' a 'queenly figure,' and a 'mouth made for kissing.'"

The scorn with which Anna uttered the last words amused her friend immensely, for the petulant beauty had never looked handsomer than at that moment.

"If any man saw you now, he 'd promise whatever you ask, no matter how absurd. But don't excite yourself, dear child; it is too warm for heroics."

Anna leaned on the wide baluster a moment, looking thoughtfully out upon the sea; and as she gazed a new expression stole over her charming face, changing its disdainful warmth to soft regret.

"This is not all a whim. I know what I covet, because I had it once," she said, with a sigh. "I had a boy friend when I was a girl, and for several years we were like brother and sister. Ah! what happy times we had together, Frank and I. We played and studied, quarrelled and made up, dreamed splendid dreams, and loved one another in our simple child fashion, never thinking of sex, rivalry, or any of the forms and follies that spoil maturer friendships."

"What became of him? Did he die angelically in his early bloom, or outgrow his Platonics with round jackets?" asked Clara.

"He went to college. I went abroad, to be 'finished off;' and when we met a year ago the old charm was all gone, for we were 'in society' and had our masks on."

"So the boy and girl friendship did not ripen into love and end the romance properly?"

"No, thank Heaven! no flirtation spoilt the pretty story. Frank was too wise, and I too busy. Yet I remember how glad I was to see him; though I hid it properly, and pretended to be quite unconscious that I was anything but a belle. I got paid for my deceit, though; for, in spite of his admiration, I saw he was disappointed in me. I should not have cared if I had been disappointed in him; but I was quick to see that he was growing one of the strong, superior men who command respect. I wanted to keep his regard, at least; and I seemed to have nothing but beauty to give in return. I think I never was so hurt in my life as I was by his not coming to see me after a week or two, and hearing him say to a friend, one night, when I thought I was at my very best, 'She is spoilt, like all the rest.' "

"I do believe you loved him, and that is why you won't love any one else," cried Clara, who had seen her friend in her moods before; but never understood them, and thought she had found a clew now.

"No," said Anna, with a quiet shake of the head. "No, I only wanted my boy friend back, and could not find him. The fence between us was too high; and I could not climb over, as I used to do when I leaped the garden-wall to sit in a tree and help Frank with his lessons."

"Has the uncivil wretch never come back?" asked Clara, interested in the affair.

"Never. He is too busy shaping his life bravely and successfully to waste his time on a frivolous butterfly like Anna West."

An eloquent little gesture of humility made the words almost pathetic. Kind-hearted Clara was touched by the sight of tears in the "heavenly eyes," and tumbling out of the hammock she embraced the "queenly figure" and warmly pressed the "lips that were made for kissing," thereby driving several approaching gentlemen to the verge of distraction.

"Now don't be tragical, darling. You have nothing to cry for, I'm sure. Young, lovely, rich, and adored, what more *can* any girl want?" said Clara, gushingly.

"Something besides admiration to live for," answered Anna, adding, with a shrug, as she saw several hats fly off and several manly countenances beam upon her, "Never mind, my fit is over now; let us go and dress for tea."

Miss West usually took a brisk pull in her own boat before breakfast; a habit which lured many indolent young gentlemen out of their beds at unaccustomed hours, in the hope that they might have the honor of splashing their legs helping her off, the privilege of wishing her "*Bon voyage*," or the rapture of accompanying her.

On the morning after her "fit," as she called the discontent of a really fine nature with the empty life she led, she was up and out unusually early; for she had kept her room with a headache all the evening, and now longed for fresh air and exercise.

As she prepared the "Gull" for a start, she was idly wondering what early bird would appear eager to secure the coveted worm, when a loud and cheerful voice was heard calling, —

"Hullo, Anna!" and a nautically attired gentleman hove in sight, waving his hat as he hailed her.

She started at the unceremonious salute and looked back. Then her whole face brightened beautifully as she sprang up the bank, saying, with a pretty mixture of hesitation and pleasure, —

"Why, Frank, is that you?"

"Do you doubt it?"

And the new-comer shook both her hands so vigorously that she winced a little as she said, laughing, —

"No, I don't. That is the old squeeze with extra power in it."

"How are you? Going for a pull? Take me along and show me the lions. There's a good soul."

"With pleasure. When did you come?" asked Anna, settling the black ribbon under the sailor collar which set off her white throat charmingly.

"Last night. I caught a glimpse of you at tea; but you were surrounded then and vanished immediately afterward. So when I saw you skipping over the rocks just now, I gave chase, and here I am. Shall I take an oar?" asked Frank, as she motioned him to get in.

"No, thank you. I prefer to row myself and don't need any help," she answered, with an imperious little wave of the hand; for she was glad to show him she could do something besides dance, dress, and flirt.

"All right. Then I 'll do the luxurious and enjoy myself." And, without offering to help her in, Frank seated himself, folded his arms, stretched out his long legs, and placidly remarked, —

"Pull away, skipper."

Anna was pleased with his frank and friendly greeting, and, feeling as if old times had come again, sprang in, prepared to astonish him with her skill.

"Might I suggest that you —" began Frank, as she pushed off.

"No suggestions or advice allowed aboard this ship. I know what I 'm about, though I *am* a woman," was the severe answer, as the boat glided from the wharf.

"Ay, ay, sir!" And Frank meekly subsided, with a twinkle of amusement in the eyes that rested approvingly on the slender figure in a blue boating suit and the charming face under the sailor hat.

Anna paddled her way dexterously out from among the fleet of boats riding at anchor in the little bay; then she seated herself, adjusted one oar, and looked about for the other rowlock. It was nowhere visible; and, after a silent search, she deigned to ask, —

"Have you seen the thing anywhere?"

"I saw it on the bank."

"Why did n't you tell me before?"

"I began to, but was quenched; so I obeyed orders."

"You have n't forgotten how to tease," said Anna, petulantly.

"Nor you to be wilful."

She gave him a look that would have desolated most men; but only made Frank smile affably as she paddled laboriously back, recovered the rowlock and then her temper, as, with a fine display of muscle, she pulled out to sea.

Getting into the current, she let the boat drift, and soon forgot time and space in the bewildering conversation that followed.

"What have you been doing since I saw you last?" she asked, looking as rosy as a milkmaid, as she stopped rowing and tied up her wind-tossed hair.

"Working like a beaver. You see" — and then, to her utter amazement, Frank entered into an elaborate statement of his affairs, quite as if she understood all about it and her opinion was valuable. It was all Greek to Anna, but she was immensely gratified; for it was just the way the boy used to tell her his small concerns in the days when each had firm faith in the other's wisdom. She tried to look as if she understood all about "investments, percentage, and long credit;" but she was out of her depth in five minutes, and dared say nothing, lest she should betray her lamentable ignorance on all matters of business.

She got out of the scrape by cleverly turning the conversation to old times, and youthful reminiscences soon absorbed them both.

The faint, far-off sound of a gong recalled her to the fact that breakfast was nearly ready; and, turning the boat, she was dismayed to see how far they had floated. She stopped talking and rowed her best; but wind and tide were against her, she was faint with hunger, and her stalwart passenger made her task doubly hard. He offered no help, however; but did the luxurious to the life, leaning back, with his hat off, and dabbling his hands in the way that most impedes the progress of a boat.

Pride kept Anna silent till her face was scarlet, her palms blistered, and her breath most gone. Then, and not till then, did she condescend to say, with a gasp, poorly concealed by an amiable smile, —

"Do you care to row? I ought to have asked you before."

"I'm very comfortable, thank you," answered Frank. Then, as an expression of despair flitted over poor Anna's face, he added bluntly, "I'm getting desperately hungry, so I don't care if I do shorten the voyage a bit."

With a sigh of relief, she rose to change seats, and, expecting him to help her, she involuntarily put out her hands, as she passed. But Frank was busy turning back his cuffs, and never stirred a finger; so that she would have lost her balance and gone overboard if she had not caught his arm.

"What's the matter, skipper?" he asked, standing the sudden grip as steadily as a mast.

"Why didn't you help me? You have no more manners than a turtle!" cried Anna, dropping into the seat with the frown of a spoiled beauty, accustomed to be gallantly served and supported at every step.

Frank only added to his offence by laughing, as he said carelessly, —

"You seemed so independent, I didn't like to interfere."

"So, if I had gone overboard, you would not have fished me out, unless I asked you to do it, I suppose?"

"In that case, I'm afraid I shouldn't have waited for orders. We can't spare you to the mermen yet."

Something in the look he gave her appeased Anna's resentment; and she sat silently admiring the strong, swift strokes that sent the "Gull" skimming over the water.

"Not too late for breakfast, after all," she said graciously, as they reached the wharf, where several early strollers stood watching their approach.

"Poor thing! You look as if you needed it," answered Frank. But he let her get out alone, to the horror of Messrs. Barlow, King, & Co.; and, while she fastened the boat, Frank stood settling his hatband, with the most exasperating unconsciousness of his duty.

"What are you going to do with yourself this morning?" she asked, as she walked up the rocky path, with no arm to lean upon.

"Fish. Will you come along?"

"No, thank you. One gets so burnt. I shall go to my hammock under the pine," was the graciously suggestive reply of the lady who liked a slave to fan or swing her, and seldom lacked several to choose from.

"See you at dinner, then. My room is in the Cottage. So by-by for the present." And, with a nod, Frank strolled away, leaving the lovely Miss West to mount the steps and cross the hall unescorted.

"The dear fellow's manners need polish. I must take him in hand, I see. And yet he is very nice, in spite of his brusque ways," thought Anna, indulgently. And more than once that morning she recalled his bluff "Hullo, Anna!" as she swung languidly in her hammock, with a devoted being softly reading Tennyson to her inattentive ears.

At dinner she appeared in unusual spirits, and kept her end of the table in a ripple of merriment by her witty and satirical sallies, privately hoping that her opposite neighbor would discover that she could talk well when she chose to do so. But Frank was deep in politics, discussing some new measure with such earnestness and eloquence that Anna, pausing to listen for a moment, forgot her lively gossip in one of the great questions of the hour.

She was listening with silent interest, when Frank suddenly appealed to her to confirm some statement he had just made; and she was ignominiously obliged to confess she knew too little about the matter to give any opinion. No compliment ever paid her was more flattering than his way of turning to her now and then, as if including her in the discussion as a matter of course; and never had she regretted anything more keenly than she did her ignorance on a subject that every man and woman should understand and espouse.

She did her best to look intelligent; racked her brain to remember facts which she had heard discussed for weeks, without paying any attention to them; and, thanks to her quick wit and womanly sympathy, she managed to hold her own, saying little, but looking much.

The instant dinner was over, she sent a servant to the reading-room for a file of late papers, and, retiring to a secluded corner, read up with a diligence that not only left her with clearer ideas on one subject, but also a sense of despair at her own deficiencies in the knowledge of many others.

"I really must have a course of solid reading. I do believe that is what I need; and I'll ask Frank where to begin. He always was an intelligent boy; but I was surprised to hear how well he talked. I was actually proud of him. I wonder where he is, by the way. Clara wants to be introduced, and I want to see how he strikes her."

Leaving her hiding-place, Anna walked forth in search of her friends, looking unusually bright and beautiful, for her secret studies had waked her up and lent her face the higher charm it needed. Clara appeared first. The new-comer had already been presented to her, and she professed herself "perfectly fascinated." "Such a personable man! Quite distinguished, you know, and so elegant in his manners. Devoted, graceful, and altogether charming."

"You like his manners, do you?" and Anna smiled at Clara's enthusiasm.

"Of course I do; for they have all the polish of foreign travel, with the indescribable something which a really fine character lends to every little act and word."

"Frank has never been abroad, and if I judged his character by his manners I should say he was rather a rough customer," said Anna, finding fault because Clara praised.

"You are so fastidious, nothing ever suits you, dear. I did n't expect to like this old friend of yours. But I frankly confess I do immensely; so, if you are tired of him, I 'll take him off your hands."

"Thank you, love. You are welcome to poor

Frank, if you can win him. Men are apt to be more loyal to friendship than women; and I rather fancy, from what I saw this morning, that he is in no haste to change old friends for new."

Anna spoke sweetly, but at heart was ill pleased with Clara's admiration of her private property, as she considered "poor Frank," and inwardly resolved to have no poaching on her preserves.

Just then the gentleman in question came up, saying to Anna, in his abrupt way, —

"Every one is going to ride, so I cannot get the best horses; but I 've secured two, and now I want a companion. Will you come for a good old-time gallop?"

Anna thought of her blistered hands, and hesitated, till a look at Clara's hopeful face decided her to accept. She did so, and rode like an Amazon for several hours, in spite of heat, dust, and a hard-mouthed horse, who nearly pulled her arms out of the sockets.

She hoped to find a chance to consult Frank about her course of useful reading; but he seemed intent on the "old-time gallop," and she kept up gallantly till the ride was over, when she retired to her room, quite exhausted, but protesting with heroic smiles that she had had a delightful time.

She did not appear at tea; but later in the evening, when an informal dance was well under way, she sailed in on the arm of a distinguished old gentleman, "evidently prepared to slay her thousands," as young Barlow said, observing the unusual brilliancy of her eyes and the elaborate toilette she had made.

"She means mischief to-night. Who is to be the victim, I wonder?" said another man, putting up his glass for a survey of the charmer.

"Not the party who came last evening. He is only an old friend, she says."

"He might be her brother or her husband, judging by the cavalier way in which he treats her. I could have punched his head this morning, when he let her pull up that boat alone," cried a youthful adorer, glaring irefully at the delinquent, lounging in a distant doorway.

"If she said he was an old friend, you may be sure he is an accepted lover. The dear creatures all fib in these matters; so I 'll lay wagers to an enormous amount that all this splendor is for the lord and master, not for our destruction," said Barlow, who was wise in the ways of women and wary as a moth should be who had burnt his wings more than once at the same candle.

Clara happened to overhear these pleasing remarks, and five minutes after they were uttered she breathed them tenderly into Anna's ear. A scornful smile was all the answer she received; but the beauty was both pleased and annoyed, and awaited with redoubled interest the approach of the old friend, who was regarded in the light of a successful lover. But he seemed in no haste to claim his privileges, and dance after dance went by, while he sat talking with the old general or absently watching the human teetotums that spun about before him.

"I can't stand this another moment!" said Anna to herself, at last, and beckoned the recreant knight to approach, with a commanding gesture.

"Why don't you dance, sir?"

"I 've forgotten how, ma'am."

"After all the pains I took with you when we had lessons together, years ago?"

"I 've been too busy to attend to trifles of that sort."

"Elegant accomplishments are not trifles, and no one should neglect them who cares to make himself agreeable."

"Well, I don't know that I do care, as a general thing."

"You ought to care; and, as a penance for that rude speech, you must dance this dance with me. I cannot let you forget all your accomplishments for the sake of business; so I shall do my duty as a friend and take you in hand," said Anna, severely.

"You are very kind; but is it worth the trouble?"

"Now, Frank, don't be provoking and ungrateful. You know you like to give pleasure, to be cared for, and to do credit to your friends; so just rub up your manners a bit, and be as well-bred as you are sensible and brave and good."

"Thank you, I'll try. May I have the honor, Miss West?" and he bowed low before her, with a smile on his lips that both pleased and puzzled Anna.

They danced the dance, and Frank acquitted himself respectably, but relapsed into his objectionable ways as soon as the trial ended; for the first thing he said, with a sigh of relief, was, —

"Come out and talk; for upon my life I can't stand this oven any longer."

Anna obediently followed, and, seating herself in a breezy corner, waited to be entertained. But Frank seemed to have forgotten that pleasing duty; for, perching himself on the wide baluster of the piazza, he not only proceeded to light a cigarette, without even saying, "By your leave," but coolly offered her one also.

"How dare you!" she said, much offended at this proceeding. "I am not one of the fast girls who do such things, and I dislike it exceedingly."

"You used to smoke sweet-fern in corn-cob pipes, you remember; and these are not much stronger," he said, placidly restoring the rejected offering to his pocket.

"I did many foolish things then which I desire to forget now."

"And some very sweet and sensible ones, also. Ah, well! it can't be helped, I suppose."

Anna sat silent a moment, wondering what he meant; and when she looked up, she found him pensively staring at her, through a fragrant cloud of smoke.

"What is it?" she asked, for his eyes seemed seeking something.

"I was trying to see some trace of the little Anna I used to know. I thought I'd found her again this morning in the girl in the round hat; but I don't find her anywhere to-night."

"Indeed, Frank, I'm not so much changed as I seem. At least, to you I am the same, as far as I can be. Do believe it, and be friends, for I want one very much," cried Anna, forgetting everything but the desire to re-establish herself in his good opinion. As she spoke, she turned her face toward the light and half extended her hand, as if to claim and hold the old regard that seemed about to be withdrawn from her.

Frank bent a little and scanned the upturned face with a keen glance. It flushed in the moonlight and the lips trembled like an anxious child's; but the eyes met his with a look both proud and wistful, candid and sweet, — a look few saw in those lovely eyes, or, once seeing, ever forgot. Frank gave a little nod, as if satisfied, and said, with that perplexing smile of his, —

"Most people would see only the beautiful Miss West, in a remarkably pretty gown; but

I think I catch a glimpse of little Anna, and I am very glad of it. You want a friend? Very good. I 'll do my best for you; but you must take me as I am, thorns and all."

"I will, and not mind if they wound sometimes. I 've had roses till I 'm tired of them, in spite of their sweetness."

As he spoke, Frank had taken the hand she offered, and, having gravely shaken it, held the "white wonder" for an instant, glancing from the little blisters on the delicate palm to the rings that shone on several fingers.

"Are you reading my fortune?" asked Anna, wondering if he was going to be sentimental and kiss it.

"After a fashion; for I am looking to see if there is a suspicious diamond anywhere about. Is n't it time there was one?"

"That is not a question for you to ask;" and Anna caught away her hand, as if one of the thorns he spoke of had suddenly pricked.

"Why not? We always used to tell each other everything; and, if we are to go on in the old friendly way, we must be confidential and comfortable, you know."

"You can begin yourself then, and I 'll see how I like it," said Anna, aroused and interested, in spite of her maidenly scruples about the new arrangement.

"I will, with all my heart. To own the truth, I 've been longing to tell you something; but I wasn't sure that you 'd take any interest in it," began Frank, eating rose-leaves with interesting embarrassment.

"I can imagine what it is," said Anna, quickly, while her heart began to flutter curiously, for these confidences were becoming exciting. "You have found your fate, and are dying to let everybody know how happy you are."

"I think I have. But I 'm not happy yet. I 'm desperately anxious, for I cannot decide whether it is a wise or foolish choice."

"Who is it?"

"Never mind the name. I have n't spoken yet, and perhaps never shall; so I may as well keep that to myself, — for the present, at least."

"Tell me what you like then, and I will ask no more questions," said Anna, coldly; for this masculine discretion annoyed her.

"Well, you see, this dear girl is pretty, rich, accomplished, and admired. A little spoilt, in fact; but very captivating, in spite of it. Now, the doubt in my mind is whether it is wise to woo a wife of this sort; for I know I shall want a companion in all things, not only a pretty sweetheart or a graceful mistress for my house."

"I should say it was *not* wise," began Anna, decidedly, then hastened to add, more quietly: "But perhaps you only see one side of this girl's character. She may have much strength and sweetness hidden away under her gay manner, waiting to be called out when the right mate comes."

"I often think so myself, and long to learn if I am the man; but some frivolous act, thoughtless word, or fashionable folly on her part dampens my ardor, and makes me feel as if I had better go elsewhere before it is too late."

"You are not madly in love, then?"

"Not yet; but I should be if I saw much of her, for when I do I rather lose my head, and am tempted to fall upon my knees, regardless of time, place, and consequences."

Frank spoke with sudden love and longing in his voice, and stretched out his arms so suggestively that Anna started. But he contented himself with gathering a rose from the clusters that hung all about, and Anna slapped an imaginary mosquito as energetically as if it had been the unknown lady, for whom she felt a sudden and inexplicable dislike.

"So you think I 'd better not say to my love, like the mad gentleman to Mrs. Nickleby, 'Be mine, be mine'?" was Frank's next question, as he sat with his nose luxuriously buried in the fragrant heart of the rose.

"Decidedly not. I 'm sure, from the way you speak of her, that she is not worthy of you; and your passion cannot be very deep if you can quote Dickens's nonsense at such a moment," said Anna, more cheerfully.

"It grows rapidly, I find; and I give you

my word, if I should pass a week in the society of that lovely butterfly, it would be all over with me by Saturday night."

"Then don't do it."

"Ah! but I want to desperately. Do say that I may, just for a last nibble at temptation, before I take your advice and go back to my bachelor life again," he prayed beseechingly.

"Don't go back, love somebody else, and be happy. There are plenty of superior women in the world who would be just the thing for you. I am sure you are going to be a man of mark, and you *must* have a good wife, — not a silly little creature, who will be a clog upon you all your life. So *do* take my advice, and let me help you, if I can."

Anna spoke earnestly, and her face quite shone with friendly zeal; while her eyes were full of unspoken admiration and regard for this friend, who seemed tottering on the verge of a precipice. She expected a serious reply, — thanks, at least, for her interest; and great was her surprise to see Frank lean back against the vine-wreathed pillar behind him, and laugh till a shower of rose-leaves came fluttering down on both their heads.

"I don't see any cause for such unseemly merriment," was her dignified reproof of this new impropriety.

"I beg your pardon. I really could n't help it, for the comical contrast between your sage counsels and your blooming face upset me. Your manner was quite maternal and most impressive, till I looked at you in your French finery, and then it was all up with me," said Frank, penitently, though his eyes still danced with mirth.

The compliment appeased Anna's anger; and, folding her round white arms on the railing in front of her, she looked up at him with a laugh as blithe as his own.

"I dare say I was absurdly sober and important; but you see it is so long since I have had a really serious thought in my head or felt a really sincere interest in any one's affairs but my own that I overdid the matter. If you don't care for my advice, I'll take it all back; and you can go and marry your butterfly as soon as you like."

"I rather think I shall," said Frank, slowly. "For I fancy she *has* got a hidden self, as you suggested, and I'd rather like to find it out. One judges people so much by externals that it is not fair. Now, you, for instance, if you won't mind my saying it, don't show half your good points; and a casual observer would consider you merely a fashionable woman, — lovely, but shallow."

"As you did the last time we met," put in Anna, sharply.

If she expected him to deny it, she was mistaken, for he said, with provoking candor, —

"Exactly. And I quite grieved about it; for I used to be very fond of my little playmate and thought she'd make a fine woman. I'm glad I've seen you again; for I find I was unjust in my first judgment, and this discovery gives me hope that I may have been mistaken in the same way about my — well, we'll say sweetheart. It's a pretty old word and I like it."

"If he only *would* forget that creature a minute and talk about something more interesting!" sighed Anna to herself. But she answered, meekly enough: "I knew you were disappointed in me, and I did not wonder, for I am not good for much, thanks to my foolish education and the life I have led these last few years. But I do sincerely wish to be more of a woman, only I have no one to tell me how. Everybody flatters me and" —

"I don't!" cried Frank, promptly.

"That's true." And Anna could not help laughing in the middle of her confessions at the tone of virtuous satisfaction with which he repelled the accusation. "No," she continued, "you are honest enough for any one; and I like it, though it startles me now and then, it is so new."

"I hope I'm not disrespectful," said Frank, busily removing the thorns from the stem of his flower.

"Oh, no! Not that exactly. But you treat me very much as if I was a sister or a — masculine friend." Anna meant to quote the expression Clara had reported; but somehow the word "wife" was hard to utter, and she finished the sentence differently.

"And you don't like it?" asked Frank, lifting the rose to hide the mischievous smile that lurked about his mouth.

"Yes, I do, — infinitely better than the sentimental homage other men pay me or the hackneyed rubbish they talk. It does me good to be a little neglected; and I don't mind it from you, because you more than atone for it by talking to me as if I could understand a man's mind and had one of my own."

"Then you don't quite detest me for my rough ways and egotistical confidences?" asked Frank, as if suddenly smitten with remorse for the small sins of the day.

"No, I rather fancy it, for it seems like old times, when you and I played together. Only then I could help you in many ways, as you helped me; but now I don't seem to know anything, and can be of no use to you or any one else. I should like to be; and I think, if you would kindly tell me what books to read, what people to know, and what faculties to cultivate, I might become something besides 'a fashionable woman, lovely but shallow.'"

There was a little quiver of emotion in Anna's voice as she uttered the last words that did not escape her companion's quick ear. But he only smiled a look of heartfelt satisfaction to the rose, and answered soberly.

"Now that is a capital idea, and I 'll do it with pleasure. I have often wondered how you bright girls *could* be contented with such an empty sort of life. We fellows are just as foolish for a time, I know, — far worse in the crops of wild oats we sow; but we have to pull up and go to work, and that makes men of us. Marriage ought to do that for women, I suppose; but it does n't seem to nowadays, and I do pity you poor little things from the bottom of my heart."

"I 'm ready now to 'pull up and go to work.' Show me how, Frank, and I 'll change your pity into respect," said Anna, casting off her lace shawl, as if preparing for immediate action; for his tone of masculine superiority rather nettled her.

"Come, I 'll make a bargain with you. I 'll give you something strong and solid to brace up your mind, and in return you shall polish my manners, see to my morals, and keep my heart from wasting itself on false idols. Shall we do this for one another, Anna?"

"Yes, Frank," she answered heartily. Then, as Clara was seen approaching, she added playfully, "All this is *sub rosa,* you understand."

He handed her the flower without a word, as if the emblem of silence was the best gage he could offer. Many flowers had been presented to the beauty; but none were kept so long and carefully as the thornless rose her old friend gave her, with a cordial smile that warmed her heart.

A great deal can happen in a week, and the seven days that followed that moonlight *tête-à-tête* seemed to Anna the fullest and the happiest she had ever known. She had never worked so hard in her life; for her new tutor gave her plenty to do, and she studied in secret to supply sundry deficiencies which she was too proud to confess. No more novels now; no more sentimental poetry, lounging in a hammock. She sat erect upon a hard rock and read Buckle, Mill, and Social Science Reports with a diligence that appalled the banished dawdlers who usually helped her kill time. There was early boating, vigorous horse exercise, and tramps over hill and dale, from which she returned dusty, brown, and tired, but as happy as if she had discovered something fairer and grander than wild flowers or the ocean in its changeful moods. There were afternoon concerts in the breezy drawing-rooms, when others were enjoying siestas, and Anna sang to her one listener as she had never sung before. But best of all were the moonlight *séances* among the roses; for there they interchanged interesting confidences and hovered about those dangerous but delightful topics that need the magic of a midsummer night to make the charm quite perfect.

Anna intended to do her part honorably; but

soon forgot to correct her pupil's manners, she was so busy taking care of his heart. She presently discovered that he treated other women in the usual way; and at first it annoyed her that she was the only one whom he allowed to pick up her own fan, walk without an arm, row, ride, and take care of herself as if she was a man. But she also discovered that she was the only woman to whom he talked as to an equal, in whom he seemed to find sympathy, inspiration, and help, and for whom he frankly showed not admiration alone, but respect, confidence, and affection.

This made the loss of a little surface courtesy too trifling for complaint or reproof; this stimulated and delighted her; and, in striving to deserve and secure it, she forgot every thing else, prouder to be one man's true friend than the idol of a dozen lovers.

What the effect of this new league was upon the other party was less evident; for, being of the undemonstrative sex, he kept his observations, discoveries, and satisfaction to himself, with no sign of especial interest, except now and then a rapturous allusion to his sweetheart, as if absence was increasing his passion.

Anna tried to quench his ardor, feeling sure, she said, that it was a mistake to lavish so much love upon a person who was so entirely unworthy of it. But Frank seemed blind on this one point; and Anna suffered many a pang, as day after day showed her some new virtue, grace, or talent in this perverse man, who seemed bent on throwing his valuable self away. She endeavored to forget it, avoided the subject as much as possible, and ignored the existence of this inconvenient being entirely. But as the week drew to an end a secret trouble looked out at her eyes, a secret unrest possessed her, and every moment seemed to grow more precious as it passed, each full of a bitter sweet delight never known before.

"I must be off to-morrow," said Frank, on the Saturday evening, as they strolled together on the beach, while the sun set gloriously and the great waves broke musically on the sands.

"Such a short holiday, after all those months of work!" answered Anna, looking away, lest he should see how wistful her tell-tale eyes were.

"I may take a longer holiday, the happiest a man can have, if somebody will go with me. Anna, I 've made up my mind to try my fate," he added impetuously.

"I have warned you, I can do no more." Which was quite true, for the poor girl's heart sunk at his words, and for a moment all the golden sky was a blur before her eyes.

"I won't be warned, thank you; for I 'm quite sure now that I love her. Nothing like absence to settle that point. I 've tried it, and I can't get on without her; so I 'm going to 'put my fortune to the touch and win or lose it all.'"

"If you truly love her, I hope you will win, and find her the wife you deserve. But think well before you put your happiness into any woman's hands," said Anna, bravely trying to forget herself.

"Bless you! I 've hardly thought of any thing else this week! I 've enjoyed myself, though; and am very grateful to you for making my visit so pleasant," Frank added warmly.

"Have I? I 'm so glad!" said Anna, as simply as a pleased child; for real love had banished all her small coquetries, vanities, and affectations, as sunshine absorbs the mists that hide a lovely landscape.

"Indeed, you have. All the teaching has not been on my side, I assure you; and I 'm not too proud to own my obligation to a woman. We lonely fellows, who have neither mother, sister, nor wife, need some gentle soul to keep us from getting selfish, hard, and worldly; and few are so fortunate as I in having one like little Anna."

"Oh, Frank! what have I done for you? I have n't dared to teach one so much wiser and stronger than myself. I 've only wanted to, and grieved because I was so ignorant, so weak, and silly," cried Anna, glowing beautifully with surprise and pleasure at this unexpected revelation.

"Your humility blinded you; yet your unconsciousness was half the charm. I 'll tell you what you did, dear. A man's moral sense gets blunted knocking about this rough-and-tumble world, where the favorite maxim is, 'Every man for himself and the Devil take the hindmost.' It is so with me; and in many of our conversations on various subjects, while I seemed to be teaching you, your innocent integrity was rebuking my worldly wisdom, your subtle instincts were pointing out the right which is above all policy, your womanly charity softening my hard judgments, and your simple faith in the good, the beautiful, the truly brave was waking up the high and happy beliefs that lay, not dead, but sleeping, in my soul. All this you did for me, Anna, and even more; for, in showing me the hidden side of your nature, I found it so sweet and deep and worshipful that it restores my faith in womankind, and shows me all the lovely possibilities that may lie folded up under the frivolous exterior of a fashionable woman."

Anna's heart was so full she could not speak for a moment; then like a dash of cold water came the thought, "And all this that I have done has only put him further from me, since it has given him courage to love and trust that woman." She tried to show only pleasure at his praise; but for the life of her she could not keep a tone of bitterness out of her voice as she answered gratefully, —

"You are too kind, Frank. I can hardly believe that I have so many virtues; but if I have, and they, like yours, have been asleep, remember you helped wake them up, and so you owe me nothing. Keep your sweet speeches for the lady you go to woo. I am contented with honest words that do not flatter."

"You shall have them;" and a quick smile passed over Frank's face, as if he knew what thorn pricked her just then, and was not ill pleased at the discovery. "Only, if I lose my sweetheart, I may be sure that my old friend won't desert me?" he asked, with a sincere anxiety that was a balm to Anna's sore heart.

She did not speak, but offered him her hand with a look which said much. He took it as silently, and, holding it in a firm, warm grasp, led her up to a cleft in the rocks, where they often sat to watch the great breakers thunder in. As she took her seat, he folded his plaid about her so tenderly that it felt like a friendly arm shielding her from the fresh gale that blew up from the sea. It was an unusual attention on his part, and coming just then it affected her so curiously that, when he lounged down beside her, she felt a strong desire to lay her head on his shoulder and sob out, —

"Don't go and leave me! No one loves you half as well as I, or needs you half so much!"

Of course, she did nothing of the sort; but began to sing, as she covertly whisked away a rebellious tear. Frank soon interrupted her music, however, by a heavy sigh; and followed up that demonstration with the tragical announcement, —

"Anna, I've got something awful to tell you."

"What is it?" she asked, with the resignation of one who has already heard the worst.

"It is so bad that I can't look you in the face while I tell it. Listen calmly till I am done, and then pitch me overboard if you like, for I deserve it," was his cheerful beginning.

"Go on." And Anna prepared herself to receive some tremendous shock with masculine firmness.

Frank pulled his hat over his eyes, and, looking away from her, said rapidly, with an odd sound in his voice,—

"The night I came I was put in a room opening on the back piazza; and, lying there to rest and cool after my journey, I heard two ladies talking. I knocked my boots about to let them know I was near; but they took no notice, so I listened. Most women's gabble would have sent me to sleep in five minutes; but this was rather original, and interested me, especially when I found by the names mentioned that I knew one of the parties. I've been trying your experiment all the week. Anna, how do you like it?"

She did not answer for a moment, being absorbed in swift retrospection. Then she colored to her hat-brim, looked angry, hurt, amused, gratified, and ashamed, all in a minute, and said slowly, as she met his laughing eyes,—

"Better than I thought I should."

"That 's good! Then you forgive me for my eavesdropping, my rudeness, and manifold iniquities? It was abominable; but I could not resist the temptation of testing your sincerity. It was great fun; but I 'm not sure that I shall not get the worst of it, after all," said Frank, sobering suddenly.

"You have played so many jokes upon me in old times that I don't find it hard to forgive this one; though I think it rather base in you to deceive me so. Still, as I have enjoyed and got a good deal out of it, I don't complain, and won't send you overboard yet," said Anna, generously.

"You always were a forgiving angel." And Frank settled the plaid again more tenderly than before.

"It was this, then, that made you so brusque to me alone, so odd and careless? I could not understand it and it hurt me at first; but I thought it was because we had been children together and soon forgot it, you were so kind and confidential, so helpful and straightforward. It *was* 'great fun,' for I always knew you meant what you said; and that was an unspeakable comfort to me in this world of flattery and falsehood. Yes, you may laugh at me, Frank, and leave me to myself again. I can bear it, for I 've proved that my whim was a possibility. I see my way now, and can go on alone to a truer, happier life than that in which you found me."

She spoke out bravely, and looked above the level sands and beyond the restless sea, as if she had found something worth living for and did not fear the future. Frank watched her an instant, for her face had never worn so noble an expression before. Sorrow as well as strength had come into the lovely features, and pain as well as patience touched them with new beauty. His own face changed as he looked, as if he let loose some deep and tender sentiment, long held in check, now ready to rise and claim its own.

"Anna," he said penitently, "I 've got one other terrible confession to make, and then my conscience will be clear. I want to tell you who my sweetheart is. Here 's her picture. Will you look at it?"

She gave a little shiver, turned steadily, and looked where he pointed. But all she saw was her own astonished face reflected in the shallow pool behind them. One glance at Frank made any explanation needless; indeed, there was no time for her to speak before something closer than the plaid enfolded her, something warmer than tears touched her cheek, and a voice sweeter to her than wind or wave whispered tenderly in her ear, —

"All this week I have been studying and enjoying far more than you; for I have read a woman's heart and learned to trust and honor what I have loved ever since I was a boy. Absence proved this to me: so I came to look for little Anna, and found her better and dearer than ever. May I ask her to keep on teaching me? Will she share my work as well as holiday, and be the truest friend a man can have?"

And Anna straightway answered, "Yes."

TRANSCENDENTAL WILD OATS

A CHAPTER FROM AN UNWRITTEN ROMANCE

ON the first day of June, 184–, a large wagon, drawn by a small horse and containing a motley load, went lumbering over certain New England hills, with the pleasing accompaniments of wind, rain, and hail. A serene man with a serene child upon his knee was driving, or rather being driven, for the small horse had it all his own way. A brown boy with a William Penn style of countenance sat beside him, firmly embracing a bust of Socrates. Behind them was an energetic-looking woman, with a benevolent brow, satirical mouth, and eyes brimful of hope and courage. A baby reposed upon her lap, a mirror leaned against her knee, and a basket of provisions danced about at her feet, as she struggled with a large, unruly umbrella. Two blue-eyed little girls, with hands full of childish treasures, sat under one old shawl, chatting happily together.

In front of this lively party stalked a tall, sharp-featured man, in a long blue cloak; and a fourth small girl trudged along beside him through the mud as if she rather enjoyed it.

The wind whistled over the bleak hills; the rain fell in a despondent drizzle, and twilight began to fall. But the calm man gazed as tranquilly into the fog as if he beheld a radiant bow of promise spanning the gray sky. The cheery woman tried to cover every one but herself with the big umbrella. The brown boy pillowed his head on the bald pate of Socrates and slumbered peacefully. The little girls sang lullabies to their dolls in soft, maternal murmurs. The sharp-nosed pedestrian marched steadily on, with the blue cloak streaming out behind him like a banner; and the lively infant splashed through the puddles with a duck-like satisfaction pleasant to behold.

Thus these modern pilgrims journeyed hopefully out of the old world, to found a new one in the wilderness.

The editors of "The Transcendental Tripod" had received from Messrs. Lion & Lamb (two of the aforesaid pilgrims) a communication from which the following statement is an extract:—

"We have made arrangements with the proprietor of an estate of about a hundred acres which liberates this tract from human ownership. Here we shall prosecute our effort to initiate a Family in harmony with the primitive instincts of man.

"Ordinary secular farming is not our object. Fruit, grain, pulse, herbs, flax, and other vegetable products, receiving assiduous attention, will afford ample manual occupation, and chaste supplies for the bodily needs. It is intended to adorn the pastures with orchards, and to supersede the labor of cattle by the spade and the pruning-knife.

"Consecrated to human freedom, the land awaits the sober culture of devoted men. Beginning with small pecuniary means, this enterprise must be rooted in a reliance on the succors of an ever-bounteous Providence, whose vital affinities being secured by this union with uncorrupted field and unworldly persons, the cares and injuries of a life of gain are avoided.

"The inner nature of each member of the Family is at no time neglected. Our plan contemplates all such disciplines, cultures, and habits as evidently conduce to the purifying of the inmates.

"Pledged to the spirit alone, the founders anticipate no hasty or numerous addition to their numbers. The kingdom of peace is entered only through the gates of self-denial; and felicity is the test and the reward of loyalty to the unswerving law of Love."

This prospective Eden at present consisted of an old red farm-house, a dilapidated barn, many acres of meadow-land, and a grove. Ten ancient apple-trees were all the "chaste supply" which the place offered as yet; but, in the firm belief that plenteous orchards were soon to be evoked from their inner consciousness, these sanguine founders had christened their domain Fruitlands.

Here Timon Lion intended to found a colony of Latter Day Saints, who, under his patriarchal sway, should regenerate the world and glorify his name for ever. Here Abel Lamb, with the devoutest faith in the high ideal which was to him a living truth, desired to plant a Paradise, where Beauty, Virtue, Justice, and Love might live happily together, without the possibility of a serpent entering in. And here his wife, unconverted but faithful to the end, hoped, after many wanderings over the face of the earth, to find rest for herself and a home for her children.

"There is our new abode," announced the enthusiast, smiling with a satisfaction quite undamped by the drops dripping from his hat-brim, as they turned at length into a cart-path that wound along a steep hillside into a barren-looking valley.

"A little difficult of access," observed his practical wife, as she endeavored to keep her various household gods from going overboard with every lurch of the laden ark.

"Like all good things. But those who earnestly desire and patiently seek will soon find us," placidly responded the philosopher from the mud, through which he was now endeavoring to pilot the much-enduring horse.

"Truth lies at the bottom of a well, Sister Hope," said Brother Timon, pausing to detach his small comrade from a gate, whereon she was perched for a clearer gaze into futurity.

"That 's the reason we so seldom get at it, I suppose," replied Mrs. Hope, making a vain clutch at the mirror, which a sudden jolt sent flying out of her hands.

"We want no false reflections here," said Timon, with a grim smile, as he crunched the fragments under foot in his onward march.

Sister Hope held her peace, and looked wistfully through the mist at her promised home. The old red house with a hospitable glimmer at its windows cheered her eyes; and, considering the weather, was a fitter refuge than the sylvan bowers some of the more ardent souls might have preferred.

The new-comers were welcomed by one of the elect precious, — a regenerate farmer, whose idea of reform consisted chiefly in wearing white cotton raiment and shoes of untanned leather. This costume, with a snowy beard, gave him a venerable, and at the same time a somewhat bridal appearance.

The goods and chattels of the Society not having arrived, the weary family reposed before the fire on blocks of wood, while Brother Moses White regaled them with roasted potatoes, brown bread and water, in two plates, a tin pan, and one mug; his table service being limited.

But, having cast the forms and vanities of a depraved world behind them, the elders welcomed hardship with the enthusiasm of new pioneers, and the children heartily enjoyed this foretaste of what they believed was to be a sort of perpetual picnic.

During the progress of this frugal meal, two more brothers appeared. One a dark, melancholy man, clad in homespun, whose peculiar mission was to turn his name hind part before and use as few words as possible. The other was a bland, bearded Englishman, who expected to be saved by eating uncooked food and going without clothes. He had not yet adopted the primitive costume, however; but contented himself with meditatively chewing dry beans out of a basket.

"Every meal should be a sacrament, and the vessels used beautiful and symbolical," observed Brother Lamb, mildly, righting the tin pan slipping about on his knees. "I priced a silver service when in town, but it was too costly; so I got some graceful cups and vases of Britannia ware."

"Hardest things in the world to keep bright. Will whiting be allowed in the community?" inquired Sister Hope, with a housewife's interest in labor-saving institutions.

"Such trivial questions will be discussed at a more fitting time," answered Brother Timon, sharply, as he burnt his fingers with a very hot potato. "Neither sugar, molasses, milk, butter, cheese, nor flesh are to be used among us, for nothing is to be admitted which has caused wrong or death to man or beast."

"Our garments are to be linen till we learn to raise our own cotton or some substitute for woollen fabrics," added Brother Abel, blissfully basking in an imaginary future as warm and brilliant as the generous fire before him.

"Haou abaout shoes?" asked Brother Moses, surveying his own with interest.

"We must yield that point till we can manufacture an innocent substitute for leather. Bark, wood, or some durable fabric will be invented in time. Meanwhile, those who desire to carry out our idea to the fullest extent can go barefooted," said Lion, who liked extreme measures.

"I never will, nor let my girls," murmured rebellious Sister Hope, under her breath.

"Haou do you cattle'ate to treat the ten-acre lot? Ef things ain't 'tended to right smart, we shan't hev no crops," observed the practical patriarch in cotton.

"We shall spade it," replied Abel, in such perfect good faith that Moses said no more, though he indulged in a shake of the head as he glanced at hands that had held nothing heavier than a pen for years. He was a paternal old soul and regarded the younger men as promising boys on a new sort of lark.

"What shall we do for lamps, if we cannot use any animal substance? I do hope light of some sort is to be thrown upon the enterprise," said Mrs. Lamb, with anxiety, for in those days kerosene and camphene were not, and gas unknown in the wilderness.

"We shall go without till we have discovered some vegetable oil or wax to serve us," replied Brother Timon, in a decided tone, which caused Sister Hope to resolve that her private lamp should be always trimmed, if not burning.

"Each member is to perform the work for which experience, strength, and taste best fit him," continued Dictator Lion. "Thus drudgery and disorder will be avoided and harmony prevail. We shall rise at dawn, begin the day by bathing, followed by music, and then a chaste repast of fruit and bread. Each one finds congenial occupation till the meridian meal; when some deep-searching conversation gives rest to the body and development to the mind. Healthful labor again engages us till the last meal, when we assemble in social communion, prolonged till sunset, when we retire to sweet repose, ready for the next day's activity."

"What part of the work do you incline to yourself?" asked Sister Hope, with a humorous glimmer in her keen eyes.

"I shall wait till it is made clear to me. Being in preference to doing is the great aim, and this comes to us rather by a resigned willingness than a wilful activity, which is a check to all divine growth," responded Brother Timon.

"I thought so." And Mrs. Lamb sighed audibly, for during the year he had spent in her family Brother Timon had so faithfully carried out his idea of "being, not doing," that she had found his "divine growth" both an expensive and unsatisfactory process.

Here her husband struck into the conversation, his face shining with the light and joy of the splendid dreams and high ideals hovering before him.

"In these steps of reform, we do not rely so much on scientific reasoning or physiological skill as on the spirit's dictates. The greater part of man's duty consists in leaving alone much that he now does. Shall I stimulate with tea, coffee, or wine? No. Shall I consume flesh? Not if I value health. Shall I subjugate cattle? Shall I claim property in any created thing? Shall I trade? Shall I adopt a form of religion? Shall I interest myself in politics? To how many of these questions — could we ask them deeply enough and could they be heard as having relation to our eternal welfare — would the response be 'Abstain'?"

A mild snore seemed to echo the last word of Abel's rhapsody, for Brother Moses had succumbed to mundane slumber and sat nodding like a massive ghost. Forest Absalom, the silent man, and John Pease, the English member, now departed to the barn; and Mrs. Lamb led her flock to a temporary fold, leaving the founders of the "Consociate Family" to build castles in the air till the fire went out and the symposium ended in smoke.

The furniture arrived next day, and was soon bestowed; for the principal property of the community consisted in books. To this rare library was devoted the best room in the house, and the few busts and pictures that still survived many flittings were added to beautify the sanctuary, for here the family was to meet for amusement, instruction, and worship.

Any housewife can imagine the emotions of Sister Hope, when she took possession of a large, dilapidated kitchen, containing an old stove and the peculiar stores out of which food was to be evolved for her little family of eleven. Cakes of maple sugar, dried peas and beans, barley and hominy, meal of all sorts, potatoes, and dried fruit. No milk, butter, cheese, tea, or meat, appeared. Even salt was considered a useless luxury and spice entirely forbidden by these lovers of Spartan simplicity. A ten years' experience of vegetarian vagaries had been good training for this new freak, and her sense of the ludicrous supported her through many trying scenes.

Unleavened bread, porridge, and water for breakfast; bread, vegetables, and water for dinner; bread, fruit, and water for supper was the bill of fare ordained by the elders. No teapot profaned that sacred stove, no gory steak cried aloud for vengeance from her chaste gridiron;

and only a brave woman's taste, time, and temper were sacrificed on that domestic altar.

The vexed question of light was settled by buying a quantity of bayberry wax for candles; and, on discovering that no one knew how to make them, pine knots were introduced, to be used when absolutely necessary. Being summer, the evenings were not long, and the weary fraternity found it no great hardship to retire with the birds. The inner light was sufficient for most of them. But Mrs. Lamb rebelled. Evening was the only time she had to herself, and while the tired feet rested the skilful hands mended torn frocks and little stockings, or anxious heart forgot its burden in a book.

So "mother's lamp" burned steadily, while the philosophers built a new heaven and earth by moonlight; and through all the metaphysical mists and philanthropic pyrotechnics of that period Sister Hope played her own little game of "throwing light," and none but the moths were the worse for it.

Such farming probably was never seen before since Adam delved. The band of brothers began by spading garden and field; but a few days of it lessened their ardor amazingly. Blistered hands and aching backs suggested the expediency of permitting the use of cattle till the workers were better fitted for noble toil by a summer of the new life.

Brother Moses brought a yoke of oxen from

his farm, — at least, the philosophers thought so till it was discovered that one of the animals was a cow; and Moses confessed that he "must be let down easy, for he could n't live on garden sarse entirely."

Great was Dictator Lion's indignation at this lapse from virtue. But time pressed, the work must be done; so the meek cow was permitted to wear the yoke and the recreant brother continued to enjoy forbidden draughts in the barn, which dark proceeding caused the children to regard him as one set apart for destruction.

The sowing was equally peculiar, for, owing to some mistake, the three brethren, who devoted themselves to this graceful task, found when about half through the job that each had been sowing a different sort of grain in the same field; a mistake which caused much perplexity, as it could not be remedied; but, after a long consultation and a good deal of laughter, it was decided to say nothing and see what would come of it.

The garden was planted with a generous supply of useful roots and herbs; but, as manure was not allowed to profane the virgin soil, few of these vegetable treasures ever came up. Purslane reigned supreme, and the disappointed planters ate it philosophically, deciding that Nature knew what was best for them, and would generously supply their needs, if they could only learn to digest her "sallets" and wild roots.

The orchard was laid out, a little grafting

done, new trees and vines set, regardless of the unfit season and entire ignorance of the husbandmen, who honestly believed that in the autumn they would reap a bounteous harvest.

Slowly things got into order, and rapidly rumors of the new experiment went abroad, causing many strange spirits to flock thither, for in those days communities were the fashion and transcendentalism raged wildly. Some came to look on and laugh, some to be supported in poetic idleness, a few to believe sincerely and work heartily. Each member was allowed to mount his favorite hobby and ride it to his heart's content. Very queer were some of the riders, and very rampant some of the hobbies.

One youth, believing that language was of little consequence if the spirit was only right, startled new-comers by blandly greeting them with "good morning, damn you," and other remarks of an equally mixed order. A second irrepressible being held that all the emotions of the soul should be freely expressed, and illustrated his theory by antics that would have sent him to a lunatic asylum, if, as an unregenerate wag said, he had not already been in one. When his spirit soared, he climbed trees and shouted; when doubt assailed him, he lay upon the floor and groaned lamentably. At joyful periods, he raced, leaped, and sang; when sad, he wept aloud; and when a great thought burst upon him in the watches of the night, he crowed like a jocund cockerel, to the great delight of the children and the great annoyance of the elders. One musical brother fiddled whenever so moved, sang sentimentally to the four little girls, and put a music-box on the wall when he hoed corn.

Brother Pease ground away at his uncooked food, or browsed over the farm on sorrel, mint, green fruit, and new vegetables. Occasionally he took his walks abroad, airily attired in an unbleached cotton *poncho,* which was the nearest approach to the primeval costume he was allowed to indulge in. At midsummer he retired to the wilderness, to try his plan where the woodchucks were without prejudices and huckleberry-bushes were hospitably full. A sunstroke unfortunately spoilt his plan, and he returned to semi-civilization a sadder and wiser man.

Forest Absalom preserved his Pythagorean silence, cultivated his fine dark locks, and worked like a beaver, setting an excellent example of brotherly love, justice, and fidelity by his upright life. He it was who helped overworked Sister Hope with her heavy washes, kneaded the endless succession of batches of bread, watched over the children, and did the many tasks left undone by the brethren, who were so busy discussing and defining great duties that they forgot to perform the small ones.

Moses White placidly plodded about, "chorin' raound," as he called it, looking like an old-time patriarch, with his silver hair and flowing beard, and saving the community from many a mishap by his thrift and Yankee shrewdness.

Brother Lion domineered over the whole concern; for, having put the most money into the speculation, he was resolved to make it pay,— as if anything founded on an ideal basis could be expected to do so by any but enthusiasts.

Abel Lamb simply revelled in the Newness, firmly believing that his dream was to be beautifully realized, and in time not only little Fruitlands, but the whole earth, be turned into a Happy Valley. He worked with every muscle of his body, for *he* was in deadly earnest. He taught with his whole head and heart; planned and sacrificed, preached and prophesied, with a soul full of the purest aspirations, most unselfish purposes, and desires for a life devoted to God and man, too high and tender to bear the rough usage of this world.

It was a little remarkable that only one woman ever joined this community. Mrs. Lamb merely followed wheresoever her husband led,—"as ballast for his balloon," as she said, in her bright way.

Miss Jane Gage was a stout lady of mature years, sentimental, amiable, and lazy. She wrote verses copiously, and had vague yearnings and graspings after the unknown, which led her to believe herself fitted for a higher sphere than any she had yet adorned.

Having been a teacher, she was set to instructing the children in the common branches. Each adult member took a turn at the infants; and, as each taught in his own way, the result was a chronic state of chaos in the minds of these much-afflicted innocents.

Sleep, food, and poetic musings were the desires of dear Jane's life, and she shirked all duties as clogs upon her spirit's wings. Any thought of lending a hand with the domestic drudgery never occurred to her; and when to the question, "Are there any beasts of burden on the place?" Mrs. Lamb answered, with a face that told its own tale, "Only one woman!" the buxom Jane took no shame to herself, but laughed at the joke, and let the stout-hearted sister tug on alone.

Unfortunately, the poor lady hankered after the fleshpots, and endeavored to stay herself with private sips of milk, crackers, and cheese, and on one dire occasion she partook of fish at a neighbor's table.

One of the children reported this sad lapse from virtue, and poor Jane was publicly reprimanded by Timon.

"I only took a little bit of the tail," sobbed the penitent poetess.

"Yes, but the whole fish had to be tortured and slain that you might tempt your carnal appetite with that one taste of the tail. Know ye not, consumers of flesh meat, that ye are nourishing the wolf and tiger in your bosoms?"

At this awful question and the peal of laughter which arose from some of the younger brethren, tickled by the ludicrous contrast between the stout sinner, the stern judge, and the naughty satisfaction of the young detective, poor Jane fled from the room to pack her trunk, and return to a world where fishes' tails were not forbidden fruit.

Transcendental wild oats were sown broadcast that year, and the fame thereof has not yet ceased in the land; for, futile as this crop seemed to outsiders, it bore an invisible harvest, worth much to those who planted in earnest. As none of the members of this particular community have ever recounted their experiences before, a few of them may not be amiss, since the interest in these attempts has never died out and Fruitlands was the most ideal of all these castles in Spain.

A new dress was invented, since cotton, silk, and wool were forbidden as the product of slave-labor, worm-slaughter, and sheep-robbery. Tunics and trowsers of brown linen were the only wear. The women's skirts were longer, and their straw hat-brims wider than the men's, and this was the only difference. Some persecution lent a charm to the costume, and the long-haired, linen-clad reformers quite enjoyed the mild martyrdom they endured when they left home.

Money was abjured, as the root of all evil. The produce of the land was to supply most of their wants, or be exchanged for the few things they could not grow. This idea had its inconveniences; but self-denial was the fashion, and it was surprising how many things one can do without. When they desired to travel, they walked, if possible, begged the loan of a vehicle, or boldly entered car or coach, and, stating their principles to the officials, took the consequences. Usually their dress, their earnest frankness, and gentle resolution won them a passage; but now and then they met with hard usage, and had the satisfaction of suffering for their principles.

On one of these penniless pilgrimages they took passage on a boat, and, when fare was demanded, artlessly offered to talk, instead of pay. As the boat was well under way and they actually had not a cent, there was no help for it. So Brothers Lion and Lamb held forth to the assembled passengers in their most eloquent style. There must have been something effective in this conversation, for the listeners were moved to take up a contribution for these inspired lunatics, who preached peace on earth and good-will to man so earnestly, with empty pockets. A goodly sum was collected; but when the captain presented it the reformers proved that they were consistent even in their madness, for not a penny would they accept, saying, with a look at the group about them, whose indifference or contempt had changed to interest and respect, "You see how well we get on without money;" and so went serenely on their way, with their linen blouses flapping airily in the cold October wind.

They preached vegetarianism everywhere and resisted all temptations of the flesh, contentedly eating apples and bread at well-spread tables, and much afflicting hospitable hostesses by denouncing their food and taking away their appetites, discussing the "horrors of shambles," the "incorporation of the brute in man," and "on elegant abstinence the sign of a pure soul." But, when the perplexed or offended ladies asked what they should eat, they got in reply a bill of fare consisting of "bowls of sunrise for breakfast," "solar seeds of the sphere," "dishes from Plutarch's chaste table," and other viands equally hard to find in any modern market.

Reform conventions of all sorts were haunted by these brethren, who said many wise things and did many foolish ones. Unfortunately, these wanderings interfered with their harvest at home; but the rule was to do what the spirit moved, so they left their crops to Providence and went a-reaping in wider and, let us hope, more fruitful fields than their own.

Luckily, the earthly providence who watched over Abel Lamb was at hand to glean the scanty crop yielded by the "uncorrupted land," which, "consecrated to human freedom," had received "the sober culture of devout men."

About the time the grain was ready to house, some call of the Oversoul wafted all the men away. An easterly storm was coming up and the yellow stacks were sure to be ruined. Then Sister Hope gathered her forces. Three little girls, one boy (Timon's son), and herself, harnessed to clothes-baskets and Russia-linen sheets, were the only teams she could command; but with these poor appliances the indomitable woman got in the grain and saved food for her young, with the instinct and energy of a mother-bird with a brood of hungry nestlings to feed.

This attempt at regeneration had its tragic as well as comic side, though the world only saw the former.

With the first frosts, the butterflies, who had sunned themselves in the new light through the summer, took flight, leaving the few bees to see what honey they had stored for winter use. Precious little appeared beyond the satisfaction of a few months of holy living.

At first it seemed as if a chance to try holy dying also was to be offered them. Timon, much disgusted with the failure of the scheme, decided to retire to the Shakers, who seemed to be the only successful community going.

"What is to become of us?" asked Mrs. Hope, for Abel was heart-broken at the bursting of his lovely bubble.

"You can stay here, if you like, till a tenant is found. No more wood must be cut, however, and no more corn ground. All I have must be sold to pay the debts of the concern, as the responsibility is mine," was the cheering reply.

"Who is to pay us for what we have lost? I gave all I had, — furniture, time, strength, six months of my children's lives, — and all are wasted. Abel gave himself body and soul, and is almost wrecked by hard work and disappointment. Are we to have no return for this, but leave to starve and freeze in an old house, with winter at hand, no money, and hardly a friend left, for this wild scheme has alienated nearly all we had. You talk much about justice. Let us have a little, since there is nothing else left."

But the woman's appeal met with no reply but the old one: "It was an experiment. We all risked something, and must bear our losses as we can."

With this cold comfort, Timon departed with his son, and was absorbed into the Shaker brotherhood, where he soon found that the order of things was reversed, and it was all work and no play.

Then the tragedy began for the forsaken little family. Desolation and despair fell upon Abel. As his wife said, his new beliefs had alienated many friends. Some thought him mad, some unprincipled. Even the most kindly thought him a visionary, whom it was useless to help till he took more practical views of life. All stood aloof, saying: "Let him work out his own ideas, and see what they are worth."

He had tried, but it was a failure. The world

was not ready for Utopia yet, and those who attempted to found it only got laughed at for their pains. In other days, men could sell all and give to the poor, lead lives devoted to holiness and high thought, and, after the persecution was over, find themselves honored as saints or martyrs. But in modern times these things are out of fashion. To live for one's principles, at all costs, is a dangerous speculation; and the failure of an ideal, no matter how humane and noble, is harder for the world to forgive and forget than bank robbery or the grand swindles of corrupt politicians.

Deep waters now for Abel, and for a time there seemed no passage through. Strength and spirits were exhausted by hard work and too much thought. Courage failed when, looking about for help, he saw no sympathizing face, no hand outstretched to help him, no voice to say cheerily, —

"We all make mistakes, and it takes many experiences to shape a life. Try again, and let us help you."

Every door was closed, every eye averted, every heart cold, and no way open whereby he might earn bread for his children. His principles would not permit him to do many things that others did; and in the few fields where conscience would allow him to work, who would employ a man who had flown in the face of society, as he had done?

Then this dreamer, whose dream was the life of his life, resolved to carry out his idea to the bitter end. There seemed no place for him here, — no work, no friend. To go begging conditions was as ignoble as to go begging money. Better perish of want than sell one's soul for the sustenance of his body. Silently he lay down upon his bed, turned his face to the wall, and waited with pathetic patience for death to cut the knot which he could not untie. Days and nights went by, and neither food nor water passed his lips. Soul and body were dumbly struggling together, and no word of complaint betrayed what either suffered.

His wife, when tears and prayers were unavailing, sat down to wait the end with a mysterious awe and submission; for in this entire resignation of all things there was an eloquent significance to her who knew him as no other human being did.

"Leave all to God," was his belief; and in this crisis the loving soul clung to this faith, sure that the All-wise Father would not desert this child who tried to live so near to Him. Gathering her children about her, she waited the issue of the tragedy that was being enacted in that solitary room, while the first snow fell outside, untrodden by the footprints of a single friend.

But the strong angels who sustain and teach perplexed and troubled souls came and went, leaving no trace without, but working miracles within. For, when all other sentiments had faded into dimness, all other hopes died utterly; when the bitterness of death was nearly over, when body was past any pang of hunger or thirst, and soul stood ready to depart, the love that outlives all else refused to die. Head had bowed to defeat, hand had grown weary with too heavy tasks, but heart could not grow cold to those who lived in its tender depths, even when death touched it.

"My faithful wife, my little girls, — they have not forsaken me, they are mine by ties that none can break. What right have I to leave them alone? What right to escape from the burden and the sorrow I have helped to bring? This duty remains to me, and I must do it manfully. For their sakes, the world will forgive me in time; for their sakes, God will sustain me now."

Too feeble to rise, Abel groped for the food that always lay within his reach, and in the darkness and solitude of that memorable night ate and drank what was to him the bread and wine of a new communion, a new dedication of heart and life to the duties that were left him when the dreams fled.

In the early dawn, when that sad wife crept fearfully to see what change had come to the patient face on the pillow, she found it smiling at her, saw a wasted hand outstretched to her, and heard a feeble voice cry bravely, "Hope!"

What passed in that little room is not to be recorded except in the hearts of those who suffered and endured much for love's sake. Enough for us to know that soon the wan shadow of a man came forth, leaning on the arm that never failed him, to be welcomed and cherished by the children, who never forgot the experiences of that time.

"Hope" was the watchword now; and, while the last logs blazed on the hearth, the last bread and apples covered the table, the new commander, with recovered courage, said to her husband, —

"Leave all to God — and me. He has done his part; now I will do mine."

"But we have no money, dear."

"Yes, we have. I sold all we could spare, and have enough to take us away from this snowbank."

"Where can we go?"

"I have engaged four rooms at our good neighbor, Lovejoy's. There we can live cheaply till spring. Then for new plans and a home of our own, please God."

"But, Hope, your little store won't last long, and we have no friends."

"I can sew and you can chop wood. Lovejoy offers you the same pay as he gives his other men; my old friend, Mrs. Truman, will send me all the work I want; and my blessed brother stands by us to the end. Cheer up, dear heart, for while there is work and love in the world we shall not suffer."

"And while I have my good angel Hope, I shall not despair, even if I wait another thirty years before I step beyond the circle of the sacred little world in which I still have a place to fill."

So one bleak December day, with their few possessions piled on an ox-sled, the rosy children perched atop, and the parents trudging arm in arm behind, the exiles left their Eden and faced the world again.

"Ah, me! my happy dream. How much I leave behind that never can be mine again," said Abel, looking back at the lost Paradise, lying white and chill in its shroud of snow.

"Yes, dear; but how much we bring away," answered brave-hearted Hope, glancing from husband to children.

"Poor Fruitlands! The name was as great a failure as the rest!" continued Abel, with a sigh, as a frost-bitten apple fell from a leafless bough at his feet.

But the sigh changed to a smile as his wife added, in a half-tender, half-satirical tone, —

"Don't you think Apple Slump would be a better name for it, dear?"

THE ROMANCE OF A SUMMER DAY

"WHAT shall we do about Rose? We have tried Saratoga, and that failed to cheer her up; we tried the seashore, and that failed; now we have tried the mountains, and they are going to fail, like the rest. See if your woman's wit can't devise something to help the child, Milly."

"Time and tenderness will work the cure; and she will be all the better for this experience, I hope."

"So do I. But I don't pretend to understand these nervous ailments; so, if air, exercise, and change of scene don't cure the vapors, I give it up. Girls did n't have such worries in my day."

And the old gentleman shook his head, as if modern ills perplexed him very much.

But Milly smiled the slow, wise smile of one who had learned much from experience; among other things, the wisdom of leaving certain troubles to cure themselves.

"Has the child expressed a wish for any thing? If so, out with it, and she shall be gratified, if it can be done," began Uncle Ben, after a moment of silence, as they sat watching the moonlight, that glorified the summer night.

"The last wish is one that we can easily gratify, if you don't mind the fatigue. The restless spirit that possesses her keeps suggesting new things. Much exercise does her good, and is an excellent way to work off this unrest. She likes to tire herself out; for then she sleeps, poor dear."

"Well, well, what does the poor dear want to do?" asked Uncle Ben, quickly.

"She said to-day that, instead of going off on excursions, as we have been doing, she would like to stroll away some pleasant morning, and follow the road wherever it led, finding and enjoying any little adventures that might come along, — as Richter's heroes do."

"Yes, I see: white butterflies, morning red, disguised counts, philosophic plowmen, and all the rest of the romantic rubbish. Bless the child, does she expect to find things of that sort anywhere out of a German novel?"

"Plenty of butterflies and morning-glories, uncle, and a girl's imagination will supply the romance. Perhaps we can get up some little surprise to add flavor to our day's adventures," said Milly, who rather favored the plan, for much romance still lay hidden in that quiet heart of hers.

"Where shall we go? What shall we do? I don't know how this sort of thing is managed."

"Do nothing but follow us. Let her choose her road; and we will merely see that she has food and rest, protection, and as much pleasure as we can make for her out of such simple materials. Having her own way will gratify her, and a day in the open air do her good. Shall we try it, sir?"

"With all my heart, if the fancy lasts till morning. I'll have some lunch put up, and order Jim to dawdle after us with the wagon full of waterproofs, and so on, in case we break down. I rather like the idea, now I fairly take it in." And Uncle Ben quite beamed with interest and good-will; for a kinder-hearted man never breathed, and, in spite of his fifty years, he was as fond of adventures as any boy.

"Then, as we must be up and away very early, I'll say good-night, sir," and Milly rose to go, looking well satisfied with the success of her suggestion.

"Good-night, my dear," and Uncle Ben rose also, flung away his cigar, and offered his hand with the old-fashioned courtesy which he always showed his niece's friend; for Milly only called him uncle to please him.

"You are sure this wild whim won't be too much for *you?* You are such a self-sacrificing soul, I'm afraid my girl will wear you out," he said, looking down at her with a fatherly expression, very becoming to his comely countenance.

"Not a bit, sir. I like it, and would gladly do any thing to please and help Rose. I 'm very fond of her, and love to pet and care for her. I 'm so alone in the world I cling to my few friends, and feel as if I could n't do enough for them."

Something in Milly's face made Uncle Ben hold her hand close in both of his a moment, and look as if he was going to stoop and kiss her. But he seemed to think better of it; for he only shook the soft hand warmly, and said, in his hearty tone, —

"I don't know what we should do without you, my dear. You are one of the women born to help and comfort others, and ask no reward but love."

As the first streaks of dawn touched the eastern sky three faces appeared at three different windows of the great hotel. One was a masculine face, a ruddy, benevolent countenance, with kind eyes, grayish hair cheerfully erect upon the head, and a smile on the lips, that softly whistled the old air of

"A southerly wind and a cloudy sky
Proclaim a hunting morning."

The second was one of those serene, sweet faces, possessing an attraction more subtle than beauty; eyes always full of silent sympathy, a little wistful sometimes, but never sad, and an expression of peace and patience that told of battles fought and victories won. A happy, helpful soul shone from that face and made it lovely, though its first bloom was past and a solitary future lay before it.

The third was rich in the charms that youth and health lend any countenance. But, in spite of the bloom on the rounded cheeks, the freshness of the lips, and the soft beauty of the eyes, the face that looked out from the bonny brown hair, blowing in the wind, was not a happy one. Discontent, unrest, and a secret hunger seemed to sadden and sharpen all its outlines, making it pathetic to those who could read the language of an unsatisfied heart.

Poor little Rose was waiting, as all women must wait, for the good gift that brightens life; and, while she waited, patience and passion were having a hard fight in the silence of her heart.

"It will be a capital day, girls," called Uncle Ben, in his cheery voice.

"I thought it would be," answered Milly, nodding back, with a smile.

"I know it will pour before night," added Rose, who saw everything just then through blue spectacles.

"Breakfast is ready for us. Come on, girls, or you 'll miss your morning red," called Uncle Ben, retiring, with a laugh.

"I lost mine six months ago," sighed Rose, as she listlessly gathered up the brown curls, that were once her pride.

"Hark! hark! the lark at Heaven's gate sings," sounded from Milly's room, in her blithe voice.

"Tiresome little bird! Why don't he stay in his nest and cheer his mate?" muttered Rose, refusing to be cheered.

"Now lead on, my dear, we'll follow till we drop," said Uncle Ben, stoutly, as they stood on the piazza, half an hour later, with no one but a sleepy waiter to watch and wonder at the early start.

"I have always wondered where that lonely road went to, and now I shall find out," answered Rose, with an imperious little gesture, as she led the way. The others followed so slowly that she felt alone, and enjoyed it, in spite of herself.

It was the most eloquent hour of the day, for all was beautiful, all was fresh; nothing was out of order, nothing disturbed eye or ear, and the world seemed to welcome her with its morning face. The road wound between forests full of the green gloom no artist can ever paint. Pines whispered, birches quivered, maples dropped grateful shadows, and a little river foamed and sparkled by, carrying its melodious message from the mountains to the sea. Glimpses of hoary peaks broke on her now and then, dappled with shadows or half-veiled in mists, floating and fading like incense from altars fit for a cathedral not built with hands. Leafy vistas opened temptingly on either side, berries blushed ripely in the grass, cow-bells tinkled pleasantly along the hillsides, and that busy little farmer, the "Peabody bird," cried from tree to tree, "Sow your wheat, Peabody! Peabody! Peabody!" with such musical energy one ceased to wonder that fields were wrested from the forest, to wave like green and golden breast-knots on the bosoms of the hills.

The fresh beauty and the healthful peace of the hour refreshed the girl like dew. The human rose lifted up her drooping head and smiled back at the blithe sunshine, as if she found the world a pleasant place, in spite of her own thorns. Presently a yellow butterfly came wandering by; and she watched it as she walked, pleasing herself with the girlish fancy that it was a symbol of herself.

At first it fluttered idly from side to side, now lighting on a purple thistle-top, then away to swing on a dewy fern; now vanishing among the low-hanging boughs overhead, then settling in the dust of the road, where a ray of light glorified its golden wings, unmindful of its lowly seat.

"Little Psyche is looking for her Cupid everywhere, as I have looked for mine. I wonder if she ever found and lost him, as I did? If she does find him again, I'll accept it as a good omen."

Full of this fancy, Rose walked quickly after her airy guide, leaving her comrades far behind.

Some tender-hearted spirit surely led that butterfly, for it never wandered far away, but floated steadily before the girl, till it came at last to a wild rose-bush, full of delicate blossoms. Above it a cloud of yellow butterflies were dancing in the sun; and from among them one flew to meet and welcome the new-comer. Together they fluttered round the rosy flowers for a moment, then rose in graceful circles, till they vanished in the wood.

Rose followed them with eyes that slowly dimmed with happy tears, for the innocent soul accepted the omen and believed it gratefully.

"He will come," she said softly to herself, as she fastened a knot of wild roses in her bosom and sat down to rest and wait.

"Tired out, little girl?" asked Uncle Ben, coming up at a great pace, rather amazed at this sudden burst of energy, but glad to see it.

"No, indeed! It was lovely!" and Rose looked up with a brighter face than she had worn for weeks.

"Upon my word, I think we have hit upon the right thing at last," said Uncle Ben, aside, to Milly. "What have you been doing to get such a look as that?" he added aloud.

"Chasing butterflies," was all the answer Rose gave; for she could not tell the foolish little fancy that had comforted her so much.

"Then, my dear, I beg you will devote yourself to that amusement. I never heard it recommended, but it seems to be immensely beneficial; so keep it up, Rosy, keep it up."

"I will, sir," and on went Rose, as if in search of another one.

For an hour or two she strolled along the woody road, gathering red raspberries, with the dew still on them, garlanding her hat with fragrant Linnæa wreaths, watching the brown brooks go singing away into the forest, and wishing the little wood creatures good-morrow, as they went fearlessly to and fro, busy with their sylvan housekeeping. At every turn of the road Rose's wistful eyes looked forward, as if hoping to see some much-desired figure approaching. At every sound of steps she lifted her head like a deer, listening and watching till the stranger had gone by; and down every green vista she sent longing looks, as if memory recalled happy hours in green nooks like those.

Presently the road wound over a bridge, below which flowed a wide, smooth river, flecked with alternate sun and shadow.

"How beautiful it is! I must float down this stream a little way. It is getting warm and I am tired, yet don't want to stop or turn back yet," said Rose; adding, as her quick eye roved to and fro: "I see a boat down there, and a man reading. I'll hire or borrow it; so come on."

Away she went into the meadow, and, accosting the countryman, who lay in the shade, she made her request.

"I get my livin' in summer by rowin' folks down to the Falls. It ain't fur. Will you go, Miss?" he said, smiling all over his brown face, as he regarded the pretty vision that so suddenly appeared beside him.

Rose accepted the proposition at once; but half regretted it a minute after, for, as the man rose, she saw that he had a wooden leg.

"I'm afraid we shall be too heavy a load for you," she began, as he stumped about, preparing his boat.

The young fellow laughed and squared his broad shoulders, with a quick look, that thanked her for the pitiful glance she gave him, as he answered, in a bluff, good-natured tone, —

"Don't be afraid. I could row a dozen of you. I look rather the worse for wear; but my old mother thinks I'm about the strongest man in the State. Now, then, give us your hand, Miss, and there you are."

With that he helped her in. The others obediently followed their capricious leader, and in a moment they were floating down the river, with a fresh wind cooling their hot faces.

"You have been in the army, I take it?" began Uncle Ben, in his social way, as he watched the man pulling with long, easy strokes.

"Pretty nigh through the war, sir," with a nod and a glance at the wooden leg.

Uncle Ben lifted his hat, and Rose turned with a sudden interest from the far-off bend of the river to the honest face before her.

"Oh! tell us about it. I love to hear brave men fight their battles over," she cried, with a look half pleading, half commanding, and wholly charming.

"Sho! It ain't much to tell. No more than the rest of 'em; not so much as some. I done my best, lost my leg, got a few bullets here and there, and ain't much use any way now."

A shadow passed over the man's face as he spoke; and well it might, for it was hard to be disabled at twenty-five with a long life of partial helplessness before him. Uncle Ben, who was steering, forgot his duty in his sympathy, and regarded the wooden leg with silent interest.

Milly showed hers by keeping the mosquitoes off him by gently waving a green bough, as she sat behind him. But Rose's soft eyes shone upon him full of persuasive interest, and a new tone of respect was in her voice as she said, with a martial salute, —

"Please tell about your last battle. I had a cousin in the war, and feel as if every soldier was my friend and comrade since then."

"Thanky, Miss. I'll tell you that with pleasure, though it ain't much, any way." And, pushing back his hat, the young man rested on his oars, as he rapidly told his little tale.

"My last battle was ——," naming one of the latest and bloodiest of the war. "We were doing our best, when there came a shell and scattered half-a-dozen of us pretty lively. I was knocked flat. But I did n't feel hurt, only mad, and jumped up to hit 'em agin; but just dropped, with an awful wrench, and the feeling that both my legs was gone."

"Did no one stop to help you?" cried Rose.

"Too busy for that, Miss. The boys can't stop to pick up their mates when there are Rebs ahead to be knocked down. I knew there was no more fighting for me; and just laid still, with the balls singing round me, and wondering where they 'd hit next."

"How did you feel?" questioned the girl, eagerly.

"Dreadful busy at first; for every thing I 'd ever said, seen, or done, seemed to go spinning through my head, till I got so dizzy trying to keep my wits stiddy that I lost 'em altogether. I did n't find 'em again till some one laid hold of me. Two of our boys were luggin' me along back; but they had to dodge behind walls and cut up and down, for the scrimmage was going on all round us. One of the fellers was hit in the shoulder and the other in the face, but not bad; and they managed to get me into a sort of a ravine, out of danger. There I begged 'em to leave me. I thought I was bleeding to death rapid, and just wanted to die in peace."

"But they did n't leave you?" And Rose's face was all alive with interest now.

"Guess they did n't," answered the man, giving a stroke or two, and looking as if he found it pleasant to tell his story to so winsome a listener. "Just as they were at their wit's end what to do with me, we come upon a young surgeon, lurking there to watch the fight or to hide, — don't know which. There he was any way, looking scared half to death. Tom Hunt, my mate, made him stop and look at me. My leg was smashed, and ought to come off right away, he said. 'Do it, then!' says Tom. He was one of your rough-and-readys, Tom was; but at heart as kind as a — well, as a woman."

And the boatman gave a smile and a nod at the one opposite him.

"Thanks; but do tell on. It is *so* interesting."

And Rose let all her flowers stray down into the bottom of the boat, as she clasped her hands and leaned forward to listen.

"Don't know as I 'd better tell this part. It ain't pleasant," began the man.

"You must. I want it all. Dreadful things do me good, and other people's sufferings teach me how to bear my own," said Rose, in her imperious way.

"You don't look as if you ought to have any."

And the man's eyes rested on the delicate face opposite, full of a pleasant blending of admiration, pity and protection.

"I have; but not like yours. Go on, please."

"Well, if you say so, here goes. The surgeon was worried, and said he could n't do nothing, — had n't got his instruments, and so on. 'Yes, you have. Out with 'em,' says Tom, rapping on a case he sees in the chap's breast-pocket. 'Can't do it without bandages,' he says next. 'Here they are, and more where they came from,' says Tom; and off came his shirt-sleeves, and was stripped up in a jiffy. 'I must have help,' says that confounded surgeon, dawdling round, and me groaning my life out at his feet. 'Here 's help, — lots of it,' says Tom, taking my head on his arm; while Parkes tied up his wounded face and stood ready to lend a hand. Seeing no way out of it, the surgeon went to work. Good Lord, but that *was* awful!"

The mere memory of it made the speaker shut his eyes with a shiver, as if he felt again the sharp agony of shattered bones, rent flesh, and pitiless knife.

"Never mind that. Tell how you got comfortable again," said Milly, shaking her head at Rose.

"I was n't comfortable for three months, ma'am. Don't mind telling about it, 'cause Tom done so well, and I 'm proud of him," said the rower, with kindling eyes. "Things of that sort are hard enough done well, with chloroform and every thing handy. But laying on the bare ground, with nothing right, and a scared boy of a surgeon hacking away at you, it 's torment and no mistake. I never could have stood it, if it had n't been for Tom. He held me close and as steady as a rock; but he cried like a baby the whole time, and that did me good. Don't know why; but it did. As for Parkes, he gave out at once and went off for help. I 'll never forget that place, if I live to be a hundred. Seems as if I could see the very grass I tore up; the muddy brook they laid me by; the steep bank, with Parkes creeping up; Tom's face, wet and white, but so full of pity; the surgeon, with his red hands; and all the while such a roar of guns I could hardly hear myself groaning for some one to shoot me and put me out of my misery."

"How did you get to the hospital?" asked Uncle Ben, anxious to get over this part of the story, for Rose was now as pale as if she actually saw the scene described.

"Don't know, sir. There come a time when I could n't bear any more, and what happened then I 've never been very clear about. I did n't know much for a day or two; then I was brought round by being put in a transport. I was packed with a lot of poor fellows, and was beginning to wish I 'd stayed queer, till I heard Tom's voice saying, 'Never mind, boys; put me down anywheres, and tend to the others. I can wait.' That set me up. I sung out, and they stowed him alongside. It was so dark down there I could hardly see his face; but his voice and ways were just as hearty and comforting as ever, and he kept up my spirits wonderful that day. I was pretty weak, and kept dozing off; but whenever I woke I felt for Tom, and he was always there.

He told me, when Parkes came with help, he saw me off, and then went back for another go at the Rebs; but got a ball in the breast, and was in rather a bad way, he guessed. He could n't lay down; but sat by me, leaning back, with his hand on my pillow, where I could find it easy. He talked to me all he could, till his voice give out; for he got very weak, and there was a dreadful groaning all around us."

"I know, I know. I went aboard one of those transports to help; but could n't stay, it was so terrible," said Uncle Ben, with a groan at the mere memory of it.

"That was a long day, and I thought it was my last; for when night came I felt so gone I reckoned I was 'most over Jordan. I gave my watch to Tom as a keepsake, and told him to say good-by to the boys for me. I had n't any folks of my own, so it was n't hard to go. Tom had a sweetheart, an old mother, and lots of friends; but he did n't repine a word, — only said: 'If you do pull through, Joel, just tell mother I done my best, and give Hetty my love.' I promised, and dropped asleep, holding on to Tom as if he was my sheet-anchor. So he was; but I can't tell all he done for me in different ways."

For a minute Joel rowed in silence, and no one asked a question. Then he pushed up his old hat again, and went on, as if anxious to be done.

"Soon 's ever I woke, next morning, I looked round to thank Tom, for his blanket was over me. He was sitting as I left him, his hand on my pillow, his face toward me, so quiet and happy-looking I could n't believe he was gone. But he was, and I have had no mate since."

"Where did he live?" asked Rose, as softly as if speaking of one she had known and loved.

"Over yonder." And Joel pointed to a little brown house on the hillside.

"Are his mother and Hetty there?"

"Hetty married a number of years ago; but the old lady is there."

"And you are visiting her?"

"I live with her. You see Tom was all she had; and, when Hetty left, it was only natural that I tried to take Tom's place. Can't never fill it of course; but I do what I can, and she 's comfortable."

"So *she* is the 'old mother' who thinks so much of you? Well she may," said Rose, giving him her brightest smile.

"Yes, she 's all I 've got now. Could n't do no less, could I, seein' how much Tom done for me?" answered the man, with a momentary quiver of emotion in his rough voice.

"You 're a trump!" said Uncle Ben, emphatically.

"Thanky, sir. Starboard, if you please. I don't care to get into the rapids just here."

Joel seemed to dislike telling this part of the story; but the three listeners beamed upon him with such approving faces that he took to his oars in self-defence, rowing with all his might, till the roar of the Falls was faintly heard.

"Now, where shall I land you, sir?"

"Let us lunch on the island," proposed Rose.

"I see a tent, and fancy some one is camping there," said Milly.

"A lot of young fellows have been there this three days," said Joel.

"Then we will go on, and take to the grove above the Fall," ordered Uncle Ben.

Alas! alas! for Rose. That decision delayed her happiness a whole half day; for on that island, luxuriously reading "The Lotus Eaters," as he lay in the long grass, was the Gabriel this modern Evangeline was waiting for. She never dreamed he was so near. And the brown-bearded student never lifted up his head as the boat floated by, carrying the lady of his love.

"I want to give him more than his fare. So I shall slip my cigar-case into the pocket of this coat," whispered Uncle Ben, as Joel was busy drawing up the boat and getting a stone or two to facilitate the ladies' landing dryshod.

"I shall leave my book for him. He was poring over an old newspaper, as if hungry for reading. The dash and daring of 'John Brent' will charm him; and the sketch of Winthrop's life in the beginning will add to its value, I know." And, hastily scribbling his name in it, Rose slipped the book under the coat.

But Milly, seeing how old that coat was,

guessed that Joel gave his earnings to the old woman to whom he dutifully played a son's part. Writing on a card "For Tom's mother and mate," she folded a five-dollar bill round it, fastened it with a little pearl cross from her own throat, and laid it in the book.

Then all landed, and, with a cordial hand-shake and many thanks, left Joel to row away, quite unconscious that he was a hero in the pretty girl's eyes, till he found the tokens of his passengers' regard and respect.

"Now that is an adventure after my own heart," said Rose, as they rustled along the grassy path toward the misty cloud that hung over the Fall.

"We have nothing but sandwiches and sherry for lunch, unless we find a house and add to our stores," said Uncle Ben, beginning to feel hungry and wondering how far his provisions would go.

"There is a little girl picking berries. Call her and buy some," suggested Milly, who had her doubts about the state of the sandwiches, as the knapsack had been sat upon.

A shout from Uncle Ben caused the little girl to approach, — timidly at first; but, being joined by a boy, her courage rose, and when the idea of a "trade" was impressed upon their minds fear was forgotten and the Yankee appeared.

"How much a quart?"

"Eight cents, sir."

"But that birch-bark thing is not full."

"Now it is," and the barefooted, tow-headed lad filled the girl's pannier from his own.

"Here 's chivalry for you," said Rose, watching the children with interest; for the girl was pretty, and the boy evidently not her brother.

"You don't pick as fast as she does," said Milly, while Uncle Ben hunted up the money.

"He 's done his stent, and was helpin' me. I 'll have to pick a lot before I git my quarter," said the girl, defending her friend, in spite of her bashfulness.

"Must you each make a quarter?"

"Yes 'm. We don't have to; but we wanter, so we can go to the circus that 's comin' to-morrer. He made his'n ketchin' trout; so he 's helpin' me," explained the girl.

"Where do you get your trout?" asked Uncle Ben, sniffing the air, as if he already smelt them cooking.

"In the brook. I ain't sold mine yet. Want to buy 'em? Six big ones for a quarter," said the boy, seeing hunger in the good man's eye and many greenbacks in the corpulent purse.

"Yes, if you 'll clean them."

"But, Uncle, we can't cook them," began Milly.

"*I* can. Let an old campaigner alone for getting up a gipsy lunch. You wanted a surprise; so I 'll give you one. Now, Billy, bring on your fish."

"My name is Daniel Webster Butterfield Brown," returned the boy, with dignity; adding, with a comical change of tone: "Them fish *is* cleaned, or you 'd a got 'em cheaper."

"Very well. Hand them over."

Off ran the boy to the brook; and the girl was shyly following, when Rose said, —

"Will you sell me that pretty bark pannier of yours? I want one for my flowers."

"No 'm. I guess I 'd ruther not."

"I 'll give you a quarter for it. Then you can go to the circus without working any more."

"Dan made this for me, real careful; and I could n't sell it, no way. He would n't go without me. And I 'll pick stiddy all day, and git my money. See if I don't!" answered the child, hugging her treasure close.

"Here 's your romance in the bud," said Uncle Ben, trying not to laugh.

"It 's beautiful!" said Rose, with energy. "What is your name, dear?"

"Gusty Medders, please 'm."

"Dan is n't your brother?"

"No 'm. He lives to the poor-house. But he 's real smart, and we play together. And him and me is going to the show. He always takes care o' me; and my mother thinks a sight of him, and so do I," returned the child, in a burst of confidence.

"Happy little Gusty!" said Rose, to herself.

"Thrice happy Dan," added Uncle Ben, producing the fat pocket-book again, with the evident intention of bestowing a fortune on the small couple.

"Don't spoil the pretty little romance. Don't rob it of its self-sacrifice and simplicity. Let them earn their money. Then they will enjoy it more," cried Milly, holding his hand.

Uncle Ben submitted, and paid Dan his price, without adding a penny.

"The lady wanted to buy my basket. But I did n't sell it, Danny; 'cause you give it as a keepsake," they heard Gusty say, as the children turned away.

"Good for you, Gus; but I 'll sell mine." And back came Dan, to dispose of his for the desired quarter. "Now we 're fixed complete, and you need n't pick a darned berry. We 've got fifty cents for the show, and eight over for peanuts and candy. Won't we have a good time, though?"

With which joyful remark Dan turned a somersault, and then the little pair vanished in the wood, with shining faces, to revel in visions of the splendors to come.

"Now you have got your elephant, what are you going to do with him?" asked Rose, as they went on again, — she with her pretty basket of fruit, and he with a string of fish wrapped in leaves.

"Come on a bit, and you will see."

Uncle Ben led them to the shade of a great

maple, on a green slope, in sight of the noisy Fall, leaping from rock to rock, till the stream went singing away through wide, green meadows below.

"Now rest and cool yourselves, while I cook the dinner." And away bustled the good man, on hospitable thoughts intent.

Plenty of dry drift-wood lay about the water-course, and soon a brisk fire burned on the rocks not far away. Shingles for plates, with pointed sticks for forks, seemed quite in keeping with the rustic feast; and when the edibles were set forth on leaves the girls were charmed, and praised the trout, as it came hot from the coals, till even the flushed cook was satisfied.

"I 'd like to live so always. It is so interesting to pick up your food as you go, and eat it when and where you like. I think I could be quite happy leading a wild life like this," said Rose, as she lay in the grass, dropping berries one by one into her mouth.

"You would soon tire of it, Miss Caprice; but, if it amuses for a single day, I am satisfied," answered Milly, with her motherly smile, as she stroked the bright head in her lap, feeling sure that happiness was in store for so much youth and beauty.

Lulled by the soft caress, and the song of the waterfall, Rose fell asleep, and for an hour dreamed blissfully, while the maple dropped its shadows on her placid face, and all the wholesome influences of the place worked their healing spell on soul and body.

" A thunder-shower is rolling up in the west, my dears. We must be getting toward some shelter, unless we are to take a drenching as part of the day's pleasure," said Uncle Ben, rising briskly after his own nap.

" I see no house anywhere; but a big barn down in the intervale, and a crowd of people getting in their hay. Let us make for that, and lie on the sweet hay-cocks till the shower comes," proposed Milly.

As they went down the steep path, Rose began to sing; and at the unwonted sound her uncle and friend exchanged glances of satisfaction, for not a note had she sung for weeks. A happy mood seemed to have taken possession of her; and when they reached the intervale she won the old farmer's heart by catching up a rake and working stoutly, till the first heavy drops began to fall. Then she rode up to the barn on a fragrant load, and was so charmed with the place that she declined his invitation to " Come up and see the old woman and set a spell," and declared that she depended on enjoying the thunder-storm where she was.

The farmer and his men went their way, and Rose was just settling herself at the upper window, where the hay had been pitched in, when a long line of gay red vans came rattling down the road, followed by carriages and gilded cars, elephants and camels, fine horses and frisky ponies, all more or less excited by the coming storm.

"It 's the circus! How I wish Gusty and Dan could see it!" cried Rose, clapping her hands like a child. "I do believe they are coming here. Now that will be charming, and the best adventure of all," she added, as a carriage and several vans turned into the grassy road leading to the barn.

A pair of elephants slowly lumbered after, with a camel or two, and the finest gilded car. The rest rattled on, hoping to reach the town in time. In a moment the quiet country scene was changed, and the big barn transformed into a theatrical Babel.

Our party retreated to a loft, and sat looking down on the show, enjoying it heartily; especially Rose, who felt as if suddenly translated into an Eastern tale. The storm came on dark and wild, rain poured, thunder rolled, and lightning gave lurid glimpses of the strange surroundings.

The elephants placidly ate hay; the tired camels lay down with gusty sighs and queer groanings; but the lion in his lonely van roared royally at intervals, and the tigers snarled and tore about their cage like restless demons.

The great golden car lit up the gloom; and in it sat, or lay, the occupants of the carriage, — a big, dark man, and a little blonde creature, with a pretty, tired, painted face. Rose soon found herself curiously attracted to this pair, for they were evidently lovers; and there was a certain frank, melodramatic air about them that took her fancy. The dark man lay on the red cushion, smoking tranquilly; while the girl hovered about him with all manner of small attentions. Presently he seemed to drop asleep, undisturbed by the thunder without or the clamor within. Then the small creature smoothed her gay yet shabby dress, and braided up her hair, as composedly as if in her own room. That done, she looked about her for amusement; and, spying Rose's interested face peering down at her from above, she nodded, and called out, in a saucy voice, —

"How do you like us? Shall I come up and make you a visit?"

"I beg you will," answered Rose, in spite of a warning touch from Milly.

Up sprang the little circus-rider; and, disdaining the ladder, skipped to the gilded dome of the car, and then took a daring leap on to the loft, landing near them with a laugh.

For a minute she eyed the others with a curious mixture of coolness and hesitation, as if it suddenly struck her that they were not country girls, to be dazzled by her audacity. Milly saw and understood the pause, liked the girl for it, and said, as courteously as if to a lady in her own parlor, —

"There is plenty of room for us all. Pray sit down and enjoy this fine view with us. The storm is passing over now, and it will soon be fair."

"Thank you!" said the girl, dropping on to the hay, with her bold, bright eyes, full of admiration, fixed on Rose, who smiled, and said quickly, —

"You belong to the troop, I suppose?"

"First lady rider," replied the girl, with a toss of the head.

"It must be very romantic to lead such a life, and go driving from place to place in this way."

"It 's a hard life, anyway; and not much romance, you 'd better believe."

"Not even for *you*." And Rose glanced at the sleeper below.

The girl smiled. Her bold eyes turned to him with a softened look, and the natural color deepened on her painted cheeks, as she said, in a lower voice, —

"Yes, Joe does make a difference for me. We 've only been married three weeks."

"What does he do?"

"He 's the lion-tamer." And the girl gave them a glance of wifely pride in her husband's prowess.

"Oh! tell me about it!" cried Rose. "I admire courage so much."

"You ought to see him do Daniel in the lion's den, then. Or his great tiger act, where he piles four of 'em up, and lays on top. It 's just splendid!"

"But very dangerous! Does he never fear them? And do they never hurt him?"

"He don't fear anything in the world," said the girl, entirely forgetting herself, in enthusiastic praise of her husband.

"Cæsar, the lion, loves him like a dog; and Joe trusts him as he does me. But them tigers are deceitful beasts, and can't be trusted a minute. Judas went at Joe once, and half killed him. He seems tame enough now; but I hate him, for they say that if a tiger once tastes a man's blood he 's sure to kill him sooner or later. So I don't have a minute's peace when Joe is in that cage." And the little woman shivered with very genuine anxiety at the thought of her husband's danger.

"And, knowing this, he runs the risk every day! What a life!" said Uncle Ben, looking down at the unconscious Joe.

"A brave life, Uncle, and full of excitement. The minutes in that cage must be splendid. I wish I could see him once!" cried Rose, with the restless look in her eyes again.

"He 'd do it, if he had his things here. He 'll do anything *I* ask him," said the girl, evidently proud of her power over the lion-tamer.

"We will come and see him to-morrow. Can't you tell us how he manages to subdue these wild animals? I always wanted to know about it," said Rose, wondering if she could not get some hints for the taming of men.

"Joe 'll tell you." And, calling from her perch, the girl waked the sleeper and ordered him up to amuse the gentle-folk.

The big man came, with comical meekness; and, lounging on the hay, readily answered the questions showered upon him. Rose enjoyed that hour intensely; for the tales Joe told were full of wild adventure, hair-breadth escapes, and feats of strength or skill, that kept his listeners half breathless with interest. The presence of the little wife gave an added charm to these stories; for it was evident that the tamer of lions was completely subdued by the small woman. His brown, scarred face softened as it turned to her. While he talked, the strong hands that clutched lions by the throat were softly stroking the blonde head at his side; and, when he told of the fierce struggle with Judas, he grew so eloquent over the account of Kitty's nursing him that it was plain to see he was prouder of the conquest of her girl's heart than of his hard-won victory over the treacherous tiger.

The man's courage lent romance to his vulgar life, and his love ennobled his whole nature for a time. Kitty ate peanuts while he thrilled his hearers with his feats; but her face was so full of pride and affection all the while that no one minded what she did, and even Milly forgave the painted cheeks and cotton velvet dress for the sake of the womanly heart underneath.

The storm passed, the circus people bestirred themselves, and in a few minutes were on their way again. Joe and Kitty said "Good-by" as heartily as if that half-hour had made them friends; and, packing themselves into the little carriage drawn by the calico tandem, dashed away as gayly as if their queer honeymoon journey had just begun. Like parts of a stage pageant, the gilded car, the elephants and camels, frisky ponies, and gay red vans vanished along the winding road, leaving the old barn to silence and the scandalized swallows twittering among the rafters.

"I feel as if I'd been to an Arabian Night's entertainment," said Rose, as they descended and turned toward home.

"It was very interesting, and I do hope that brave Joe won't get eaten up by the tigers. What would poor Kitty do?" returned Milly, warmly.

"It would be sad and dreadful; but she would have the comfort of knowing how much he loved her. Some women don't even have that," added Rose, under her breath.

"A capital fellow and a nice little woman. We'll go and see them to-morrow; though I fancy I shall not like Mrs. Kitty half so well in gauze and spangles, jumping through hoops and over banners on horseback, as I did on the hayloft. And I shall be desperately anxious till Joe is safely out of the tiger's cage," said Uncle Ben, who had been as interested as a boy in the wild tales told them.

For an hour they walked back along the river-side, enjoying the wood odors brought out by the shower, the glories of the sunset sky, and the lovely rainbow that arched overhead, — a bow of promise to those who seemed passing under it from the old life to a new one, full of tender promise.

"I see a nice old woman in that kitchen, and I want to stop and ask for some new milk. Perhaps she will give us our supper, and then we can go on by moonlight," said Rose, as they came to a weather-beaten farm-house, standing under an ancient elm, with its door hospitably open, and a grandmotherly figure going to and fro within.

Rose's request was most graciously received, for the old woman seemed to regard them as most welcome cheerers of her solitude, and bustled about with an infectious cordiality that set them at their ease directly.

"Do tell! Caught in the shower? It come so suddin', I mistrusted some folks would get a duckin'. You kin hev supper jest as wal as not. 'Tain't a mite o' trouble, ef you don't mind plain vittles. Enos and me lives alone, and he ain't no gret of an eater; but I allers cattle'ate to hev a good store of pervision on hand this time a year, there 's such a sight of strangers round the mountains. The table 's all sot; and I 'll jest add a pinch of tea and a couple of pies, and there we be. Now draw right up, and do the best you kin."

The cheery old soul was so hospitable that her presence gave a grace to her homely table and added flavor to her plain fare. Uncle Ben's eyes twinkled when he saw dainty Rose eating brown-bread and milk out of a yellow bowl, with the appetite of a dairy-maid; and Milly rejoiced over the happy face opposite, wishing that it might always wear that self-forgetful look.

Enos was a feeble, bed-ridden, old man, who lay in a small room opening from the kitchen. A fretful invalid he seemed to be, hard to suit and much given to complaint. But the tender old wife never lost patience with him; and it was beautiful to see how cheerfully she trotted to and fro, trying to gratify every whim, without a reproachful word or thought of weariness.

After tea, as Rose wanted to wait till moonrise, Uncle Ben went in to chat with the invalid, while Milly insisted on wiping the cups for the old lady; and Rose sat on the doorstep, listening to their chat, and watching twilight steal softly up the valley. Presently her attention was fixed by something the old lady said in answer to Milly's praises of the quaint kitchen.

" Yes, dear, I 've lived here all my days. Was born in that bed-room; and don't ask no better than to die there when my time comes."

"Most people are not fortunate enough to keep their old home when they marry. It must be very dear to you, having spent both your maiden and married life here," said Milly, interested in her hostess.

"Wal, you see my maiden life lasted sixty year; and my married life ain't but jest begun," answered the old lady, with a laugh as gay as a girl's.

Seeing curiosity in the quick glance Rose involuntarily gave her, the chatty old soul went on, as if gossip was dear to her heart, and her late-coming happiness still so new that she loved to tell it.

"I s'pose that sounds sing'lar to you young things; but, you see, though me and Enos was engaged at twenty or so, we warn't married till two year ago. Things was dreadful con'try, and we kep' a waitin' and a waitin', till I declare for 't I really did think I should die an old maid." And she laughed again, as if her escape was the best joke in the world.

"And you waited forty years?" cried Rose, with her great eyes full of wonder.

"Yes, dear. I had other chances; but somehow they did n't none of them suit, and the more unfort'nate Enos was the more I kinder held on to him. He was one of them that 's allers tryin' new things, and did n't never seem to make a fortin out of any on 'em. He kept a tryin' because he had nothin', and would n't marry till he was wal off. My mother was dead, and left a family to be took care on. I was the oldest gal, and so I nat'rally kept house for father till he died, and the children grew up and married off. So I warn't idle all them years, and got on first-rate, allers hopin' Enos's luck would turn. But it did n't (them cups goes in the right-hand corner, dear); and so I waited and waited, and hoped and hoped."

"Oh! how could you?" sighed Rose, from the soft gloom of the doorway.

"'Pears to me strength is give us most wonderful to bear trials, if we take 'em meek. I used to think I could n't bear it no way when I was left here alone, while Enos was in Californy; and I did n't know for seven year whether he was dead or alive. His folks give him up; but I never did, and kept on hopin' and prayin' for him till he come back."

"How happy you were then!" cried Rose, as if she could sympathize heartily with that joy.

"No, I warn't, dear. That was the hardest part on 't; for Enos was married to a poor, shiftless thing, that was a burden to him for ten year."

"That *was* hard," and Rose gave a groan, as if a new trouble had suddenly come upon her.

"I done my best for 'em, in their ups and downs, till they went West. Then I settled down to end my days here alone. My folks was all dead or fur away, and it was uncommon lonesome. But I kinder clung to the old place, and had it borne in upon me strong that Enos would turn up agin in time. I wanted him to find me here, ready to give him a helpin' hand whenever and however he come."

"And he did, at last?" asked Rose, with a sympathetic quiver in her voice that went to the old woman's heart.

"Yes, my deary; he did come at last," she said, in a voice full of a satisfaction that was almost solemn in its intensity. "Ruther mor 'n two years ago he knocked at that door, a poor, broken-down old man, without wife, or child, or money, or home, — nothin' in the wide world but me. He did n't think I 'd take him in, he was so mis'able. But, Lord love him, what else had I been a waitin' for them forty year? It warn't the Enos that I loved fust; but that did n't matter one mite. And when he sat sobbin' in that chair, and sayin' he had no friend but me, why I just answered back: 'My home is your'n, Enos; and I give it jest as hearty as I did when you fust pupposed, under the laylock bushes, in the back garden. Rest here, my poor dear, and let Becky take care on you till she dies.'"

"So he stayed?" said Milly, with tears in her voice, for Rose's head was down on her knees, so eloquent had been the pathos of that old voice, telling its little tale of faithful love.

"Certin. And we was married, so no one

need make no talk. Folks said it was a dreadful poor match, and took on about my doin' on 't; for I 'm wal off, and Enos had n't a cent. But we was satisfied, and I ain't never repented of that day's work; for he took to his bed soon after, and won't quit it, the doctor says, till he 's took to his grave."

"You dear soul, I must kiss you for that lovely deed of yours, and thank you from my heart for this lesson in fidelity." And, obeying an irresistible impulse, Rose threw her arms round the old lady's neck, kissing the wrinkled cheek with real reverence and tenderness.

"Sakes alive! Wal, I never did see sech a soft-hearted little creter. Why, child, what I done warn't nothin' but a pleasure. We women are such queer things, we don't care how long we wait, ef we only hev our way at last."

As she spoke, the old woman hugged the blooming girl with a motherly warmth, most sweet and comfortable to see; yet the longing look, the lingering touch, betrayed how much the tender old heart would have loved to pillow there a child of its own.

Just then Uncle Ben appeared, and the early moon peeped over the mountain-top, plainly hinting that it was time for the wanderers to turn homeward. Bidding their hospitable hostess good night, they came again into the woody road, now haunted with soft shadows and silvery with falling dew. The brown brooks were singing lullabies, the pines whispering musically in the wind, the mellow moonlight was falling everywhere, and the world was full of the magical beauty of a midsummer's night.

"Go on, please, and let me follow alone. I want to think over my pleasant day, and finish it with waking dreams, as I go through this enchanted wood," said Rose, whose mind was full of sweet yet sober thoughts; for she had gathered herbs of grace while carelessly pulling wayside flowers, and from the simple adventures of the day had unconsciously received lessons that never were forgotten.

The others walked on, and the girl followed, living over again the happy winter during which she had learned to know and love the young neighbor who had become the hero of her dreams. She had felt sure he loved her, though the modest youth had never told her so, except with eloquent glances and tender devotion. She believed in him, loved him truly, and waited with maidenly patience to hear the words that would unseal her lips. They did not come, and he had left her with no hope but such as she could find in the lingering pressure of his hand and the warmly uttered "I shall see you again."

Since then, no line, no word; and all through the lovely spring she had looked and waited for the brown-bearded student, — looked and waited in vain. Then unrest took possession of her, anxiety tormented her, and despair made her young face pathetic. Only the sad, simple old story, but as bitter to live through now as in poor Dido's day; more bitter, perhaps, because we cannot erect funeral pyres and consume the body with a flame less fierce than that which burns away the soul unseen.

Now in the silence of that summer night a blessed peace seemed to fall on the girl's unquiet heart, as she trod thoughtfully along the shadowy road. Courage and patience seemed to spring up within her. To wait and hope and love without return became a possibility; and, though a few hot tears rolled down the cheeks, that had lost their roses, the eyes that shed them were more tender for the tears, and the heart that echoed the old wife's words — "Strength is given us to bear our trials, if we take them meekly" — was worthier of life's best blessing, love, because of its submission.

As she paused a moment to wipe away the tell-tale drops, before she joined the others, the sound of far-off music came on the wings of the wind, — a man's voice, singing one of the love-lays that are never old. As if spell-bound, Rose stood motionless in the broad streak of light that fell athwart the road. She knew the voice, the sweet old song seemed answering her prayer, and now it needed no golden butterfly to guide her to her lover.

Nearer and nearer came the singer, pouring out his lay as if his heart was in it. Brighter and brighter glowed the human rose, as the featherless nightingale told his tale in music, unconsciously approaching the happy sequel with each step.

Out from the gloom he came, at last; saw her waiting for him in the light; seemed to read the glad truth in her face, and stretched both hands to her without a word. She took them; and what followed who shall say? For the moon, best friend of lovers, discreetly slipped behind a cloud, and the pines whispered their congratulations as they wrapped the twain in deepest shadow.

When, half an hour later, they joined the other pair (who, strange to say, had quite forgotten their charge), Uncle Ben exclaimed, as he welcomed the new-comer with unusual cordiality: "Why, Rose! You look quite glorified in this light and as well as ever. We must try this cure again."

"No need, sir. I have done with the heart-ache, and here is my physician," answered Rose, with a look at her lover which told the story better than the best chosen words.

"And here is mine," echoed Milly, leaning on Uncle Ben's arm as if it belonged to her; as it did, for the moonlight had been too much for the old bachelor, and, in spite of his fifty years, he had wooed and won Milly as ardently as any boy. So the lonely future she had accepted so cheerfully suddenly bloomed with happy hopes;

and the older couple looked as blissfully content as the young pair, who greeted with the blithest laughter that ever woke the echoes of the wood, this fit ending to the romance of a summer day.

MY ROCOCO WATCH

ALL three of us were inspired with an intense desire to possess one of these quaint watches, the moment we saw one hanging at the side of a certain lovely woman at a party where it created a great sensation.

Imitations we would not have, and the genuine article could not be found even in Geneva, the paradise of time-pieces. My sisters soon ceased to pine for the impossible, and contented themselves with other antiques. Fan rejoiced in a very ugly Cinque-Cento ring like a tiny coffin, and Mary was the proud possessor of a Roman necklace composed of gods and goddesses.

I, however, remained true to my first love and refused to be satisfied with anything but a veritable rococo watch, for that, I maintained, united the useful and the beautiful. Resisting the temptations of Rome, Paris, and Geneva, I skilfully lured my unsuspecting party into all sorts of out-of-the-way places under pretence of studying up the old French cathedrals.

The girls did the churches faithfully, but I

shirked them and spent my shining hours poking about dirty streets and staring in at the windows of ancient jewelry shops, patiently seeking for the watch of my dreams. I was rallied unmercifully upon my mania, and many jokes were played upon me by the frolicksome girls, who more than once sent me posting off by reports of some remarkable trinket in some almost unattainable place.

But, nothing daunted, I continued my vain search all through France, and never relinquished my hope till we left St. Malo on our way to Brest, whence we were to sail for home. Then I despaired, and, having nothing more to toil for, began to enjoy myself with a free mind, and then it was that capricious fortune chose to smile upon me and reward my long quest.

Finding that we had a day before us, we explored the queer old town, and, as our tastes varied, each went a different way. I roamed about the narrow streets, seeking some odd souvenir to carry away, and was peering into a dark lane, attracted by some fine shells, when suddenly I was arrested by a sight which caused me to pause in the middle of a puddle, exclaiming dramatically, "At last! at last!"

Yes, there, in the dusty window of a pawnbroker's shop, hung the most enchanting watch, crystal ball, silver chains, enamelled medallions, and cluster of charms, all encrusted with pearls, garnets, and turquoises set in the genuine antique style. One long gaze, one rapturous exclamation, and I skipped from the puddle to the door-step, bent on securing the prize at any and all costs.

Bouncing in upon a withered little man, who was taking coffee in a shadowy recess, I demanded the price of the watch. Of course the little man was on the alert at once, and began by protesting that it was not for sale; but I saw the fib in his eye, and sweetly insisted that I must have it. Then he improvised a mournful tale about a family of rank reduced by misfortune and forced to dispose of their cherished relics in some private manner. I affected to believe the touching romance, and offered a handsome sum for the watch, which, on closer inspection, struck me as rather more antique than even I desired.

Instantly the little man clasped his hands and protested that it was an insult to propose such a paltry price for so beautiful and perfect a treasure. Double the sum might be a temptation, but not a sou less.

This was so absurd that I tried to haggle a little; but I never succeeded in that line, so my attempt ended in both of us getting angry, when the little man tore the watch from my hands, and I left the shop as precipitately as I entered it.

Retiring to the square to cool my indignation, I was reposing on a bench, when I beheld the little man approaching with the blandest expression, and, bowing profoundly, he resumed the subject as if we had parted amicably.

"If madame would allow him to consult the owner of this so charming watch, the affair might yet be arranged in a satisfactory manner. If madame would leave her address, he would report to her in a few hours, and have the happiness of obliging the dear lady."

I consented, but preferred to return to his shop later in the day, for I wished to astonish the girls by producing my prize at some opportune moment, and I much feared if I told them of my discovery that the bargain would never be made.

I suffered agonies of suspense for hours, but basely attributed my restlessness to the heat and weariness. Five o'clock and dinner, but I declined going down, and slipped away to my tryst with the little old man. He was ready for me with another romance of the noble owner's reluctance to part with an heirloom for less than the price he had named. In vain I talked, wheedled, and protested; the crafty little man saw that I meant to have that watch, and was firm. At last I pretended to give it up, and, thanking him for his trouble, retired mournfully, hoping he would follow me again, for I had told him that I should leave in the steamer expected next day.

But the evening passed, and no little man appeared, although I sat on the balcony till the moon rose. Morning came, and with it the steamer, but still no watch arrived, as other coveted articles had often done when we firmly refused to be imposed upon.

My secret agitation increased, and my temptation waxed stronger and stronger as the hour of departure approached. The girls thought me nervous about the voyage, but were too busy to heed my preoccupation, while I was too much ashamed of my infatuation to confess it and ask advice.

Fifteen minutes before we started for the wharf, I gave in, and muttering something about looking up the carriage, I flew around the corner, demanded the watch, paid an abominable price for it, and sneaked back, knowing I had been cheated by the sly old fellow, who had evidently expected me, and whom I left chuckling over his bargain, as well he might, the rascal!

The moment the deed was done my spirits returned, and I beamed upon my sisters as benignly as if I carried a boundless supply of good humor in my pocket instead of that costly watch packed up in a shabby little box.

We sailed, and for several days I forgot every thing but my own woe; then came a calm, and then choosing a moment when the girls were comparing their treasures with those of other returning voyagers, I proudly produced my watch. The effect was superb. Cries of admiration greeted it from all but my sisters, who looked at one another in comic dismay and burst into fits of laughter.

"We saw it and tried to get it, but it cost so much we gave it up, and never told lest Penelope should be tempted beyond her strength. We might have spared our pains, for it was to be, and it is vain to fight against fate, only do tell us if you paid that Shylock what he asked us?" said Mary, naming a smaller sum than my first handsome offer.

"I did not pay that, and I shall never tell what it cost, for you would n't believe me if I did. It was a good bargain, I assure you — for Shylock," I added to myself, and kept my secret jealously, knowing I never should hear the last of it if the awful truth was known.

My treasure was so much admired that I was afraid it would be ravished from me, and I hid it in all sorts of places, like a magpie with a stolen spoon. I never went on deck without taking it with me for safe keeping. I never woke in the morning without burrowing under my mattress to see if it was safe, and never turned in for the night without seeing that I was prepared for shipwreck by having my life-preserver handy and half-a-dozen ship biscuits, a bottle of water, and the precious box lashed firmly together, for with that dearly bought watch I was resolved to sink or swim, live or die.

Being permitted to reach land in safety, I prepared to eclipse Fan's ring and Mary's necklace with my rich and rare rococo watch. But I found it impossible to set it going, though I tried all the keys in the house, so I took it to an experienced watchmaker and left it to be regulated. Every one knows what that means, and can imagine my impatience as week after week went by and still that blessed thing was not done. It came at last, however, and with it a bill that startled me; but I could not dispute it, for the job was a difficult one, owing to the antiquity of the works and the skill required to set a watch going that probably had not been wound up for half a century.

It went for a week, and then stopped for ever; for the general verdict was that no modern tinkering would restore its tone, since the springs of life were broken and the venerable wheels at a dead lock.

"Well, it is ornamental if not useful, only I am sorry I gave away my good old watch, thinking this would be all I needed," I said, making the best of what I alone knew to be a bad bargain.

So I hung the silent thing to my girdle and went forth to awaken the envy and admiration of all beholders. But, alas! the second time I wore it, one of the medallions was lost, could not be found, and its place had to be filled with a modern one, entirely out of keeping with the others. Bill the second was paid with much lamentation, and again I tried to enjoy my watch. But the fates seemed to be against me, for presently it was stolen by a maid who admired mediæval jewelry as well as her mistress.

What a state of excitement we were in then, to be sure! Cousin Dick took the matter in hand, and searched for the lost watch with the patience, if not the skill, of a detective. Mysterious men came to examine the servants, dreadful questions as to its value were put to me, and, worst of all, I knew that this sort of hide-and-go-seek was a fearfully expensive game, and of course I was n't going to let Dick pay for it.

It was found at last, and restored to me somewhat the worse for the rough handling of curious admirers. Bill the third was paid with the calmness of despair, for I really began to think some evil spell was hidden in that crystal ball; a spell which attracted, then infatuated, and now controlled me, leading me slowly and surely, through tribulation after tribulation, to the poorhouse in the end.

The accidents that befell that fatal watch would fill a chapter, and the narrow escapes it had would make a thrilling tale. Babies half choked themselves with the charms, little Tommy was discovered trying to divest it of all incumbrances that he might use it as a "jolly big marble." It was always falling off, catching in buttons, or bobbing wildly about when I danced, and more than once I was cut to the soul by hearing benighted people wonder at Miss Pen's bad taste in wearing Salom jewelry. Salom, be it known to the ignorant, is a man who deals in mock ornaments of great brilliancy and cheapness.

Soon the jewels began to fall out, and I scattered pearls about me like the young lady in the fairy tale. Then the chain broke, and the charms were lost. In one of the many falls, the crystal got cracked; the silver tarnished till it looked like dingy lead, and at last no beauty remained to reconcile me to its utter uselessness. My poor watch was the standing joke of the family, and kept every one merry but its owner. To me it was a disgrace, and I suffered endless disappointments and delays by having no trusty timekeeper at hand. Pride prevented my applying to others, and bitterly I mourned in secret for the true old friend I had deserted when the false new one came.

I ceased to wear the hollow mockery, and hoped people would forget it, but the girls still displayed their more successful ornaments; and I was forced to tell the sad tale of my mortifying failure in reply to the natural question, —

"And what charming old trinket did Pen get?"

But this was not the worst of it. Like little Rosamond in the moral tale, I had to wear my old shoes when the purple jar proved a delusion and a snare. I had overrun my allowance by that rash purchase, and had to economize just when I most wished to be fine. "Beauty unadorned," and that sort of thing, is all nonsense when a woman burns to look her loveliest in the eyes of certain persons, and the anguish I endured when I looked at that rubbishy old watch, and thought what sweet things could have been bought with the money recklessly lavished upon it, can better be imagined than described.

Fain would I have sold my treasure for a quarter what I gave for it, but who would buy the ruined relic now? And the mere idea of having it even partially repaired made my blood run cold. So I laid it away as a warning example of woman's folly, and began to save up, that I might replace it by a modern watch with all the improvements procurable for money.

I was effectually cured of my passion for antiquities, and hated the sound of the word *rococo*. Nothing could be too new for me now, and I privately studied up on watches, being bound never to buy another, which, though it might last to all eternity, yet had no connection with time.

Slowly the memory of that temptation and fall seemed to fade from all minds but my own; slowly my little hoard increased at the expense of many an ungratified whim, inviting bargain, or girlish vanity, and slowly I decided what sort of watch would most entirely combine the solid virtues and modest graces I desired to possess in the new one I intended to choose so wisely and well.

But just as my hundred dollars was nearly completed, I discovered that Dick's younger brother, Geordie, had got himself into a boyish scrape, and was planning to run away to sea as the best means of settling the difficulty. I was immediately possessed with an intense desire to help the poor lad, and, having won his confidence in a desponding moment, I offered my little hoard as a loan, to be paid in time, if he would accept it on no other condition.

I really don't think I could have done it for any one but Dick's brother, and I did not desire any praise for it, since I made the boy take a solemn vow that it should be a secret between us for ever. It was reward enough to know that I had spared dear Dick another care, and done something to be more worthy of him, though it was only a little sacrifice like this.

So Geordie was a free man again, and my devoted slave from that day forth, causing much merry wonderment in the family, and actually making Dick jealous by his grateful gallantry.

My sacrifice cost me something more than the loss of my watch, however, for with a part of the money I had planned to get a fine Christmas gift for some one, and now I was obliged to content myself with such a poor little offering that the girls called me mean, and nearly broke my heart by insisting that I did not care for somebody who cared a great deal for me. I bore it all and kept Geordie's secret faithfully; but I will confess that, in a paroxysm of anger with myself, I dashed that hateful rococo watch upon the floor and trampled on it as the only adequate vent for the conflicting emotions which possessed me.

But the good fairies who fly about at Christmas time set every thing right, and broke the evil spell cast over me by the Breton magician in his gloomy cell. As we sat about the breakfast-table, talking over our gifts on the morning of that happy day, Dick and Geordie came in to see how we were after the fatigues of a grand family frolic the night before.

"Here's a new conundrum; guess it, girls," said Geordie, who had the Dundreary fever upon him just at that time. "I was sent to India and stopped there; I came back because I did not go there. Now what was it?"

We puzzled over it, but gave it up at last, and when Geordie answered, "A watch," there was a general laugh, for since my ruinous speculation that word always produced a sensation among us.

"The place mentioned should have been Brittany, not India, hey, Pen?" said Dick, with a wicked twinkle of the eye.

"Don't," I began, pathetically, as the girls giggled, and Mary added, with mock sympathy, "Hush, boys, and let that sacred sorrow be for ever hidden in Pen's own breast."

"Watch and pray, dear, watch and pray, for I'm sure you have need of both," cried Fan, seeing my rising wrath.

"Put your hands before your face but don't

strike, I beg of you," cut in Geordie, trying to be witty.

"It is a sad case, but I think I have a key that will wind up the affair and set all going right," began Dick, still twinkling with fun.

To have him join the enemy was too much for me, because he had always been very careful to avoid that tender point.

"If you say another word, I 'll throw the horrid thing into the fire, for I 'm sick to death of hearing bad jokes made on it," I cried, feeling a strong desire to shake them all round.

"No doubt; give it to me, and you shall never see or hear of it again. I like old trinkets, and I 'll never tell the story of that one, on my honor as a gentleman," said Dick, in a tone that appeased my wrath at once.

"Do you really want it?" I asked, pleased and surprised, yet still a little suspicious of some new joke.

"I do, because, although it will never go again, it will always remind me of some of the happiest hours and minutes of my life, Pen."

There was no fun in Dick's eyes as he said that, and I was glad to hide the sudden color in my cheeks by running away to get the poor old watch. But I found there *was* a surprise, and a very pleasant one, in store for me; for, as I thrust the shabby box into Dick's pocket, he handed me a little parcel prettily tied up with white ribbons, saying in his most captivating way, "Fair exchange is no robbery, you know, so you must take this, and then we shall be square."

"It looks like wedding cake," I said, surveying it with curiosity, and wondering why Geordie and the girls did not stop to see the mystery unfolded.

"No, that comes later, dear," answered Dick, in a tone that made me devote myself to the white ribbons with sudden zeal.

A blue velvet case appeared, and I could not resist saying, in a voice more tender than reproachful, "You extravagant man! I know it is something costly and beautiful in return for the disgracefully mean gift I gave you."

"Bless your innocent heart, did you think you could hide any thing from me? Geordie could n't keep a secret, and I 'm only paying his debt, Pen dear, with the sort of interest women like," Dick answered, with an audacious arm around my waist and a brown beard close to my cheek.

As I did not refuse the offered interest, he added, in a softer tone, "My own debt I never can settle unless with all my worldly goods I thee endow; my heart you have had for years. Say yes, dear, and be my little *châtelaine*."

Never mind what I said, but I assure you if it had not been for Dick's arm I should have gone under the table, when, a few minutes later, I lifted the blue velvet lid and saw a dainty watch luxuriously lying on its white satin bed.

BY THE RIVER

A LEGEND OF THE ASSABET

CHAPTER I

IN the shadow of the bridge a boy lay reading on the grass, — a slender lad, broad-browed and clear-eyed, barefooted and clad in homespun, yet happy as a king; for health sat on his sunburned cheeks, a magic book lay open before him, and sixteen years of innocence gave him a passport to the freshest pleasures life can offer.

"Nat! Nat! come here and see!" cried a shrill voice from among the alders by the riverside.

But Nat only shook his head as if a winged namesake had buzzed about his ears, and still read on. Presently a twelve-years child came scrambling up the bank, dragging a long rod behind her with a discontented air.

"I wish you'd come and help me. The fish won't bite and my line is in a grievous snarl. Don't read any more. I'm tired of playing all alone."

"I forgot you, Ruthy, and it was ill done of

me. Sit here and rest while I undo the tangle," and Nat looked up good-naturedly at the small figure before him, with its quaint pinafore, checked linen gown, and buckled shoes; for this little maid lived nearly a hundred years ago and this lad had seen Washington face to face.

"Now tell me a story while I wait. Not out of that stupid play-book you are always reading, but about something that really happened, with naughty children and nice folks in it, and have it end good," said Ruth, beginning a dandelion chain; for surely it is safe to believe that our honored grandmothers enjoyed that pretty pastime in their childhood.

Nat lay in the grass, dreamily regarding the small personage who ruled him like a queen and whom he served with the devotion of a loyal heart. Now the royal command was for a story, and, stifling a sigh, this rustic gentleman closed the book, whose magic had changed the spring morning to a Midsummer Night's Dream for an hour, and set himself to gratify the little damsel's whim.

"You liked the last tale about the children who were lost. Shall I tell one about a child who was found? It really happened, and you never heard it before," he asked.

"Yes; but first put your head in my lap, for there are ants in the grass and I like to see your eyes shine when you spin stories. Tell away."

"Once upon a time there was a great snow-storm," began Nat, obediently pillowing his head on the blue pinafore.

"Whereabouts?" demanded Ruth.

"Don't spoil the story by interrupting. It was in this town, and I can show you the very house I 'm going to tell about."

"I like to know things straight along, and not bounce into a snow-storm all in a minute. I 'll be good. Go on."

"Well, it snowed so hard that people stayed indoors till the storm had beat and blown itself away. Right in the worst of it, as a farmer and his wife sat by the fire that night, they heard a cry at the door. You see they were sitting very still, the man smoking his pipe and the woman knitting, both thinking sorrowfully of their only son, who had just died."

"Don't have it doleful, Nat," briskly suggested Ruth, working busily while the narrator's hands lay idle, and his eyes looked as if they actually saw the little scene his fancy conjured up.

"No, I won't; only it really was like that," apologized Nat, seeing that sentiment was not likely to suit his matter-of-fact auditor. "When the cry came a second time, both of these people ran to the door. No one was to be seen, but on the wide step they saw a little mound not there an hour before. Brushing off the snow, they found a basket; and, when they opened it, there lay a little baby, who put out its arms with a pitiful cry, that went to their hearts. The woman hugged it close, fed it, and hushed it to sleep as if it had been her own. Her husband let her do as she liked, while he tried to find where it came from; but no trace appeared, and there was no name or mark on the poor thing's clothes."

"Did they keep it?" asked Ruth, tickling Nat's nose with a curly dandelion stem, to goad him on, as he lay silent for a moment.

"Yes, they kept it; for their hearts were sore and empty, and the forlorn baby seemed to fill them comfortably. The townsfolk gossiped awhile, but soon forgot it; and it grew up as if it had been born in the farmer's house. I 've often wondered if it was n't the soul of the little son who died, come back in another shape to comfort those good people."

"Now don't go wandering off, Nat; but tell me if he was a pretty, nice, smart child," said Ruth, with an eye to the hero's future capabilities.

"Not a bit pretty," laughed Nat, "for he grew up tall and thin, with big eyes and a queer brow. He was n't 'nice,' either, if you mean good, for he got angry sometimes and was lazy; but he tried, — oh! yes, he truly tried to be a dutiful lad. He was n't 'smart,' Ruth; for he hated to study, and only loved story books, ballads, and plays, and liked to wander round alone in the woods better than to be with other boys.

People laughed at him because of his queersome ways; but he could n't help it, — he was born so, and it would come out."

"He was what Aunt Becky calls shiftless, I guess. She says you are; but I don't mind as long as you take care of me and tell me stories."

The boy sighed and shook his head as if a whole swarm of gnats were annoying him now. "He was grateful, anyhow, this fellow I 'm telling about; for he loved the good folks and worked on the farm with all his might to pay them for their pity. He never complained; but he hated it, for delving day after day in the dirt made him feel as if he was nothing but a worm."

"We are all worms, Deacon Hurd says; so the boy need n't have minded," said Ruth, trying to assume a primly pious expression, that sat very ill upon her blooming little face.

"But some worms can turn into butterflies, if they get a chance; so the boy did mind, Ruthy." And Nat looked out into the summer world with a longing glance, which proved that he already felt conscious of the folded wings and was eager to try them.

"Was he a God-fearing boy?" asked Ruth, with a tweak of the ear; for her friend showed signs of "wandering off" again into a world where her prosaic little mind could not follow him.

"He did n't *fear* God; he loved Him. Perhaps it was wrong; but somehow he could n't believe in a God of wrath when he saw how good and beautiful the world was and how kind folks were to him. He felt as if the Lord was his father, for he had no other; and when he was lonesomest that thought was right comfortable and helpful to him. Was it wrong?" asked Nat of the child.

"I'm afraid Aunt Becky would think so. She's awful pious, and boxed my ears with a psalm-book last Sabbath, when I said I wished the lions would bite Daniel in the den, I was so tired of seeing them stare and roar at him. She would n't let me look at the pictures in the big Bible another minute, and gave me a long hymn to learn, shut up in the back bedroom. She's a godly woman, Deacon Hurd says; but I think she's uncommon strict."

"Shall I tell any more, or are you tired of this stupid boy?" said Nat, modestly.

"Yes, you may as well finish. But do have something happen. Make him grow a great man, like Whittington, or some of the story-book folks, it's so nice to read about," answered Ruth, rather impatiently.

"I hope he did something better than trade cats and be lord mayor of London. But that part of the story has n't come yet; so I'll tell you of two things that happened, one sad and one merry. When the boy was fourteen, the good woman died, and that nearly broke his heart; for she had made things easy for him, and he loved her dearly. The farmer sent for his sister to keep house, and then the boy found it harder than ever to bear his life; for the sister was a notable woman, well-meaning, but as strict as Aunt Becky, and she pestered the lad as Aunt pesters me. You see, Ruthy, it grew harder every year for him to work on the farm, for he longed to be away somewhere quiet among books and learned folk. He was not like those about him, and grew more unlike all the time, and people often said: 'He 's come of gentle blood. That 's plain to see.' He loved to think it was true, — not because he wanted to be rich and fine, but to find his own place and live the life the Lord meant him to. This feeling made him so unhappy that he was often tempted to run away, and would have done it but for the gratitude that kept him."

"Lack-a-daisy! What a bad boy, when he had good clothes and victuals and folks were clever to him! But did he ever find his grand relations?" asked Ruth, curiosity getting the better of the reproof she thought it her duty to administer.

"I don't know yet. But he did find something that made him happier and more contented. Listen now; for you 'll like this part, I know. One night, as he came home with the cows, watching the pretty red in the sky, hearing the crickets chirp, and picking flowers along the way, because he liked to have 'em in his room, he felt uncommon lonesome, and kept wishing he 'd meet a fairy who 'd give him all he wanted. When he got to the house, he thought the fairy had really come; for there on the door-stone stood a little lass, looking at him. A right splendid little lass, Ruth, with brown hair long upon her shoulders, blue eyes full of smiles, and a face like one of the pink roses in Madam Barrett's garden."

"Did she have good clothes?" demanded Ruth, eagerly, for this part of the tale did interest her, as Nat foretold.

"Let me see. Yes, nice clothes; but sad-colored, for the riding-cloak that hung over her white dimity frock was black. Yet she stood on a pair of the trimmest feet ever seen, wearing hose with fine clocks, and silver buckles in the little shoes. You may believe the boy stared well, for he had never seen so pretty a sight in all his days, and before he knew it he had given her his nosegay of sheepsbane, fern, and honeysuckle. She took it, looking pleased, and made him as fine a courtesy as any lady; whereat he turned red and foolish, being shy, and hurried off into the barn. But she came skipping after, and peeped at him as he milked, watched how he did it for a bit, and then said, like a little queen, 'Boy, get up and let me try.' That pleased him mightily; so, taking little madam on his knee, he let her try. But something went amiss, for all at once Brindle kicked over the pail, away went the three-legged stool, and both the milkers lay in the dirt."

"Why, Nat! why, Nat! that was you and I," cried Ruth, clapping her hands delightedly, as this catastrophe confirmed the suspicions which had been growing in her mind since the appearance of the child.

"Hush! or I'll never tell how they got up," said Nat, hurrying on with a mirthful face. "The boy thought the little maid would cry over her bruised arm or go off in a pet at sight of the spoilt frock. But no; she only laughed, patted old Brindle, and sat down, saying stoutly, 'I shall try again and do it right.' So she did, and while she milked she told how she was an orphan and had come to be Uncle Dan's girl all her life. That was a pleasant hearing for the lad, and he felt as if the fairy had done better by him than he had hoped. They were friends at once, and played cat's cradle on the kitchen settle all the evening. But, when the child was put to bed in a strange room, her little heart failed her, and she fell a-sobbing for her mother. Nothing would comfort her till the boy went up and sang her to sleep, with her pretty hand in his and all her tears quite gone. That was nigh upon two years ago; but from that night they were fast friends, and happier times began for the boy, because he had something to love and live for besides work. She was very good to him, and nowhere in all the world was there a dearer, sweeter lass than Nat Snow's little maid."

During the latter part of this tale "founded upon fact," Ruth had been hugging her playmate's head in both her chubby arms, and when he ended by drawing down the rosy face to kiss it softly on the lips it grew a very April countenance, as she exclaimed, with a childish burst of affection, curiosity, and wonder, —

"Dear Nat, how good you were to me that night and ever since! Did you really come in a basket, and don't you know anything about your folks? Good lack! And to think you may turn out a lord's son, after all!"

"How could I help being good to you, dear? Yes, I 'll show you the very basket, if Aunt Becky has not burnt it up as rubbish. I know nought about my folk, and have no name but Snow. Uncle Dan gave me that because I came in the storm, and the dear mother added Nathaniel, her own boy's name, since I was sent to take his place, she said. As for being a lord's son, I 'd rather be a greater man than that."

And Nat rose up with sudden energy in his voice, a sudden kindling of the eyes, that pleased Ruth, and made her ask, with firm faith in the possibility of his being anything he chose, —

"You mean a king?"

"No, a poet!"

"But that 's not fine at all!" and Ruth looked much disappointed.

"It is the grandest thing in the world! Look now, the man who wrote this play was a poet, and, though long dead, he is still loved and honored, when the kings and queens he told about would be forgotten but for him. Who cares for them, with all their splendor? Who does not worship William Shakespeare, whose genius made him greater than the whole of them!" cried Nat, hugging the dingy book, his face all aglow with the beautiful enthusiasm of a true believer.

"Was Master Shakespeare rich and great?" asked Ruth, staring at him with round eyes.

"Never rich or great in the way you mean, or even famous, till after he was dead."

"Then I'd rather have you like Major Wild, for he owns much land, lives in a grand house, and wears the finest-laced coat in all the town. Will you be like him, please, Nat?"

"No, I won't!" answered the lad, with emphatic brevity, as the image of the red-faced, roystering Major passed before his mind's eye.

His bluntness ruffled his sovereign's temper for a moment, and she asked with a frown, —

"What do you think Aunt Becky said yesterday, when we found ever so many of your verses hidden in the clothes-press, where we went to put lavender among the linen?"

"Something sharp, and burnt the papers, I'll warrant," replied Nat, with the resignation of one used to such trials.

"No, she kept 'em to cover jam-pots with, and she said you were either a fool or a genus. Is a genus very bad, Nat?" added Ruth, relenting as she saw his dreamy eyes light up with what she fancied was a spark of anger.

"Aunt Becky thinks so; but I don't, and, though I may not be one, sooner or later folks shall see that I'm no fool, for I feel, I know, I was not born to hoe corn and feed pigs all my life."

"What will you do?" cried Ruth, startled by the almost passionate energy with which he spoke.

"Till I'm twenty-one I'll stay to do my duty. When the time comes, I'll break away and try my own life, for I shall have a right to do it then."

"And leave me? Nay, I'll not let you go." And Ruth threw her dandelion chain about his neck, claiming her bondsman with the childish tyranny he found so sweet.

He laughed and let her hold him, seeing how frail the green links were; little dreaming how true a symbol it was of the stronger tie by which she would hold him when the time came to choose between liberty and love.

"Five years is a long time, Ruth. You will get tired of my odd ways, and be glad to have me go. But never fret about it; for, whatever happens, I'll not forget you."

Quite satisfied with this promise, the little

maid fell to sticking buttercups in the band of the straw hat her own nimble fingers had braided, as if bent on securing one crown for her friend. But Nat, leaning his head upon his hand, sat watching the sunshine glitter on the placid stream that rippled at his feet, with such intentness that Ruth presently disturbed him by demanding curiously, —

"What is it? A kingfisher or a turtle?"

"It's the river, dear. It seems to sing to me as it goes by. I always hear it, yet I never understand what it says. Do you?"

Ruth fixed her blue eyes on the bluer water, listened for an instant, then laughed out blithely, and sprung up, saying, —

"It sings: 'Come and fish, Nat. Come and fish!'"

The boy's face fell, and the dreamy look faded, and, with a patient sort of sigh, he rose and followed her, leaving his broken dream with his beloved book among the buttercups. But, though he sat by Ruth in the shadow of the alder-bushes, his rod hung idly from his hand, for he was drawing bright fancies from a stream she never saw, was dimly feeling that he had a harder knot to disentangle than his little friend's, and faintly hearing a higher call than hers, in the ripple of the river.

CHAPTER II

FIVE years later Ruth was in the dairy making up butter, surrounded by tier above tier of shining pans, whence proceeded a breath as fresh and fragrant as if the ghosts of departed king-cups and clover still haunted the spot. Standing before a window where morning-glories rung their colored bells in the balmy air, she was as pleasant a sight as any eye need wish to see upon a summer's day; for the merry child had bloomed into a sprightly girl, rich in rustic health and beauty. All practical virtues were hers; and, while they wore so comely a shape, they possessed a grace that hid the lack of those finer attributes which give to womanhood its highest charm. The present was all in all to Ruth. Its homely duties were her world, its petty griefs and joys her life, and her ambition was bounded by her desire to show her mates the finest yarn, the sweetest butter, the gayest cardinal, and the handsomest sweetheart, in the town. An essentially domestic character, cheery as the blaze upon the hearth, contented as the little kettle singing there, and so affectionate, discreet, and diligent that she was the model damsel of the town, the comfort of Uncle Daniel's age, the pride of Aunt Becky's heart, the joy of Nat's life, and the desire of his eyes.

Unlike as ever, the pair were still fast friends. Nay, more, for the past year had been imperceptibly transforming that mild sentiment into a much warmer one by the magic of beauty, youth, and time. Year after year Nat had patiently toiled on, for gratitude controlled ambition, and Ruth's presence made his life endurable. But Nature was stronger than duty or love, and as the boy ripened into the man he looked wistfully beyond the narrow present into the great future, which allures such as he with vague, sweet prophecies, hard to be resisted. Silently the struggle went on, steadily the inborn longing strengthened, and slowly the resolution was fixed to put his one gift to the test and learn if it was a vain delusion or a lovely possibility. Each year proved to himself and those about him that their world was not his world, their life his life; for, like Andersen's young swan, the barnyard was no home to him, and when the other fowls cackled, hissed, and scolded, he could only put his head under his wing and sigh for the time when he should join "the beautiful white birds among the rushes of the stream that flowed through the poet's garden, where the sun shone and the little children played."

Ruth knew his dreams and desires; but, as she could not understand them, she tried to cure them by every innocent art in her power, and nursed him through many a fit of the heart-sickness of hope deferred as patiently as she would have done through any less occult disease that flesh is heir to. She was thinking of him as she worked that day, and wishing she could mould his life as easily as she did the yellow lumps before her, stamping them with her own mark, and setting them away for her own use. She felt that some change was about to befall Nat, for she had listened to the murmur of voices as the old man and the young sat talking far into the night. What the result had been was as yet unknown; for Uncle Daniel was unusually taciturn that morning, and Nat had been shut up in his room since breakfast, though spring work waited for him all about the farm.

An unwonted sobriety sat on Ruth's usually cheerful face, and she was not singing as she worked, but listening intently for a well-known step to descend the creaking stairs. Presently it came, paused a moment in the big kitchen, where Aunt Becky was flying about like a domestic whirlwind, and Ruth heard Nat ask for her with a ring in his voice that made her heart begin to flutter.

"She 's in the dairy. But for landsake where are you a-going, boy? I declare for 't, you look so fine and chirk I scursely knew yer," answered the old lady, pausing in her work to stare at the astonishing spectacle of Nat in his Sunday best upon a week day.

"I 'm going to seek my fortune, Aunty. Won't you wish me luck?" replied Nat, cheerily.

Aunt Becky had a proverb for every occasion, and could not lose this opportunity for enriching the malcontent with a few suited to his case.

"Yes, child, the best of lucks; but it 's my opinion that, if we 'get spindle and distaff ready, the Lord will send the flax,' without our goin' to look for 't. 'Every road has its puddle,' and 'he that prieth into a cloud may get struck by lightenin'.' God bless you, my dear, and remember that 'a handful of good life is wuth a bushel of learnin'.'"

"I will, Ma'am; and also bear in mind that 'he who would have eggs must bear the cackling of hens,'" with which return shot Nat vanished, leaving the old lady to expend her energies and proverbs upon the bread she was kneading with a vigor that set the trough rocking like a cradle.

Why Ruth began to sing just then, and why she became so absorbed in her oleaginous sculpture as to seem entirely unconscious of the appearance of a young man at the dairy door, are questions which every woman will find no difficulty in answering. Actuated by one of the whims which often rule the simplest of the sex, she worked and sang as if no anxiety had ruffled her quiet heart; while Nat stood and watched her with an expression which would have silenced her, had she chosen to look up and meet it.

The years that had done much for Ruth had been equally kind to Nat, in giving him a generous growth, for the figure leaning in the doorway seemed full of the vigor of wholesome country life. But the head that crowned it was such as one seldom sees on a farmer's shoulders; for the brown locks, gathered back into a ribbon, after the fashion of the time, showed a forehead of harmonious outline, overarching eyes full of the pathos and the passion that betray the presence of that gift which is divine when young. The mouth was sensitive as any woman's, and the lips were often folded close, as if pride controlled the varying emotions that swayed a nature ardent and aspiring as a flame of fire. Few could read the language of this face, yet many felt the beauty that it owed to a finer source than any grace of shape or color, and wondered where the subtle secret lay.

"Ruth, may I tell you something?"

"Of course you may. Only don't upset the salt-box or sit down upon the churn."

Nat did neither, but still leaned in the doorway and still watched the trim figure before him, as if it was very pleasant to his eyes; while Ruth, after a brief glance over her shoulder, a nod and a smile, spatted away as busily as ever.

"You know I was twenty-one yesterday?"

"I 'm not like to forget it, after sewing my eyes out to work a smart waistcoat as a keepsake."

"Nor I; for there 's not such another in the town, and every rosebud is as perfect as if just pulled from our bush yonder. See, I 've put it on as knights put on their armor when they went to fight for fortune and for their ladies' love."

As he spoke, Nat smilingly thrust his hands into the pockets of a long-flapped garment, which was a masterpiece of the needlework in vogue a century ago. Ruth glanced up at him with eyes full of hearty admiration for the waistcoat and its wearer. But something in those last words of his filled her with a trouble both sweet and bitter, as she asked anxiously, —

"Are you going away, Nat?"

"For a week only. Uncle has been very kind, and given me a chance to prove which road it 's best for me to take, since the time has come when I must choose. I ride to Boston this afternoon, Ruth, carrying my poems with me, that I may submit them to the criticism of certain learned gentlemen, who can tell me if I deceive myself or not. I have agreed to abide by their decision, and if it is in my favor — as God grant it be — Uncle leaves me free to live the life I love, among my books and all that makes this world glorious. Think, Ruth, — a poet in good truth, to sing when I will, and delve no more! Will you be pleased and proud if I come back and tell you this?"

"Indeed, I will, if it makes you happy. And yet"— She paused there, looking wistfully into his face, now all aglow with the hope and faith that are so blissful and so brief.

"What is it, lass? Speak out and tell me all that's in your heart, for I mean to show you mine," he said in a commanding tone seldom heard before, for he seemed already to have claimed the fair inheritance that makes the poet the equal of the prince.

Ruth felt the change with a thrill of pride, yet dared suggest the possibility of failure, as a finer nature would have shrunk from doing in such a happy, hopeful hour as that.

"If the learned gentlemen decide that the poems have no worth, what then?"

He looked at her an instant, like one fallen from the clouds, then squared his shoulders, as if resettling the burden put off for a day, and answered bravely, though a sudden shadow crossed his face,—

"Then I give up my dream and fall to work again,—no poet, but a man, who will do his best to be an honest one. I have promised Uncle to abide by this decision, and I'll keep my word."

"Will it be very hard, Nat?" and Ruth's eyes grew pitiful, for in his she read how much the sacrifice would cost him.

"Ay, lass, very hard," he said briefly; then

added, with an eloquent change in voice and face, "unless you help me bear it. Sweetheart, whichever road I take, I had no thought to go alone. Will you walk with me, Ruth? God knows I'll make the way as smooth and pleasant as a faithful husband can."

The busy hands stopped working there, for Nat held them fast in his, and all her downcast eyes could see were the gay flowers her needle wrought, agitated by the beating of the man's heart underneath. Her color deepened beautifully and her lips trembled, in spite of the arch smile they wore, as she said half-tenderly, half-wilfully, —

"But I should be afeared to marry a poet, if they are such strange and delicate creatures as I've heard tell. 'T would be like keeping house for a butterfly. I tried to cage one once; but the poor thing spoilt its pretty wings beating against the bars, and when I let it go it just dropped down and died among the roses there."

"But if I be no poet, only a plain farmer, with no ambition except how I may prosper and make my wife a happy woman, what answer then, Ruth?" he asked, feeling as the morning-glories might have felt if a cold wind had blown over them.

"Dear lad, it's this!" and, throwing both arms about his neck, the honest little creature kissed his brown cheek heartily.

After that no wonder if Ruth forgot her work,

never saw an audacious sunbeam withering the yellow roses she had caused to bloom, never heard the buzz of an invading fly, nor thought to praise the labor of her hands, though her plump cheek was taking off impressions of the buttons on the noble waistcoat. While to Nat the little dairy had suddenly become a Paradise, life for a moment was all poetry, and nothing in the wide world seemed impossible.

"Ruth! Ruth! The cat 's fell into the pork-kag, and my hands is in the dough. For massy sake, run down suller and fish her out!"

That shrill cry from Aunt Becky broke the spell, dissolved the blissful dream, for, true to her instincts, Ruth forgot the lover in the housewife, and vanished, leaving Nat alone with his love — and the butter-pats.

CHAPTER III

HE rode gallantly away to Boston that afternoon, and ten days later came riding slowly home again, with the precious manuscript still in his saddle-bag.

"What luck, boy?" asked Uncle Dan, with a keen glance from under his shaggy brows, as the young man came into the big kitchen, where they all sat together when the day's work was done.

"Pretty much what you foretold, sir," answered Nat, trying to smile bravely as he took his place beside Ruth on the settle, where she sat making up cherry-colored breast-knots by the light of one candle.

"Fools go out to shear and come home shorn," muttered Aunt Becky from the chimney-corner, where she sat reeling yarn and brooding over some delectable mess that simmered on the coals.

Nat did not hear the flattering remark; for he was fingering a little packet that silently told the story of failure in its dog-eared leaves, torn wrappers, and carelessly knotted string.

"Yes," he said rapidly, as if anxious to have a hard task over, "I showed my poems to sundry gentlemen, as I proposed. One liked them much, and said they showed good promise of better things; but added that it was no time for such matters now, and advised me to lay them by till I was older. A very courteous and friendly man this was, and I felt much beholden to him for his gracious speeches. The second criticized my work sharply, and showed me how I should mend it. But, when he was done, I found all the poetry had gone out of my poor lines, and nothing was left but fine words; so I thanked him and went away, thinking better of my poems than when I entered. The third wise man gave me his opinion very briefly, saying, as he handed back the book, 'Put it in the fire.'"

"Nay! but that was too harsh. They are very pretty verses, Nat, though most of them are far beyond my poor wits," said Ruth, trying to lighten the disappointment that she saw weighed heavily on her lover's spirit.

"In the good gentleman's study, I had a sight of some of the great poets of the world, and while he read my verses I got a taste of Milton, Spenser, and my own Shakespeare's noble sonnets. I saw what mine lacked; yet some of them rang true, so I took heart and trimmed them up in the fashion my masters set me. Let me read you one or two, Ruth, while you tie your true lover's knots."

And, eagerly opening the beloved book, Nat began to read by the dim light of the tallow candle, blind to the resigned expression Ruth's face assumed, deaf to Aunt Becky's muttered opinion that "an idle brain is the devil's workshop," and quite unconscious that Uncle Dan spread a checked handkerchief over his bald pate, ready for a nap. Absorbed in his delightful task, the young poet went on reading his most perfect lines, with a face that brightened blissfully, till, just as he was giving a love-lay in his tenderest tone, a mild snore checked his heavenward flight, and brought him back to earth with a rude shock. He started, paused, and looked about him, like one suddenly wakened from a happy dream. Uncle Dan was sound asleep, Aunt Becky busily counting her tidy skeins, and Ruth, making a mirror of one of the well-scoured pewter platters on the dresser, was so absorbed in studying the effect of the gay breast-knots that she innocently betrayed her inattention by exclaiming, with a pretty air of regret, —

"And that 's the end?"

"That is the end," he answered, gently closing the book which no one cared to hear, and, hiding his reproachful eyes behind his hand, he sat silent, till Uncle Dan, roused by the cessation of the melodious murmur that had soothed his ear, demanded with kindly bluntness, —

"Well, boy, which is it to be, moonshine or money? I want you to be spry about decidin', for things is gittin' behindhand, and I cattle'ate to hire if you mean to quit work."

"Sakes alive! No man in his senses would set long on the fence when there's a good farm and a smart wife a-waitin' on one side and nothin' but poetry and starvation on the other!" ejaculated Aunt Becky, briskly clattering the saucepan-lid, as if to add the savory temptations of the flesh to those of filthy lucre.

Ruth said nothing, but looked up at Nat with the one poetic sentiment of her nature shining in her eyes and touching her with its tender magic, till it seemed an easy thing to give up liberty for love. The dandelion chain the child wove round the boy had changed to a flowery garland now, but the man never saw the thorns among the roses, and let the woman fetter him again; for, as he looked at her, Nat flung the cherished book into the fire with one hand, and with the other took possession of the only bribe that could win him from that other love.

"I decide as you would have me, sir. Not for the sake of the farm you promise me, but for love of her who shall one day be its happy mistress, please God."

"Now that's sensible and hearty, and I'm waal pleased, my boy. You jest buckle to for a year stiddy and let your ink-horn dry, and we'll have as harnsome a weddin' as man could wish, — always providin' Ruth don't change her mind," said Uncle Dan, beaming benignantly at the young pair through a cloud of tobacco smoke; while Aunt Becky poked the condemned manuscript deeper into the coals, as if anxious to exorcise its witchcraft by fire, in the good old fashion.

But even in Ruth's arms Nat cast one longing, loving glance at his first-born darling on its funeral-pyre; then turned his head resolutely away, and whispered to the girl, —

"Never doubt that I love you, sweetheart, since for your sake I have given up the ambition of my life. I don't regret it, but be patient with me till I learn to live without my 'moonshine,' as you call it."

"Sunshine is better, and I'll make it for you, if I can. So cheer up, dear lad, fall to work like a man, and you'll soon forget your pretty nonsense," answered Ruth, with firm faith in the cure she proposed.

"I'll try."

And, folding his wings, Pegasus bent his neck to the yoke and fell to ploughing.

Nat kept his word and did try manfully, working early and late, with an energy that delighted Uncle Dan, made Aunt Becky bestir herself to bleach her finest webs for the wedding outfit, and caused Ruth to believe that he had forgotten the "pretty nonsense;" for the pen lay idle and he gave all his leisure to her, discussing house-gear and stock with as deep an interest as herself apparently. All summer long he toiled like one intent only on his crops; all winter he cut wood and tended cattle, as if he had no higher hope than to sell so many cords and raise likely calves for market.

Outwardly he was a promising young farmer, with a prosperous future and a notable wife awaiting him. But deep in the man's heart a spark of the divine fire still burned, unquenched by duty, love, or time. The spirit that made light in Milton's darkness, walked with Burns beside the plough, and lifted Shakespeare higher than the royal virgin's hand, sang to Nat in the airy whisper of the pines, as he labored in the wintry wood, smiled back at him in every ox-eyed daisy his scythe laid low along the summer fields, and solaced him with visions of a fairer future than any buxom Ruth could paint. It would not leave him, and he learned too late that it was the life of his life, a gift that could not be returned, a blessing turned into a curse; for, though he had burned the little book, from its ashes rose a flame that consumed him, since it could find no vent. Even the affection, for which he had made a costlier sacrifice than he knew, looked pale and poor beside the loftier loveliness that dawned upon him in the passionate struggle, ripening heart and soul to sudden manhood; and the life that lay before him seemed very bleak and barren when he returned from playing truant in the enchanted world Imagination opens to her gifted children.

Ruth vaguely felt the presence of this dumb despair, dimly saw its shadow in the eyes that sometimes wore a tragic look, and fancied that the hand working so faithfully for her was slipping from her hold, it grew so thin and hot with the inward fever, which no herb in all her garden could allay. She vainly tried to rise to his level; but the busy sparrow could not follow the aspiring lark, singing at heaven's gate. It could only chirp its little lay and build its nest, with no thought beyond a straw, a worm, and the mate that was to come.

Nat never spoke of the past, and Ruth dared not, for she grew to feel that he did "regret it" bitterly, though too generous for a word of reproach or complaint.

"I 'll make it up to him when we are married; and he will learn to love the farm when he has little lads and lasses of his own to work for," she often said to herself, as she watched her lover sit among them, after his day's work, listening to their gossip with a pathetic sort of patience, or, pleading a weariness there was no need to feign, lie on the old settle, lost in thoughts that made his face shine like one who talked with angels.

So the year rolled round, and May came again. Uncle Dan was well satisfied, Aunt Becky's preparations were completed, and Ruth had not "changed her mind."

"Settle about the weddin' as soon as you like,

my girl, and I'll see that it is a merry one," said the old man, coming in from work, as Ruth blew the horn from the back porch one night at sunset.

"Nat must decide that. Where is he, Uncle?" asked the girl, looking out upon the quiet landscape, touched with spring's tenderest green.

"Down in the medder, ploughin'. It 's a toughish bit, and he 'll be late, I reckon; for he took a long noon-spell, and I give him a piece of my mind about it, so I 'll venter to say he won't touch a bit of victuals till the last furrow is laid," answered Uncle Dan, plodding away to wash his hands at the horse-trough.

"Nay, Uncle, it is his birthday, and surely he had a right to a little rest, for he works like a slave, to please us, though far from well, I 'm thinking." And, waiting for no reply, Ruth hurried in, filled a tankard with cider, and tripped away to bring her lover home, singing as she went, for Nat loved to hear her voice.

Down the green lane toward the river the happy singer stepped, thinking in what sweet words she could give the old man's message. But the song died on her lips and the smiling eyes grew wistful suddenly; for, passing by the willow-trees, she saw the patient oxen standing in the field alone.

"Nat is hunting violets for me," she thought, with a throb of pleasure; for she was jealous of a viewless rival, and valued every token of fidelity her lover gave her.

But as she drew nearer Ruth frowned; for Nat lay beside the river, evidently quite forgetful of scolding, supper, and sweetheart. No, not of the latter; for a little nosegay of violets lay ready near the paper on which he seemed to be writing a song or sonnet to accompany the gift.

Seeing this, the frown faded, as the girl stole noiselessly across the grass, to peep over his shoulder, with a soft rebuke for his imprudence and delay.

Alas for Ruth! One glance at the placid face, pillowed on his arm, told her that this birthday was Nat's last; for the violets were less white than the cheek they touched, the pencil had fallen from nerveless fingers, and Death's hand had written "Finis" to both life and lay. With a bitter cry, she gathered the weary head into her arms, fearing she had come too late to say good-by. But the eyes that opened were so tranquil, and the pale lips that answered wore such a happy smile, she felt that tears would mar his peace, and hushed her sobs, to listen as he whispered brokenly, with a glance that brightened as it turned from the wide field where his last hard day's work lay finished, to the quiet river, whose lullaby was soothing him to sleep.

"Tell Uncle I did not stop till the job was done, nor break my promise; for the year is over now, and it was so sweet to write again that I forgot to go home till it was too late."

"O Nat, not too late. You shall work no more, but write all day, without a care. We have been too hard upon you, and you too patient with our blindness. Dear lad, forgive us, and come home to live a happier year than this has been," cried Ruth, trying with remorseful tenderness to keep the delicate spirit that was escaping from her hold, like the butterfly that died among her roses with broken wings.

But Nat had no desire to stay; for he *was* going home, to feel hunger, thirst, and weariness no more, to find a love Ruth could not give, and to change earth's prose to heaven's immortal poetry. Yet he lingered on the threshold to look back and whisper gently: "It is better so, sweetheart. There was no place for me here, and I was homesick for my own friends and country. I 'm going to find them, and I 'm quite content. Forget me and be happy; or remember me only in the springtime, when the world is loveliest and my birthday comes. See, this is all I had to give you; but my heart was in it."

He tried to lift the unfinished song and give it to her; but it fluttered down upon his breast, and the violets dropped after, lying there unstirred by any breath, for with the words a shadow deeper than that twilight laid upon the fields stole over the face on Ruth's bosom, and all the glory of the sunset sky could only touch it with a pathetic peace, as the poet lay asleep beside the river.

He lies there still, the legend says, under the low green mound, where violets bloom earliest, where the old willows drop their golden tassels in the spring, and blackbirds fill the air with their melodious ecstasy. No song of his lived after him; no trace of him remains, except that nameless grave; and few ever heard of one who came and went like the snow for which they christened him. Yet it seems as if his gentle ghost still haunted those sunny meadows, still listened to the enchanted river, and touched with some mysterious charm the places that knew him once. For strangers find a soft attraction in the quiet landscape; lovers seek those green solitudes to tell the story that is always new; and poets muse beside the shadowy stream, hearing, as he heard, a call to live the life that lifts them highest by unwavering fidelity to the gift Heaven sends.

LETTY'S TRAMP

LETTY sat on the doorstep one breezy summer day, looking down the road and wishing with all her heart that something pleasant would happen. She often did this; and one of her earliest delights when a lonely child was to sit there with a fairy book upon her knee, waiting and watching in all good faith for something wonderful to happen.

In those days, Cinderella's golden coach dashing round the corner to carry her away was the favorite dream; but at eighteen one thinks more of the prince than either golden coach or splendid ball. But no prince as yet had cut his way through the grove of "laylocks" round the gate, and the little beauty still dreamed waking dreams on the doorstep, with her work forgotten in her lap.

Behind her in the quaint, quiet room Aunt Liddy dozed in her easy chair, the clock ticked, the bird chirped, old Bran snapped lazily at the flies, and nothing else broke the hush that brooded over the place. It was always so, and

Letty often felt as if an earthquake would be a blessed relief to the dreadful monotony of her life.

To-day it was peculiarly trying, for a slight incident had ruffled the calm; and, though it lasted but a moment, it had given Letty a glimpse into that lovely "new world which is the old." A carriage containing a gay young couple on their honeymoon trip had stopped at the gate, for the bride had a fancy for a draught from the mossy well, and the bridegroom blandly demanded that her whim be gratified.

Letty served them, and while one pretty girl slaked her thirst the other watched her with admiring eyes and a tender interest, touched by envy. It was all over in a minute. Then bonny bride and enamoured bridegroom rolled away on that enchanted journey which is taken but once in a lifetime, leaving a cloud of dust behind and a deeper discontent in Letty's heart.

With a long sigh she had gone back to her seat, and, closing her eyes upon a world that could offer her so little, fell a-dreaming again, till a rough voice startled her wide awake.

"I say, miss, can you give a poor fellow a bite and a sup?"

Opening her eyes, she saw a sturdy tramp leaning over the low gate, so ragged, dusty, worn, and weary that she forgave the look of admiration in the bold black eyes which had been fixed on her longer than she knew. Before she could answer, however, Aunt Liddy, a hospitable old soul, called out from within, —

"Certin, certin. Set right down on the door-step and rest a spell, while we see what we can do about vittles."

Letty vanished into the pantry, and the man threw himself down in the shady porch, regardless of Bran's suspicious growl. He pulled off his hat, stretched out his tired limbs, and leaned his rough head back among the woodbine leaves, with a long breath, as if nearly spent.

When Letty brought him a plate of bread and meat, he took it from her so eagerly and with such a ravenous look that she shrank back involuntarily. Seeing which he said, with a poor attempt at a laugh, —

"You need n't be afraid. I look like a rough customer; but I won't hurt you."

"Lawful sakes! We ain't no call to be afraid of no one, though we be lone women; for Bran is better 'n a dozen men. A lamb to them he knows; but let any one try to pester Letty, and I never see a fercer beast," said Aunt Liddy, as the girl went back for more food, seeing the stranger's need.

"He knows *I'm* all right, and makes friends at once, you see," answered the tramp, with a satisfied nod, as Bran, after a brief investigation, sat down beside him, with a pacific wag of the tail.

"Well, I never! He don't often do that to

strangers. Guess you 're fond of dumb critters," said Aunt Liddy, much impressed by Bran's unusual condescension.

" They 've been my best friends, and I don't forget it," returned the man, giving the dog a bone, though half-starved himself.

Something in the tone, the act, touched Letty's tender heart, and made her own voice very sweet and cordial as she said, —

" Please have some milk. It 's nice and cold."

The tramp put up both hands to take the bowl, and as he did so looked into a face so full of compassion that it seemed like an angel's leaning down to comfort a lost and weary soul. Hard as life had been to the poor fellow, it had not spoiled him yet, as was plainly proved by the change that softened his whole face like magic, and trembled in the voice that said, as if it were a sort of grace, " God bless you, Miss," as he bent his head and drank.

Only a look of human sympathy and human gratitude; yet, in the drawing of a breath, it cast out Letty's fear, and made the stranger feel as if he had found friends, for it was the touch of Nature that makes the whole world kin. Every one seemed to feel its influence. Bran turned his benevolent eyes approvingly from his mistress to his new friend: the girl sat down confidingly; and the old lady began to talk, for, being fond of chat, she considered a stranger as a special providence.

" Where be you travellin'? "

" Nowhere in particular."

" Where did you come from, then? " continued Aunt Liddy, undaunted by the short answer.

" California."

" Do tell! Guess you 've been one of the rovin' sort, ain't you? "

" Have n't done much else."

" It don't appear to have agreed with you remarkable well," said the blunt old lady, peering at him over her spectacles.

" If I had n't had the devil's own luck, I 'd have been a rich man, instead of a beggar," answered the tramp, with a grim look and an ireful knitting of his black brows.

" Been unfort'nate, have you? I 'm sorry for that; but it 'pears to me them as stays to home and works stiddy does better than them that goes huntin' after luck," observed Aunt Liddy, feeling it her duty to give a word of advice.

" Should n't wonder if you were right, ma'am. But some folks have n't got any home to stay in; and fellows of my sort have to hunt after luck, for it won't come to 'em."

" Ain't you got no friends, young man? "

" Not one. Lost the last yesterday."

" Took suddin, I suppose? " and the old lady's face was full of interest as she put the question.

" Drowned."

"Merciful sakes! How did it happen?"

"Got hurt, could n't be cured, so I drowned him, and" —

"What!" shrieked Aunt Liddy, upsetting her footstool with a horrified start.

"Only a dog, ma'am. I could n't carry him, would n't leave him to suffer; so put him out of pain and came on alone."

The tramp had ceased eating, and sat with his head on his hand in a despondent attitude, that told his story better than words. His voice was gruffer than ever as he spoke of his dog; but the last word was husky, and he put his hand on Bran's head with a touch that won the good creature's heart entirely, and made him lick the downcast face, with a little whine of sympathy and satisfaction.

Letty's eyes were full, and Aunt Liddy took snuff and settled her footstool, feeling that something must be done for one who showed signs of being worth the saving.

"Poor creter! And you was fond of him?" she said in a motherly tone; for the man of five or six and twenty was but a boy to her.

"I 'd have been a brute if I was n't fond of him, for he stuck to me when all the other fellows cut me, and tried to drag himself along with a broken leg, rather than leave me. Talk about friends! Give me a dumb animal if you want one worth having."

A bitter tone was in the man's voice and a

wrathful spark kindled in his eyes, as if wrong as well as want had made him what he was.

"Rest a little, and tell us about California. A neighbor went there, and we like to hear news of that great, splendid place."

Letty spoke, and the half-eager, half-timid voice was very winning, especially to one who seldom heard such now. Seeing her kindly interest, and glad to pay for his meal in the only way he could, the man told some of his adventures in brief but graphic words, while the old woman plied him with questions and the young one listened with a face so full of pretty wonder that the story-teller was inspired to do his best.

Aunt Liddy's cap-frills stood erect with horror at some of the hair-breadth escapes recounted; but to Letty it was better than any romance she had ever read to listen to tales full of danger and hardship, told by a living voice and face to face with the chief actor in them all, who unconsciously betrayed that he possessed many of the manly attributes women most admire.

"After adventures like these, I don't wonder it seems hard to settle down, as other folks do," she said warmly, when the man stopped short, as if ashamed of talking so much of his own affairs.

"I would n't mind trying it, though," he answered, as he glanced about the sunny little room, so homelike and reposeful, and so haunted by all the sweet influences that touch men's hearts when most forlorn.

"You 'd better," said Aunt Liddy, decidedly. "Git work and stick to it; and, if luck don't come, bread and butter will, and in a world of woe mebby that 's about as much as any one on us ought to expect."

"I have tried to get it. But I 'm such a hard-looking chap no one wants me; and I don't blame 'em. Look at that hat, now! Ain't that enough to spoil a man's chance, let alone his looks?" The young fellow held up a battered object with such a comical mixture of disgust and indignation that Letty could not help laughing; and the blithe sound was so contagious that the wanderer joined in it, cheered already by rest and food and kindly words.

"It 's singular what store men-folks do set by their hats. My Moses could n't never read his paper till he 'd put on his 'n, and as for drivin' a nail bare-headed, in doors or out, he 'd never think of such a thing," said Aunt Liddy, with the air of one well versed in the mysterious ways of men-folks.

But Letty clapped her hands, as if a brilliant idea had flashed upon her, and, running to the back entry, returned with a straw hat, brown and dusty, but shady, whole, and far more appropriate to the season than the ragged felt the man was eying hopelessly.

"It is n't very good; but it might do for a time. We only keep it to scare folks, and I don't feel afraid now. Would you mind if I gave it to you?" stammered Letty, coloring up, as she tried to offer her poor gift courteously.

"Mind! I guess I'd be glad to get it, fit or no fit," and, dropping the old hat, the tramp clapped on the new one, making his mirror of the bright eyes before him.

"It does nicely, and you're very welcome," said the girl, getting rosier still, for there was something beside gratitude in the brown face that had lost the dogged, dangerous look it wore at first.

"Now, if you was to wash up and smooth that hair of yourn a trifle, you'd be a likely-looking young man; and, if you're civil-spoken and willin' to lend a hand anywheres, you'll git work, I ain't a doubt," observed Aunt Liddy, feeling a growing interest in the wayfarer, and, woman-like, acknowledging the necessity of putting the best foot foremost.

Letty ran for basin and towel, and, pointing to the well, modestly retired into the kitchen, while Aunt Liddy watched the vigorous scrubbing that went on in the yard; for the tramp splashed the water about like a Newfoundland dog, and Bran assisted at the brief toilet with hospitable zeal.

It seemed as if a different man came out from that simple baptism; for the haggard cheek had a glow upon it, the eyes had lost their hopelessness, and something like courage and self-respect shone in the face that looked in at the door as the stranger gave back basin and towel, saying, with a wave of the old straw hat, —

"I 'm heartily obliged, ma'am. Would you kindly tell me how far it is to the next big town?"

"Twenty miles. The cars will take you right there, and the deepo ain't fur," answered Aunt Liddy, showing the way.

The man glanced at his ragged shoes, then squared his broad shoulders, as if bracing himself for the twenty long hot miles that his weary feet must carry him, since his pockets were empty, and he could not bring himself to ask for any thing but food enough to keep life in him.

"Good-by, ma'am, and God bless you." And, slouching the hat over his eyes, he limped away, escorted to the gate by Bran.

At the turn of the road he stopped and looked back as wistfully as ever Letty had done along the shadowy road, and as he looked it seemed as if he saw a younger self setting off with courage, hope, and energy upon the journey, which alas! had ended here. His eye went to the old well, as if there had been some healing in its water; then turned to the porch, where he had been fed and comforted, and lingered there as if some kindly memory warmed his solitary heart.

Just then a little figure in blue gingham ran out and came fluttering after him, accompanied by Bran, in a state of riotous delight. Rosy and breathless, Letty hurried to him, and, looking up with a face full of the innocent compassion that never can offend, she said, offering a parcel neatly folded up, —

"Aunt Liddy sends you some dinner; and this, so that you need n't walk, unless you like, you are so lame."

As if more touched than he cared to show, the man took the food, but gently put away the little roll of greenbacks, saying quickly, —

"Thank you for this; but I can't take your money."

"We ain't rich, but we love to help folks. So you need n't be proud about it." And Letty looked ruffled at his refusal.

"I 'll take something else, if you don't mind," said the tramp, pulling off his hat, with a sudden smile that made his face look young and comely.

"What is it?" And Letty looked up so innocently that it was impossible to resist the impulse of a grateful heart.

His answer was to stoop and kiss the blooming cheek, that instantly grew scarlet with girlish shame and anger as she turned to fly. Catching her by the hand, he said penitently, —

"I could n't help it, you 're so good to me. Don't begrudge me a kiss for luck. I need it, God knows!"

The man's real destitution and despair broke out in these words, and he grasped the little hand as if it was the only thing that kept him from the manifold temptations of a desperate mood.

It thrilled the girl like a cry for help, and made her forget every thing except that a fellow-creature suffered. She shook the big hand warmly, and said, with all her heart, —

"You 're welcome, if it helps you. Good-by and good luck to you!" and ran away as fast as she had come.

The man stood motionless, and watched her till she vanished, then turned and tramped sturdily on, muttering to himself, with a suspicious gruffness in his voice, —

"If I had a little mate like that alongside, I know my luck would turn."

CHAPTER II

A WILD December night, with bitter wind and blinding snow, reigned outside the long, rude building, lighted only by furnace fires, that went roaring up the tall chimneys, whence poured clouds of smoke and showers of sparks, like beacons through the storm. No living thing appeared in that shadowy place except a matronly gray cat, sitting bolt upright upon an old rug spread over a heap of sand near one of the fires. A newspaper and a tin pail were beside her, and she seemed to have mounted guard, while the watchman of the Foundry went his rounds.

A door stood half-open upon the sheltered side of the building; and suddenly, as if blown thither like a storm-driven bird, a little figure came fluttering in, breathless, half-frozen, and quite bewildered by a long struggle with the pitiless gale. Feebly brushing away the snow that blinded her, the poor thing looked about her with frightened eyes; and, seeing no one but the cat, seemed to take courage and crept toward the fire, suffering for the moment conquering fear.

"Oh! Pussy, let me warm myself one minute, for I 'm perished with the cold," she whispered, stretching two benumbed hands to the blaze.

The cat opened her yellow eyes, and, evidently glad to meet one of her own sex, began to purr hospitably as she rustled across the newspaper to greet her guest. There was something inexpressibly comforting in the sound; and, reassured by it, the girl pushed back her drenched hat, shook her snowy garments, and drew a long breath, like one nearly spent. Yet, even while she basked in the warmth that was salvation, her timid eyes glanced about the great, gloomy place, and her attitude was that of one ready to fly at a moment's warning.

Presently a step sounded on a flight of stairs leading to some loft above. The wanderer started like a hare, and, drawing nearer to the door, paused as if to catch a glimpse of the approaching face before she fled away into the storm, that howled just then with a violence which might well daunt a stouter heart.

A tall man, in a rough coat, with grizzled hair and beard under an old fur cap, came slowly down the steps, whistling softly to himself, as he swung his lantern to and fro.

"An old man, and the cat is fond of him. I guess I 'll dare to ask my way, or I 'll never get home," thought the girl, as her eye scanned the new-comer with a woman's quickness.

An involuntary rustle of her dress caught his ear, and, lifting the lantern, he saw her at once; but did not speak, as if afraid of frightening her still more, for her pale face and the appealing gesture of the outstretched hand told her fear and need better than her hurried words, —

" Oh! please, I 've lost my way and am nearly frozen. Could I warm myself a bit and find out where I am?"

" Of course, you may. Why, bless your heart, I would n't turn a dog out such a night as this, much less a poor little soul like you," answered the man, in a hearty tone, that rang true on the listening ear of the girl.

Then he hung up the lantern, put a stool nearer the fire, and beckoned her to approach. But even the kindly words and act failed to win the timid creature; for she drew back as he advanced, gave a glance at the door, and said, as if appealing to the best instincts of the man, whom she longed yet feared to trust, —

" Thank you; but it 's getting late, and I ought to be getting on, if I knew the way. Perhaps you 've got some girls of your own, so you can understand how scared I am to be lost at night and in such a strange place as this."

The man stared, then laughed, and, shaking the snow from his curly hair and beard, showed himself to be a young and pleasant-looking fellow, with a merry eye, an honest brown face, and a hearty voice.

"You thought I was an old chap, did you? Wish I was, if it would be any comfort to you. I 've got no little girls, neither, more 's the pity; but you need n't be afraid of me, though it *is* late and lonely. Why, Lord love you, child, I 'm not a brute! Sit down and thaw out, while you tell me where you want to go."

The half-indignant tone of the man made his guest feel as if she had insulted him; and she obeyed with a docility which appeased his anger at once. Seating herself upon the stool, she leaned toward the fire with an irrepressible shiver, and tried to keep her teeth from chattering as she told her little story.

"I want work badly, and went a long way, hoping to get some. But I did n't find it, and that discouraged me very much. I had no money, so had to walk, and the storm got so bad I lost my way. Then I was scared and half-frozen, and so bewildered I think I'd have died if I had n't seen the light and come in here."

"I guess you would. And the best thing you can do now is to stop till the storm lifts. Should n't wonder if it did about midnight," said the man, stirring up the red embers, as if anxious to do something for her comfort.

"But that is so late, and I must be ever so far away from home; for I came over the wrong bridge. Oh, me! What shall I do?" And the poor thing wrung her hands in dismay.

"Won't your folks go to look for you?"

"I have n't any one in the world to care for me. The woman where I board won't trouble herself; or she 'll think I 've run away, because I owe her money. I might be dead in the river, and no one would mind!" sighed the girl, leaning her head on her hands, while some bright, dishevelled hair fell over her face, as if to hide its youth and innocence from a world that seemed to have no shelter for either.

"That 's hard! But don't you be down-hearted, child. Things often mend when they seem worst. I know; for I 've been through the mill, and had friends raised up to me when I 'd about done with living, as a bad job. I can't leave here until sunrise; but I 'll do the best I can for you till then. Sam will be along early, and he 'll see to you, if you can't trust me; for he is as gray as a badger, and he 's got six girls of his own, if that 's a recommendation. I 've got nothing but a cat; and she trusts me. Don't you, old Sally?"

As he spoke, the man sat down upon the sand-heap, and Sally leaped to his knee, rubbing her head against his cheek, with a soft sound of confidence and contentment which seemed to afford her friend great satisfaction. The girl smiled faintly, and said, in an apologetic tone, for there had been something like reproach in the man's voice, as he asked the dumb animal to vouch for his character, —

"I don't believe I 'd have dared to come in

here if I had n't seen Pussy. But I thought any one who was good to her would be good to me; and now I 'm sure of it."

"That 's right. You see, I 'm a lonesome sort of a chap and like something to pet. So I took old Sally, and we get on capitally. She won't let the other fellows touch her, but always comes and sits with me when I am alone here nights. And it 's surprising what good company she is."

He laughed as he spoke, as if half-ashamed of the amiable weakness, yet anxious to put his guest at her ease. He evidently succeeded; for she stretched two shabby little boots toward the fire and leaned her head against a grimy beam, saying, with a sigh of weariness, —

"It is very comfortable; but the heat makes me feel queer and dizzy."

"You 're just about used up; and I 'm going to give you a sup of hot coffee. That 'll bring you round in a jiffy. It 's time for supper. Hey, Sally?"

As he spoke, the man set his pail in the hot ashes, unfolded a parcel of bread and meat, and, laying a rude sandwich on a clean bit of paper, offered it with a hospitable, —

"Have a bit. Do, now. You 've had a hard pull and need something to set you up."

Leaning forward to give and take, two faces came into the clear red glow of the furnace-fire, and a look of recognition flashed into each so suddenly that it startled both man and maid into involuntary frankness of expression.

"Why, it's little Letty!"

"And you are my tramp!"

A change so rapid as to be almost ludicrous came over the pair in the drawing of a breath. She smoothed back her hair and hid the shabby boots, yet sat more erect upon the stool, as if she had a right there and felt no longer any fear. He pulled off his cap, with a pleasant mixture of respect, surprise, and satisfaction in his manner, as he said, in a half-proud, half-humble tone, —

"No, miss; for, thanks to you, I'm a decent man now."

"Then you did find work and get on?" she exclaimed, with a bright, wistful look, that touched him very much.

"Did n't you get my letter?" he asked eagerly. "I sent you the first dollar I earned, and told you and the old lady I was all right."

Letty shook her head, and all the light passed out of her face, leaving it pathetic in its patient sorrow.

"Aunt Liddy died a week after you were there, so suddenly that every thing was in confusion, and I never got a letter. I wish *she* had known of it, because it would have pleased her so. We often talked about you and hoped you'd do well. We led such quiet lives, you see, that any little thing interested us for a long time."

"It was a little thing to you, I dare say; but it was salvation to me. Not the money or the food only, but the kindness of the old lady, and — and the look in your sweet face, miss. I 'd got so far down, through sickness and bad luck, that there did n't seem any thing left for me but deviltry or death. That day it was a toss-up between any bad job that came along first and drowning, like my dog. That seemed sort of mean, though, and I felt more like being revenged somehow on the world, that had been so hard on me."

He stopped short, breathing hard, with a sudden spark in his black eyes and a nervous clenching of the strong hands that made Letty shrink; for he seemed to speak in spite of himself, as if the memory of that time had left its impress on his life.

"But you did n't do anything bad. I 'm sure you did n't; for Aunt Liddy said there was the making of a man in you, because you were so quick to feel a little bit of kindness and take good advice."

The soft, eager voice of the girl seemed to work the miracle anew, for a smile broke over his face, the angry spark was quenched, and the clenched hand opened to offer again all it had to give, as he said, with a characteristic mingling of fun and feeling in his voice, —

"I don't know much about angels; but I felt as if I 'd met a couple that day, for they saved me from destruction. You cast your bread upon the waters, and it 's come back when, maybe, you need it 'most as much as I did then. 'T is n't half as nice as yours; but perhaps a blessing will do as well as butter."

Letty took the brown bread, feeling that he had said the best grace over it; and while she ate he talked, evidently moved to open his heart by the memory of the past, and eager to show that he had manfully persisted in the well-doing his angels had advised.

"That was nearly two years ago, you know, and I 've been hard at it ever since. I took anything that come along, and was glad to get it. The hat did that, I firmly believe." And he laughed a short laugh, adding soberly, "But I did n't take to work at first, for I 'd been a rover and liked it; so it took a long pull and a strong pull and a pull all together before I settled down steady. The hat and the" — he was going to say "kiss;" but a look at the lonely little creature sitting there so confidingly made him change the word to — "the money seemed to bring me luck; and I followed the advice of the good old lady, and stuck to my work till I got to liking it. I 've been here more than a year now, and am getting on so well I shall be overseer before long. I 'm only watchman for a short time. Old Sam has been sick, and they wanted some one they could trust, so they chose me."

It was good to see him square his broad shoulders and throw back his head as he said that; and pretty to see Letty nod and smile with sincerest pleasure in his success, as she said, —

"It looks dark and ugly now; but I 've seen a foundry when they were casting, and it was splendid to watch the men manage the furnaces and do wonderful things with great hammers and moulds and buckets of red-hot melted iron. I like to know you do such things, and now I 'm not afraid. It seems sort of romantic and grand to work in this place, where every one must be strong and brave and skilful to get on."

"That 's it. That 's why I like it; don't you see?" he answered, brightening with pleasure at her artless praise. "You just come some casting day, and I 'll show you sights you won't forget in a hurry. If there was n't danger and noise and good hard work wrastling with fire and iron, and keeping a rough set of fellows in order, I should n't stay; for the restless fit comes on sometimes, and I feel as if I must cut away somewhere. Born so, and can't help it. Maybe I could, if I had something to anchor me; but, as you say, 'Nobody would care much if I was in the river,' and that 's bad for a chap like me."

"Sally would care," said the girl, quite soberly; for she sympathized now with the man's loneliness as she could not have done two years ago.

"So she would; but I 'll take her with me when I leave — not for the river, mind you. I 'm in no danger of that nonsense now. But, if I go on a tramp (and I may, if the fit gets too strong for me), she shall go too; and we 'll be Dick Whittington and his cat over again."

He spoke in a devil-may-care tone, and patted the plump Tabby with a curious mixture of boyish recklessness and a man's sad knowledge of life in his face.

"Don't go," pleaded Letty, feeling that she had a certain responsibility in the matter. "I should mind, as well as Sally; for, if Aunt Liddy and I helped put you in a good way, it would be a disappointment to have you go wrong. Please stop here, and I 'll try and come to see you work some day, if I can get time. I 'm likely to have plenty of it, I 'm afraid."

She began eagerly, but ended with a despondent droop of the whole figure, that made her new friend forget himself in interest for her.

"I 'll stop, honor bright. And you come and look after me now and then. That 'll keep me steady. See if it don't. But tell me how you are getting on? Little down on your luck just now, I guess? Come, I 've told my story, you tell yours, and maybe I can lend a hand. I owe you a good turn, you know; and I 'm one that likes to pay his debts, if he can."

"You did pay yours; but I never got the letter, for I came away after Aunty died. You see I was n't her own niece, — only sort of a distant relation; and she took me because my own people were gone. Her son had all she left, — it was n't much; and she told him to be good to me. But I soon saw that I was a burden, and could n't bear to stay. So I went away, to take care of myself. I liked it at first; but this winter, times are so hard and work so scarce, I don't get on at all."

"What do you do, miss?" asked Whittington, with added respect; because in her shabby dress and altered face he read the story of a struggle Letty was too proud to tell.

"I sew," she answered briefly, smoothing out her wet shawl with a hand so thin and small it was pathetic to see, when one remembered that nothing but a needle in those slender fingers kept want and sin at bay.

The kindly fellow seemed to feel that; and, as his eye went from his own strong right arm to the sledge-hammer it often swung, the instinct of protection so keen in manly men made him long to stand between poor Letty and the hard world he knew so well. The magnetism of sympathy irresistibly attracted iron to steel, while little needle felt assured that big hammer would be able to beat down many of the obstacles which now seemed insurmountable, if she only dared to ask for aid. But help came without the asking.

"Been after work, you say? Why, we could give you heaps of it, if you don't mind its being coarse and plain. This sort of thing, you know," touching his red shirt with a business-like air. "Our men use 'em altogether, and like 'em strong in the seams. Some ain't, and buttons fly off just looking at 'em. That makes a fellow mad, and swearing comes easy."

But Letty shook her head, though she could n't help smiling at his sober way of explaining the case and its sad consequences.

"I 've tried that work, and it does n't pay. Six cents for a shirt, and sometimes only four, is n't enough to earn one's board and clothes and fire, even if one made half a dozen a day. *You* can't get them for that, and somebody grows rich while *we* starve."

"Hanged if I ever buy another! See here, you make me enough for a year, and we 'll have a fair bargain between us. That is, if you can't do better and don't mind," he added, suddenly abating his warmth and looking almost bashful over the well-meant proposal.

"I 'd love to do it. Only you must n't pay too much," said Letty, glad of anything to keep her hands and thoughts busy, for life was very bare and cold just then.

"All right. I 'll see to it directly, and nobody be the wiser," returned her new employer, privately resolving to order a bale of red flannel on the morrow, and pay fabulous prices for the work of the little friend who had once kept him from worse than starvation.

It was not much to offer, and red flannel was not a romantic subject of conversation; but something in the prompt relief and the hearty good-will of the man went to Letty's heart, already full to overflowing with many cares and troubles. She tried to thank him, but could only cover up her face and sob. It was so sweet and comfortable to find any one who cared enough for her to lift her out of the slough of despond, which was to her as dangerous a mood as the desperate one he had known. There were hands enough to beckon the winsome creature to the wrong side of the quagmire, where so many miss the stepping-stones; but she felt that this was the right side, and the hand an honest one, though rough and grimy with hard work. So the tears were glad and grateful tears, and she let them flow, melting the fatal frost that had chilled her hope and faith in God and man.

But the causer of them could not bear the sight, for the contrast between this forlorn girl and the blithe, blooming Letty of that memorable day was piteous. Manlike, he tried to express his sympathy in deeds as well as words, and, hastily filling a tin cup from the coffee-can, pressed it upon her with a fatherly stroke of the bent head and a soothing, —

"Now, my dear, just take a sip of this, and don't cry any more. We'll straighten things out. So cheer up, and let me lend a hand anywhere, anyhow."

But hunger and fear, weariness and cold, had been too much for poor Letty; and, in the act of lifting up her wet face to thank him, the light left her eyes, and she would have slipped to the ground, if he had not caught her.

In a minute she was herself again, lying on the old rug, with snow upon her forehead and some one fanning her with a newspaper.

"I thought I was going to die," she whispered, looking about her in a dazed sort of way.

"Not a bit of it! You 're going to sleep. That 's what you want, and old Sally 's going to sit by while you do it. It 's a hardish pillow; but I 've put my handkerchief over it, and, being Monday, it 's spick-and-span clean."

Letty smiled as she turned her cheek to the faded silk handkerchief laid over the rolled-up coat under her head, for Pussy was nestling close beside her, as if her presence was both a comfort and defence. Yet the girl's eyes filled even while she smiled, for, when most desolate, a friend had been raised up to her; and, though the face bending over her was dark and shaggy, there was no fear in her own, as she said half-appealingly, half-confidingly, —

"I don't believe I could go if I tried, I 'm so worn out. But you 'll take care of me, and in the morning show me the way home?"

"Please God, I will!" he answered, as solemnly as if taking an oath, adding, as he stepped back to the stool she had left: "I shall stay here and read my paper. Nothing shall scare you; so make yourself comfortable, and drop off with an easy mind."

Sitting there, he saw her lay her hands together, as if she said some little prayer; then, turning her face from the light, she fell asleep, lulled by the drowsy purr of the humble friend to whom she clung even in her dreams. He only looked a minute, for something that was neither the shimmer of firelight nor the glitter of snow-dust made the quiet group dance mistily before his eyes; and, forgetting his paper, he fell to drying Letty's hat.

It was both comical and pleasant to see how tenderly he touched the battered thing, with what interest he surveyed it, perched on his big hand, and how carefully he smoothed out the ribbons, evidently much bewildered as to which was the front and which the back. Giving up the puzzle, he hung it on the handle of the great hammer, and, leaning his chin on his hand, began to build castles in the air and watch the red embers, as if he saw in them some vision of the future that was very pleasant.

Hour after hour struck from the city clocks across the river; the lantern burned itself out, untrimmed; the storm died away; and a soft, white silence followed the turmoil of the night. Still Letty slept like a tired child; still old Sally, faithful to her trust, lay in the circle of the girl's arm; and still the watchman sat before the fire, dreaming waking dreams, as he had often done before; but never any half so earnest, sweet, and hopeful as those that seemed to weave a tender romance about the innocent sleeper, to whom he was loyally paying a debt of gratitude with such poor hospitality as he could show.

Dawn came up rosy and clear along the east; and the first level ray of wintry sunlight, as it struck across the foundry walls, fell on Letty's placid face, with the bright hair shining like a halo round it.

Feeling very much as if he had entertained an angel unaware, the man stood enjoying the pretty picture, hesitating to wake her, yet fearing that a gruff hallo from old Sam might do it too suddenly. Somehow he hated to have her go; for the gloomy foundry seemed an enchanted sort of place this morning, with a purer heaven and earth outside, and within the "little mate" whom he felt a strong desire to keep "always alongside," for something better than luck's sake.

He was smiling to himself over the thought, yet half ashamed to own how it had grown and strengthened in a night, when Letty opened wide a pair of eyes full of the peace sleep brings and the soft lustre that comes after tears. Involuntarily the man drew back, and waited silently for her to speak. She looked bewildered for a moment, then remembered, and sprang up, full of the relief and fresh gratitude that came with her first waking thought.

"How long I 've slept! How kind you were to me! I can go now, if you will start me right."

"You are heartily welcome! I can take you home at once, unless you'd rather wait for Sam," he answered, with a quick look toward the door, as if already jealous of the venerable Samuel.

"I'd rather go before any one comes. But perhaps you ought not to leave yet? I would n't like to take you from your duty," began Letty, looking about her for her hat.

"Duty be — hanged! I'm going to see you safe home, if you'll let me. Here's your hat. I dried it; but it don't look quite shipshape somehow." And taking the shabby little object from the nail where it hung, he presented it with such respectful care that a glimmer of the old mirthfulness came into Letty's face, as she said, surveying it with much disfavor, —

"It is almost as bad as the one I gave you; but it must do."

"I've got that old thing up at my place now. Keep it for luck. Wish I had one for you. Hold on! Here's a tippet — nice and warm. Have it for a hood. You'll find it cold outside."

He was so intent on making her comfortable that Letty could not refuse, and tied on the tippet, while he refilled the cup with hot coffee, carefully saved for her.

"Little Red Riding Hood! Blest if you ain't!" he exclaimed admiringly, as he turned to her again, and saw the sweet face in its new head-gear.

"But you are not the wolf," she answered, with a smile like sunshine, bending to drink from the cup he held.

As she lifted her head, the blue eyes and the black exchanged again the subtle glance of sympathy that made them friends before; only now the blue ones looked up full of gratitude, and the black ones looked down soft with pity. Neither spoke; but Letty stooped, and, gathering old Sally in her arms, kissed the friendly creature, then followed her guide to the door.

"How beautiful!" she cried, as the sun came dazzling down upon the snow, that hid all dark and ugly things with a veil of purity.

"Looks kind of bridal, don't it?" said the man, taking a long breath of the frosty air, and straightening himself up, as if anxious to look his best by daylight.

He never had looked better, in spite of the old coat and red shirt; for the glow of the furnace-fire still seemed to touch his brown face, the happy visions of the night still shone in his eyes, and the protective kindliness of a generous nature gave dignity to the rough figure, as he strode into the snow and stretched his hand to Letty, saying cheerily, —

"Pretty deep, but hold on to me, and I'll get you through. Better take my hand; I washed it a-purpose."

Letty did take it in both her little ones; and they went away together through the deserted streets, feeling as if they were the only pair alive in the still white world that looked so lovely in the early sunshine.

The girl was surprised to find how short the way seemed; for, in spite of drifts, she got on bravely, with a strong arm to help and a friendly voice to encourage her. Yet when she reached the last corner she stopped, and said, with a sudden shyness which he understood and liked, —

"I 'd best go on alone now. But I 'm very grateful to you! Please tell me your name. I 'd love to know who my friend is, though I never shall forget his kindness."

"Nor I yours. Joe Stone is my name. But I 'd rather you called me your tramp till we get something better," he answered, with a laugh in his eyes, as he bent toward her for a hearty shake of the slender hand that had grown warm in his.

"I will! Good-by, good-by!" And, suddenly remembering how they parted before, Letty blushed like a rose, and ran away as fast as the drifts would let her.

"And I 'll call you my Letty some day, if I 'm not much mistaken," Joe said to himself, with a decided nod, as he went back to the foundry, feeling that the world looked more "sort of bridal" than ever.

He was not mistaken; for, when spring budded, his dream came true, and in the little sewing-girl, who bound him with a silken thread so soft and strong it never broke, he found an anchor that held him fast to happiness and home. To Letty something wonderful happened at last. The prince came when most she needed him; and, though even when the beggar's rags fell off his only crown was the old hat, his royal robes red flannel and fustian, his sceptre a sledge-hammer, she knew and loved him, for

"The man was a man for a' that."

SCARLET STOCKINGS

CHAPTER I

HOW THEY WALKED INTO LENNOX'S LIFE

"COME out for a drive, Harry?"

"Too cold."

"Have a game of billiards?"

"Too tired."

"Go and call on the Fairchilds?"

"Having an unfortunate prejudice against country girls, I respectfully decline."

"What will you do, then?"

"Nothing, thank you."

And, settling himself more luxuriously upon the couch, Lennox closed his eyes, and appeared to slumber tranquilly. Kate shook her head, and stood regarding her brother despondently, till a sudden idea made her turn toward the window, exclaiming abruptly, —

"Scarlet stockings, Harry!"

"Where?" and, as if the words were a spell to break the deepest day-dream, Lennox hurried to the window, with an unusual expression of interest in his listless face.

"I thought that would succeed! She is n't

there, but I 've got you up, and you are not to go down again," laughed Kate, taking possession of the sofa.

"Not a bad manœuvre. I don't mind: it 's about time for the one interesting event of the day to occur, so I 'll watch for myself, thank you," and Lennox took the easy chair by the window with a shrug and a yawn.

"I 'm glad anything does interest you," said Kate, petulantly. "I don't think it amounts to much, for, though you perch yourself at the window every day to see that girl pass, you don't care enough about it to ask her name."

"I 've been waiting to be told."

"It 's Belle Morgan, the doctor's daughter, and my dearest friend."

"Then, of course, she is a blue-belle?"

"Don't try to be witty or sarcastic with her, for she will beat you at that."

"Not a dumb-belle, then?"

"Quite the reverse: she talks a good deal, and very well, too, when she likes."

"She is very pretty: has anybody the right to call her 'Ma belle'?"

"Many would be glad to do so, but she won't have anything to say to them."

"A Canterbury belle, in every sense of the word, then?"

"She might be, for all Canterbury loves her; but she is n't fashionable, and has more friends among the poor than among the rich."

"Ah, I see, a diving-bell, who knows how to go down into a sea of troubles, and bring up the pearls worth having."

"I 'll tell her that, it will please her. You are really waking up, Harry," and Kate smiled approvingly upon him.

"This page of 'Belle's Life' is rather amusing, so read away," said Lennox, glancing up the street, as if he awaited the appearance of the next edition with pleasure.

"There is n't much to tell; she is a nice, bright, energetic, warm-hearted dear; the pride of the doctor's heart, and a favorite with every one, though she is odd."

"How odd?"

"Does and says what she likes, is very blunt and honest, has ideas and principles of her own, goes to parties in high dresses, won't dance round dances, and wears red stockings, though Mrs. Plantagenet says it 's fast."

"Rather a jolly little person, I fancy. Why have n't we met her at some of the tea-fights and muffin-worries we 've been to lately?"

"It may make you angry, but it will do you good, so I 'll tell. She did n't care enough about seeing the distinguished stranger to come; that 's the truth."

"Sensible girl, to spare herself hours of mortal dulness, gossip, and dyspepsia," was the placid reply.

"She has seen you, though, at church, and

dawdling about town, and she called you 'Sir Charles Coldstream,' on the spot. How does that suit?" asked Kate, maliciously.

"Not bad; I rather like that. Wish she'd call some day, and stir us up."

"She won't; I asked her, but she said she was very busy, and told Jessy Tudor she was n't fond of peacocks."

"I don't exactly see the connection."

"Stupid boy! she meant you, of course."

"Oh, I'm peacocks, am I?"

"I don't wish to be rude, but I really do think you *are* vain of your good looks, elegant accomplishments, and the impression you make wherever you go. When it's worth while, you exert yourself, and are altogether fascinating; but the 'I come-see-and-conquer' air you put on spoils it all for sensible people."

"It strikes me that Miss Morgan has slightly infected you with her oddity, as far as bluntness goes. Fire away! it's rather amusing to be abused when one is dying of ennui."

"That's grateful and complimentary to me, when I have devoted myself to you ever since you came. But everything bores you, and the only sign of interest you've shown is in those absurd red hose. I *should* like to know what the charm is," said Kate, sharply.

"Impossible to say; accept the fact calmly as I do, and be grateful that there is one glimpse of color, life, and spirit in this aristocratic tomb of a town."

"You are not obliged to stay in it!" fiercely.

"Begging your pardon, my dove, but I am. I promised to give you my enlivening society for a month, and a Lennox keeps his word, even at the cost of his life."

"I 'm sorry I asked such a sacrifice; but I innocently thought that, after being away for five long years, you might care to see your orphan sister," and the dove produced her handkerchief with a plaintive sniff.

"Now, my dear creature, don't be melodramatic, I beg of you!" cried her brother, imploringly. "I wished to come, I pined to embrace you, and, I give you my word, I don't blame you for the stupidity of this confounded place."

"It never was so gay as since you came, for every one has tried to make it pleasant for you," cried Kate, ruffled at his indifference to the hospitable efforts of herself and friends. "But you don't care for any of our simple amusements, because you are spoilt by the flattery, gayety, and nonsense of foreign society. If I did n't know it was half affectation, I should be in despair, you are so *blasé* and absurd. It 's always the way with men: if one happens to be handsome, accomplished, and talented, he puts on as many airs, and is as vain as any silly girl."

"Don't you think if you took breath you 'd get on faster, my dear?" asked the imperturbable gentleman, as Kate paused with a gasp.

"I know it 's useless for me to talk, as you

don't care a straw what I say; but it 's true, and some day you 'll wish you had done something worth doing all these years. I was so proud of you, so fond of you, that I can't help being disappointed to find you with no more ambition than to kill time comfortably, no interest in anything but your own pleasures, and only energy enough to amuse yourself with a pair of scarlet stockings."

Pathetic as poor Kate's face and voice were, it was impossible to help laughing at the comical conclusion of her lament. Lennox tried to hide the smile on his lips by affecting to curl his moustache with care, and to gaze pensively out as if touched by her appeal. But he was n't, — oh, bless you, no! she was only his sister, and, though she might have talked with the wisdom of Solomon and the eloquence of Demosthenes, it would n't have done a particle of good. Sisters do very well to work for one, to pet one, and play confidante when one's love affairs need feminine wit to conduct them; but when they begin to reprove, or criticise, or moralize, it won't do, and can't be allowed, of course. Lennox never snubbed anybody, but blandly extinguished them by a polite acquiescence in all their affirmations, for the time being, and then went on in his own way as if nothing had been said.

"I dare say you are right; I 'll go and think over your very sensible advice," and, as if roused to unwonted exertion by the stings of an accusing conscience, he left the room abruptly.

"I do believe I 've made an impression at last! He 's actually gone out to think over what I 've said. Dear Harry, I was sure he had a heart, if one only knew how to get at it!" and with a sigh of satisfaction Kate went to the window to behold the "Dear Harry" going briskly down the street after a pair of scarlet stockings. A spark of anger kindled in her eyes as she watched him, and when he vanished she still stood knitting her brows in deep thought, for a grand idea was dawning upon her.

It *was* a dull town; no one could deny that, for everybody was so intensely proper and well-born that nobody dared to be jolly. All the houses were square, aristocratic mansions with Revolutionary elms in front and spacious coach-houses behind. The knockers had a supercilious perk to their bronze or brass noses, the dandelions on the lawns had a highly connected air, and the very pigs were evidently descended from "our first families." Stately dinner-parties, decorous dances, moral picnics, and much tea-pot gossiping were the social resources of the place. Of course, the young people flirted, for that diversion is apparently irradicable even in the "best society," but it was done with a propriety which was edifying to behold.

One can easily imagine that such a starched state of things would not be particularly attractive to a travelled young gentleman like Lennox, who, as Kate very truly said, *had* been spoilt by the flattery, luxury, and gayety of foreign society. He did his best, but by the end of the first week ennui claimed him for its own, and passive endurance was all that was left him. From perfect despair he was rescued by the scarlet stockings, which went tripping by one day as he stood at the window, planning some means of escape.

A brisk, blithe-faced girl passed in a gray walking suit with a distracting pair of high-heeled boots and glimpses of scarlet at the ankle. Modest, perfectly so, I assure you, were the glimpses; but the feet were so decidedly pretty that one forgot to look at the face appertaining thereunto. It was n't a remarkably lovely face, but it was a happy, wholesome one, with all sorts of good little dimples in cheek and chin, sunshiny twinkles in the black eyes, and a decided yet lovable look about the mouth that was quite satisfactory. A busy, bustling little body she seemed to be, for sack-pockets and muff were full of bundles, and the trim boots tripped briskly over the ground, as if the girl's heart were as light as her heels. Somehow this active, pleasant figure seemed to wake up the whole street, and leave a streak of sunshine behind it, for every one nodded as it passed, and the primmest faces relaxed into smiles, which lingered when the girl had gone.

"Uncommonly pretty feet, — she walks well, which American girls seldom do, — all waddle or prance, — nice face, but the boots are French, and it does my heart good to see them."

Lennox made these observations to himself as the young lady approached, nodded to Kate at another window, gave a quick but comprehensive glance at himself and trotted round the corner, leaving the impression on his mind that a whiff of fresh spring air had blown through the street in spite of the December snow. He did n't trouble himself to ask who it was, but fell into the way of lounging in the bay-window at about three P. M., and watching the gray and scarlet figure pass with its blooming cheeks, bright eyes, and elastic step. Having nothing else to do, he took to petting this new whim, and quite depended on the daily stirring up which the sight of the energetic damsel gave him. Kate saw it all, but took no notice till the day of the little tiff above recorded; after that she was as soft as a summer sea, and by some clever stroke had Belle Morgan to tea that very week.

Lennox was one of the best-tempered fellows in the world, but the "peacocks" did rather nettle him, because there was some truth in the insinuation; so he took care to put on no airs or try to be fascinating in the presence of Miss Belle. In truth, he soon forgot himself entirely, and enjoyed her oddities with a relish, after the prim proprieties of the other young ladies who had simpered and sighed before him. For the first time in his life, the "Crusher," as his male friends called him, got crushed; for Belle, with the subtle skill of a quick-witted, keen-sighted girl, soon saw and condemned the elegant affectations which others called foreign polish. A look, a word, a gesture from a pretty woman, is often more eloquent and impressive than moral essays or semi-occasional twinges of conscience; and in the presence of one satirical little person Sir Charles Coldstream soon ceased to deserve the name.

Belle seemed to get over her hurry and to find time for occasional relaxation, but one never knew in what mood he might find her, for the weathercock was not more changeable than she. Lennox liked that, and found the muffin-worries quite endurable with this *sauce piquante* to relieve their insipidity. Presently he discovered that he was suffering for exercise, and formed the wholesome habit of promenading the town about three P. M.; Kate said, to follow the scarlet stockings.

CHAPTER II

WHERE THEY LED HIM

"WHITHER away, Miss Morgan?" asked Lennox, as he overtook her one bitter cold day.

"I 'm taking my constitutional."

"So am I."

"With a difference," and Belle glanced at the blue-nosed, muffled-up gentleman strolling along beside her with an occasional shiver and shrug.

"After a winter in the south of France, one does not find arctic weather like this easy to bear," he said, with a disgusted air.

"I like it, and do my five or six miles a day, which keeps me in what fine ladies call 'rude health,'" answered Belle, walking him on at a pace which soon made his furs a burden.

She was a famous pedestrian, and a little proud of her powers; but she outdid all former feats that day, and got over the ground in gallant style. Something in her manner put her escort on his mettle; and his usual lounge was turned into a brisk march, which set his blood dancing, face glowing, and spirits effervescing as they had not done for many a day.

"There! you look more like your real self now," said Belle, with the first sign of approval she had ever vouchsafed him, as he rejoined her after a race to recover her veil, which the wind whisked away over hedge and ditch.

"Are you sure you know what my real self is?" he asked, with a touch of the "conquering hero" air.

"Not a doubt of it. I always know a soldier when I see one," returned Belle, decidedly.

"A soldier! that 's the last thing I should expect to be accused of," and Lennox looked both surprised and gratified.

"There 's a flash in your eye and a ring to your voice, occasionally, which made me suspect that you had fire and energy enough if you only chose to show it, and the spirit with which you have just executed the 'Morgan Quickstep' proves that I was right," returned Belle, laughing.

"Then I am not altogether a 'peacock'?" said Lennox, significantly, for during the chat, which had been as brisk as the walk, Belle had given his besetting sins several sly hits, and he could n't resist one return shot, much as her unexpected compliment pleased him.

Poor Belle blushed up to her forehead, tried to look as if she did not understand, and gladly hid her confusion behind the recovered veil without a word.

There was a decided display both of the "flash" and the "ring," as Lennox looked at the suddenly subdued young lady, and, quite satisfied with his retaliation, gave the order, "Forward, march!" which brought them to the garden-gate breathless, but better friends than before.

The next time the young people met, Belle was in such a hurry that she went round the corner with an abstracted expression which was quite a triumph of art. Just then, off tumbled the lid of the basket she carried; and Lennox, rescuing it from a puddle, obligingly helped re-adjust it over a funny collection of bottles, dishes, and tidy little rolls of all sorts.

"It 's very heavy, may n't I carry it for you?" he asked, in an insinuating manner.

"No, thank you," was on Belle's lips; but, observing that he was dressed with unusual elegance to pay calls, she could n't resist the temptation of making a beast of burden of him, and took him at his word.

"You may, if you like. I 've got more bundles to take from the store, and another pair of hands won't come amiss."

Lennox lifted his eyebrows, also the basket; and they went on again, Belle very much absorbed in her business, and her escort wondering where she was going with all that rubbish. Filling his unoccupied hand with sundry brown paper parcels, much to the detriment of the light glove that covered it, Belle paraded him down the main street before the windows of the most aristocratic mansions, and then dived into a dirty back-lane, where the want and misery of the town was decorously kept out of sight.

"You don't mind scarlet fever, I suppose?" observed Belle, as they approached the unsavory residence of Biddy O'Brien.

"Well, I'm not exactly partial to it," said Lennox, rather taken aback.

"You need n't go in if you are afraid, or speak to me afterwards, so no harm will be done — except to your gloves."

"Why do *you* come here, if I may ask? It is n't the sort of amusement I should recommend," he began, evidently disapproving of the step.

"Oh, I'm used to it, and like to play nurse where father plays doctor. I'm fond of children and Mrs. O'Brien's are little dears," returned Belle, briskly, threading her way between ash-heaps and mud-puddles as if bound to a festive scene.

"Judging from the row in there, I should infer that Mrs. O'Brien had quite a herd of little dears."

"Only nine."

"And all sick?"

"More or less."

"By Jove! it's perfectly heroic in you to visit this hole in spite of dirt, noise, fragrance, and infection," cried Lennox, who devoutly wished that the sense of smell if not of hearing were temporarily denied him.

"Bless you, it's the sort of thing I enjoy, for there's no nonsense here; the work you do is pleasant if you do it heartily, and the thanks you get are worth having, I assure you."

She put out her hand to relieve him of the basket, but he gave it an approving little shake, and said briefly, —

"Not yet, I'm coming in."

It's all very well to rhapsodize about the exquisite pleasure of doing good, to give carelessly of one's abundance, and enjoy the delusion of having remembered the poor. But it is a cheap charity, and never brings the genuine satisfaction which those know who give their mite with heart as well as hand, and truly love their neighbor as themselves. Lennox had seen much fashionable benevolence, and laughed at it even while he imitated it, giving generously when it was n't inconvenient. But this was a new sort of thing entirely; and in spite of the dirt, the noise, and the smells, he forgot the fever, and was glad he came when poor Mrs. O'Brien turned from her sick babies, exclaiming, with Irish fervor at sight of Belle, —

"The Lord love ye, darlin', for remimberin' us when ivery one, barrin' the doctor, and the praste, turns the cowld shouldther in our throuble!"

"Now if you really want to help, just keep this child quiet while I see to the sickest ones," said Belle, dumping a stout infant on to his knee, thrusting an orange into his hand, and leaving him aghast while she unpacked her little messes, and comforted the maternal bird.

With the calmness of desperation, her aid-de-camp put down his best beaver on the rich soil which covered the floor, pocketed his gloves, and, making a bib of his cambric handkerchief, gagged young Pat deliciously with bits of orange whenever he opened his mouth to roar. At her first leisure moment, Belle glanced at him to see how he was getting on, and found him so solemnly absorbed in his task that she went off into a burst of such infectious merriment that the O'Briens, sick and well, joined in it to a man.

"Good fun, is n't it?" she asked, turning down her cuffs when the last spoonful of gruel was administered.

"I 've no doubt of it, when one is used to the thing. It comes a little hard at first, you know," returned Lennox, wiping his forehead, with a long breath, and seizing his hat as if quite ready to tear himself away.

"You 've done very well for a beginner; so kiss the baby and come home," said Belle approvingly.

"No, thank you," muttered Lennox, trying

to detach the bedaubed innocent. But little Pat had a grateful heart, and, falling upon his new nurse's neck with a rapturous crow, clung there like a burr.

"Take him off! Let me out of this! He 's one too many for me!" cried the wretched young man in comic despair.

Being freed with much laughter, he turned and fled, followed by a shower of blessings from Mrs. O'Brien.

As they came up again into the pleasant highways, Lennox said, awkwardly for him, —

"The thanks of the poor *are* excellent things to have, but I think I 'd rather receive them by proxy. Will you kindly spend this for me in making that poor soul comfortable?"

But Belle would n't take what he offered her; she put it back, saying earnestly, —

"Give it yourself; one can't buy blessings, — they must be *earned* or they are not worth having. Try it, please, and, if you find it a failure, then I 'll gladly be your almoner."

There was a significance in her words which he could not fail to understand. He neither shrugged, drawled, nor sauntered now, but gave her a look in which respect and self-reproach were mingled, and left her, simply saying, "I 'll try it, Miss Morgan."

"Now is n't she odd?" whispered Kate to her brother, as Belle appeared at a little dance at Mrs. Plantagenet's in a high-necked dress, knitting away on an army-sock, as she greeted the friends who crowded round her.

"Charmingly so. Why don't you do that sort of thing when you can?" answered her brother, glancing at her thin, bare shoulders, and hands rendered nearly useless by the tightness of the gloves.

"Gracious, no! It 's natural to her to do so, and she carries it off well; I could n't, therefore I don't try, though I admire it in her. Go and ask her to dance, before she is engaged."

"She does n't dance round dances, you know."

"She is dreadfully prim about some things, and so free and easy about others: I can't understand it, do you?"

"Well, yes, I think I do. Here 's Forbes coming for you, I 'll go and entertain Belle by a quarrel."

He found her in a recess out of the way of the rushing and romping, busy with her work, yet evidently glad to be amused.

"I admire your adherence to principle, Miss Belle; but don't you find it a little hard to sit still while your friends are enjoying themselves?" he asked, sinking luxuriously into the lounging chair beside her.

"Yes, very," answered Belle with characteristic candor. "But father does not approve of that sort of exercise, so I console myself with something useful till my chance comes."

"Your work can't exactly be called ornamental," said Lennox, looking at the big sock.

"Don't laugh at it, sir; it is for the foot of the brave fellow who is going to fight for me and his country."

"Happy fellow! May I ask who he is?" and Lennox sat up with an air of interest.

"My substitute: I don't know his name, for father has not got him yet; but I'm making socks, and towels, and a comfort-bag for him, so that when found he may be off at once."

"You really mean it?" cried Lennox.

"Of course I do; I can't go myself, but I *can* buy a pair of strong arms to fight for me, and I intend to do it. I only hope he'll have the right sort of courage, and be a credit to me."

"What do you call the right sort of courage?" asked Lennox, soberly.

"That which makes a man ready and glad to live or die for a principle. There's a chance for heroes now, if there ever was. When do you join your regiment?" she added, abruptly.

"Have n't the least idea," and Lennox subsided again.

"But you intend to do so, of course?"

"Why should I?"

Belle dropped her work. "Why should you? What a question! Because you have health, and strength, and courage, and money to help on the good cause, and every man should give his best, and not *dare* to stay at home when he is needed."

"You forget that I am an Englishman, and

we rather prefer to be strictly neutral just now."

"You are only half English; and for your mother's sake you should be proud and glad to fight for the North," cried Belle warmly.

"I don't remember my mother, —"

"That 's evident!"

"But, I was about to add, I 've no objection to lend a hand if it is n't too much trouble to get off," said Lennox indifferently, for he liked to see Belle's color rise, and her eyes kindle while he provoked her.

"Do you expect to go South in a bandbox? You 'd better join one of the kid-glove regiments; they say the dandies fight well when the time comes."

"I 've been away so long, the patriotic fever has n't seized me yet; and, as the quarrel is none of mine, I think perhaps I 'd better take care of Kate, and let you fight it out among yourselves. Here 's the Lancers, may I have the honor?"

But Belle, being very angry at this lukewarmness, answered in her bluntest manner, —

"Having reminded me that you are a 'strictly neutral' Englishman, you must excuse me if I decline; *I* dance only with loyal Americans," and, rolling up her work with a defiant flourish, she walked away, leaving him to lament his loss and wonder how he could retrieve it. She did not speak to him again till he stood in the hall waiting for Kate; then Belle came down in a charming little red hood, and going straight up to him with her hand out, a repentant look and a friendly smile, said frankly, —

"I was rude; I want to beg pardon of the English, and shake hands with the American, half."

So peace was declared, and lasted unbroken for the remaining week of his stay, when he proposed to take Kate to the city for a little gayety. Miss Morgan openly approved the plan, but secretly felt as if the town was about to be depopulated, and tried to hide her melancholy in her substitute's socks. They were not large enough, however, to absorb it all; and, when Lennox went to make his adieu, it was perfectly evident that the Doctor's Belle was out of tune. The young gentleman basely exulted over this, till she gave him something else to think about by saying gravely:

"Before you go, I feel as if I ought to tell you something, since Kate won't. If you are offended about it please don't blame her; she meant it kindly, and so did I." Belle paused as if it was not an easy thing to tell, and then went on quickly, with her eyes upon her work.

"Three weeks ago Kate asked me to help her in a little plot; and I consented, for the fun of the thing. She wanted something to amuse and stir you up, and, finding that my queer ways diverted you, she begged me to be neighborly and let you do what you liked. I did n't care particularly about amusing you, but I did think you needed rousing; so for her sake I tried to do it, and you very good-naturedly bore my lecturing. I don't like deceit of any kind, so I confess; but I can't say I 'm sorry, for I really think you are none the worse for the teasing and teaching you 've had."

Belle did n't see him flush and frown as she made her confession, and when she looked up he only said, half gratefully, half reproachfully, —

"I 'm a good deal the better for it, I dare say, and ought to be very thankful for your friendly exertions. But two against one was hardly fair, now, was it?"

"No, it was sly and sinful in the highest degree, but we did it for your good; so I know you 'll forgive us, and as a proof of it sing one or two of my favorites for the last time."

"You don't deserve any favor; but I 'll do it, to show you how much more magnanimous men are than women."

Not at all loth to improve his advantages, Lennox warbled his most melting lays *con amore,* watching, as he sung, for any sign of sentiment in the girlish face opposite. But Belle would n't be sentimental; and sat rattling her knitting-needles industriously, though "The Harbor Bar was moaning" dolefully, though "Douglas" was touchingly "tender and true," and the "Wind of the Summer Night" sighed romantically through the sitting-room.

"Much obliged. Must you go?" she said, without a sign of soft confusion as he rose.

"I must; but I shall come again before I leave the country. May I?" he asked, holding her hand.

"If you come in a uniform."

"Good night, Belle," tenderly. — "Good-by, Sir Charles," with a wicked twinkle of the eye, which lasted till he closed the hall-door, growling irefully, —

"I thought I 'd had some experience, but one never *can* understand these women!"

Canterbury did become a desert to Belle after her dear friend had gone (of course the dear friend's brother had nothing to do with the desolation); and as the weeks dragged slowly Belle took to reading poetry, practising plaintive ballads, and dawdling over her work at a certain window which commanded a view of the railway station and hotel.

"You 're dull, my dear; run up to town with me to-morrow, and see your young man off," said the Doctor one evening, as Belle sat musing with a half-mended red stocking in her hand.

"My young man?" she ejaculated, turning with a start and a blush.

"Your substitute, child. Stephens attended to the business for me, and he 's off to-morrow. I began to tell you about the fellow last week, but you were wool-gathering, so I stopped."

"Yes, I remember, it was all very nice. Goes to-morrow, does he? I 'd like to see him; but do you think we can both leave home at once?

Some one might come you know, and I fancy it 's going to snow," said Belle, putting her face behind the curtain to inspect the weather.

"You 'd better go, the trip will do you good; you can take your things to Tom Jones, and see Kate on the way: she 's got back from Philadelphia."

"Has she? I 'll go, then; it will please her, and I do need change. You are a dear, to think of it;" and, giving her father a hasty glimpse of a suddenly excited countenance, Belle slipped out of the room to prepare her best array, with a most reckless disregard of the impending storm.

It did not snow on the morrow, and up they went to see the —th regiment off. Belle did not see "her young man," however, for while her father went to carry him her comforts and a patriotic nosegay of red and white flowers, tied up with a smart blue ribbon, she called on Kate. But Miss Lennox was engaged, and sent an urgent request that her friend would call in the afternoon. Much disappointed and a little hurt, Belle then devoted herself to the departing regiment, wishing she was going with it, for she felt in a warlike mood. It was past noon when a burst of martial music, the measured tramp of many feet, and enthusiastic cheers announced that "the boys" were coming. From the balcony where she stood with her father, Belle looked down upon the living stream that flowed by like a broad river, with a steely glitter above the blue. All her petty troubles vanished at the sight; her heart beat high, her face glowed, her eyes filled, and she waved her handkerchief as zealously as if she had a dozen friends and lovers in the ranks below.

"Here comes your man; I told him to stick the posy where it would catch my eye, so I could point him out to you. Look, it 's the tall fellow at the end of the front line," said the Doctor in an excited tone, as he pointed and beckoned.

Belle looked and gave a little cry, for there, in a private's uniform, with her nosegay at his buttonhole, and on his face a smile she never forgot, was Lennox! For an instant she stood staring at him as pale and startled as if he were a ghost; then the color rushed into her face, she kissed both hands to him, and cried bravely, "Good-by, good-by; God bless you, Harry!" and immediately laid her head on her father's shoulder, sobbing as if her heart was broken.

When she looked up, her substitute was lost in the undulating mass below, and for her the spectacle was over.

"Was it really he? Why was n't I told? What does it all mean?" she demanded, looking bewildered, grieved, and ashamed.

"He 's really gone, my dear. It 's a surprise of his, and I was bound over to silence. Here, this will explain the joke, I suppose," and the Doctor handed her a cocked-hat note, done up like a military order.

"A Roland for your Oliver, Mademoiselle! I came home for the express purpose of enlisting, and only delayed a month on Kate's account. If I ever return, I will receive my bounty at your hands. Till then please comfort Kate, think as kindly as you can of 'Sir Charles,' and sometimes pray a little prayer for

"Your unworthy

"SUBSTITUTE."

Belle looked very pale and meek when she put the note in her pocket, but she only said, "I must go and comfort Kate;" and the Doctor gladly obeyed, feeling that the joke was more serious than he had imagined.

The moment her friend appeared, Miss Lennox turned on her tears, and "played away," pouring forth lamentations, reproaches, and regrets in a steady stream.

"I hope you are satisfied now, you cruel girl!" she began, refusing to be kissed. "You 've sent him off with a broken heart to rush into danger and be shot, or get his arms and legs spoiled. You know he loved you and wanted to tell you so, but you would n't let him; and now you 've driven him away, and he 's gone as an insignificant private with his head shaved, and a heavy knapsack breaking his back, and a horrid gun that will be sure to explode: and he *would* wear those immense blue socks you sent, for he adores you, and you only teased and laughed at him, my poor, deluded, deserted brother!" And, quite overwhelmed by the afflicting picture, Kate lifted up her voice and wept again.

"I *am* satisfied, for he 's done what I hoped he would; and he 's none the less a gentleman because he 's a private and wears my socks. I pray they will keep him safe, and bring him home to us when he has done his duty like a man, as I know he will. I 'm proud of my brave substitute, and I 'll try to be worthy of him," cried Belle, kindling beautifully as she looked out into the wintry sunshine with a new softness in the eyes that still seemed watching that blue-coated figure marching away to danger, perhaps death.

"It 's ill playing with edged tools; we meant to amuse him, and we may have sent him to destruction. I 'll never forgive you for your part, never!" said Kate, with the charming inconsistency of her sex.

But Belle turned away her wrath by a soft answer, as she whispered, with a tender choke in her voice, —

"We both loved him, dear; let 's comfort one another."

CHAPTER III

WHAT BECAME OF THEM

PRIVATE LENNOX certainly *had* chosen pretty hard work, for the —th was not a "kid-glove" regiment by any means; fighting in mid-winter was not exactly festive, and camps do not abound in beds of roses even at the best of times. But Belle was right in saying she knew a soldier when she saw him, for, now that he was thoroughly waked up, he proved that there was plenty of courage, energy, and endurance in him.

It is my private opinion that he might now and then have slightly regretted the step he had taken, had it not been for certain recollections of a sarcastic tongue and a pair of keen eyes, not to mention the influence of one of the most potent rulers of the human heart; namely, the desire to prove himself worthy the respect, if nothing more, of somebody at home. Belle's socks did seem to keep him safe, and lead him straight in the narrow path of duty. Belle's comfort-bag was such in very truth, for not one of the stout needles on the tri-colored cushion but what seemed to wink its eye approvingly at him; not one of the tiny balls of thread that did not remind him of the little hand he coveted, and the impracticable scissors were cherished as a good omen, though he felt that the sharpest steel that ever came from Sheffield could n't cut his love in twain. And Belle's lessons, short as they had been, were not forgotten, but seemed to have been taken up by a sterner mistress, whose rewards were greater, if not so sweet, as those the girl could give. There was plenty of exercise nowadays, and of hard work that left many a tired head asleep for ever under the snow. There were many opportunities for diving "into the depths and bringing up pearls worth having" by acts of kindness among the weak, the wicked, and the suffering all about him. He learned now how to earn, not buy, the thanks of the poor, and unconsciously proved in the truest way that a private *could* be a gentleman. But best of all was the steadfast purpose "to live and die for a principle," which grew and strengthened with each month of bitter hardship, bloody strife, and dearly bought success. Life grew earnest to him, time seemed precious, self was forgotten, and all that was best and bravest rallied round the flag on which his heart inscribed the motto, "Love and Liberty."

Praise and honor he could not fail to win, and

had he never gone back to claim his bounty he would have earned the great "Well done," for he kept his oath loyally, did his duty manfully, and loved his lady faithfully, like a knight of the chivalrous times. He knew nothing of her secret, but wore her blue ribbon like an order, never went into battle without first, like many another poor fellow, kissing something which he carried next his heart, and with each day of absence felt himself a better man, and braver soldier, for the fondly foolish romance he had woven about the scarlet stockings.

Belle and Kate did comfort one another, not only with tears and kisses, but with womanly work which kept hearts happy and hands busy. How Belle bribed her to silence will always remain the ninth wonder of the world; but, though reams of paper passed between brother and sister during those twelve months, not a hint was dropped on one side in reply to artful inquiries from the other. Belle never told her love in words; but she stowed away an unlimited quantity of the article in the big boxes that went to gladden the eyes and — alas for romance! — the stomach of Private Lennox. If pickles could typify passion, cigars prove constancy, and gingerbread reveal the longings of the soul, then would the above-mentioned gentleman have been the happiest of lovers. But camp-life had doubtless dulled his finer intuitions: for he failed to understand the new language of love, and gave away these tender tokens with lavish prodigality. Concealment preyed a trifle on Belle's damask cheek, it must be confessed, and the keen eyes grew softer with the secret tears that sometimes dimmed them; the sharp tongue seldom did mischief now, but uttered kindly words to every one, as if doing penance for the past; and a sweet seriousness toned down the lively spirit, which was learning many things in the sleepless nights that followed when the "little prayer" for the beloved substitute was done.

"I 'll wait and see if he is all I hope he will be, before I let him know. I shall read the truth the instant I see him, and if he has stood the test I 'll run into his arms and tell him every thing," she said to herself, with delicious thrills at the idea; but you may be sure she did nothing of the sort when the time came.

A rumor flew through the town one day that Lennox had arrived; upon receipt of which joyful tidings, Belle had a panic and hid herself in the garret. But when she had quaked, and cried, and peeped, and listened for an hour or two, finding that no one came to hunt her up, she composed her nerves and descended to pass the afternoon in the parlor and a high state of dignity. All sorts of reports reached her: he was mortally wounded; he had been made a major or a colonel or a general, no one knew exactly which; he was dead, was going to be married, and had n't come at all. Belle fully expiated all her small sins by the agonies of suspense she suffered that day, and when at last a note came from Kate, begging her "to drop over to see Harry," she put her pride in her pocket and went at once.

The drawing-room was empty and in confusion, there was a murmur of voices upstairs, a smell of camphor in the air, and an empty wine-glass on the table where a military cap was lying. Belle's heart sunk, and she covertly kissed the faded blue coat as she stood waiting breathlessly, wondering if Harry had any arms for her to run into. She heard the chuckling Biddy lumber up and announce her, then a laugh, and a half-fond, half-exulting, "Ah, ha, I thought she'd come!"

That spoilt it all; Belle took out her pride instanter, rubbed a quick color into her white cheeks, and, snatching up a newspaper, sat herself down with as expressionless a face as it was possible for an excited young woman to possess. Lennox came running down. "Thank Heaven, his legs are safe!" sighed Belle, with her eyes glued to the price of beef. He entered with both hands extended, which relieved her mind upon another point; and he beamed upon her, looking so vigorous, manly, and martial, that she cried within herself, "My beautiful brown soldier!" even while she greeted him with an unnecessarily brief, "How do you do, Mr. Lennox?"

The sudden eclipse which passed over his joyful countenance would have been ludicrous, if it had n't been pathetic; but he was used to hard knocks now, and bore this, his hardest, like a man. He shook hands heartily; and, as Belle sat down again (not to betray that she was trembling a good deal), he stood at ease before her, talking in a way which soon satisfied her that he *had* borne the test, and that bliss was waiting for her round the corner. But she had made it such a very sharp corner she could n't turn it gracefully, and while she pondered how to do so he helped her with a cough. She looked up quickly, discovering all at once that he was very thin, rather pale in spite of the nice tan, and breathed hurriedly as he stood with one hand in his breast.

"Are you ill, wounded, in pain?" she asked, forgetting herself entirely.

"Yes, all three," he answered, after a curious look at her changing color and anxious eyes.

"Sit down — tell me about it — can I do anything?" and Belle began to plump up the pillows on the couch with nervous eagerness.

"Thank you, I 'm past help," was the mournful reply, accompanied by a hollow cough which made her shiver.

"Oh, don't say so! Let me bring father; he is very skilful. Shall I call Kate?"

"He can do nothing; Kate does n't know this, and I beg you won't tell her. I got a shot in the breast and made light of it, but it will finish me sooner or later, I don't mind telling you, for you are one of the strong, cool sort, you know, and are not affected by such things. But Kate is so fond of me, I don't want to shock and trouble her yet awhile. Let her enjoy my little visit, and after I 'm gone you can tell her the truth."

Belle had sat like a statue while he spoke with frequent pauses and an involuntary clutch or two at the suffering breast. As he stopped and passed his hand over his eyes, she said slowly, as if her white lips were stiff, —

"Gone, where?"

"Back to my place. I 'd rather die fighting than fussed and wailed over by a parcel of women. I expected to stay a week or so, but a battle is coming off sooner than we imagined, so I 'm away again to-morrow. As I 'm not likely ever to come back, I just wanted to ask you to stand by poor Kate when I 'm finished, and to say good-by to you, Belle, before I go." He put out his hand, but, holding it fast in both her own, she laid her tearful face down on it, whispering imploringly, —

"Oh, Harry, stay!"

Never mind what happened for the next ten minutes; suffice it to say that the enemy having surrendered, the victor took possession with great jubilation and showed no quarter.

"Bang the field-piece, toot the fife, and beat the rolling drum, for ruse number three has succeeded. Come down, Kate, and give us your blessing!" called Lennox, taking pity on his sister, who was anxiously awaiting the *dénouement* on the stairs.

In she rushed, and the young ladies laughed and cried, kissed and talked tumultuously, while their idol benignantly looked on, vainly endeavoring to repress all vestiges of unmanly emotion.

"And you are not dying, really, truly?" cried Belle, when fair weather set in after the flurry.

"Bless your dear heart, no! I'm as sound as a nut, and have n't a wound to boast of, except this ugly slash on the head."

"It's a splendid wound, and I'm proud of it," and Belle set a rosy little seal on the scar, which quite reconciled her lover to the disfigurement of his handsome forehead. "You've learned to fib in the army, and I'm disappointed in you," she added, trying to look reproachful and failing entirely.

"No, only the art of strategy. You quenched me by your frosty reception, and I thought it was all up till you put the idea of playing invalid into my head. It succeeded so well that I piled on the agony, resolving to fight it out on that line, and if I failed again to make a masterly retreat. You gave me a lesson in deceit once, so don't complain if I turned the tables and made your heart ache for a minute, as you've made mine for a year."

Belle's spirit was rapidly coming back, so she gave him a capital imitation of his French shrug, and drawled out in his old way, —

"I have my doubts about that, *mon ami*."

"What do you say to this — and this — and this?" he retorted, pulling out and laying before her with a triumphant flourish a faded blue ribbon, a fat pincushion with a hole through it, and a daintily painted little picture of a pretty girl in scarlet stockings.

"There, I 've carried those treasures in my breast-pocket for a year, and I 'm firmly convinced that they have all done their part toward keeping me safe. The blue ribbon bound me fast to you, Belle; the funny cushion caught the bullet that otherwise might have finished me; and the blessed little picture was my comfort during those dreadful marches, my companion on picket-duty with treachery and danger all about me, and my inspiration when the word 'Charge!' went down the line, for in the thickest of the fight I always saw the little gray figure beckoning me on to my duty."

"Oh, Harry, you won't go back to all those horrors, will you? I 'm sure you 've done enough, and may rest now and enjoy your reward," said Kate, trying not to feel that "two is company, and three is none."

"I 've enlisted for the war, and shall not rest till either it or I come to an end. As for my reward, I had it when Belle kissed me."

"You are right, I 'll wait for you, and love you all the better for the sacrifice," whispered Belle. "I only wish I could share your hardships, dear, for while you fight and suffer I can only love and pray."

"Waiting is harder than working to such as

you; so be contented with your share, for the thought of you will glorify the world generally for me. I 'll tell you what you *can* do while I 'm away: it 's both useful and amusing, so it will occupy and cheer you capitally. Just knit lots of red hose, because I don't intend you to wear any others hereafter, Mrs. Lennox."

"Mine are not worn out yet," laughed Belle, getting merry at the thought.

"No matter for that; those are sacred articles, and henceforth must be treasured as memorials of our love. Frame and hang them up; or, if the prejudices of society forbid that flight of romance, lay them carefully away where moths can't devour nor thieves steal them, so that years hence, when my descendants praise me for any virtues I may possess, any good I may have done, or any honor I may have earned, I can point to those precious relics and say proudly, —

"My children, for all that I am, or hope to be, you must thank your honored mother's scarlet stockings."

INDEPENDENCE:

A CENTENNIAL LOVE STORY

CHAPTER I.

MISS DOLLY

"STUPID - LOOKING old place! Dare say I shall have to waste half an hour listening to centennial twaddle before I get what I want! The whole thing is a bore, but I can't quarrel with my bread and butter, so here goes;" and, with an air of resignation, the young man applied himself to the rusty knocker.

"Rather a nice old bit; may be useful, so I 'll book it;" and, whipping out a sketch-book, the stranger took a hasty likeness of the griffin's head on the knocker.

"Deaf as posts; try, try, try again;" and, pocketing his work, the artist gave an energetic rat, tat, tat, that echoed through the house.

Having rashly concluded that the inhabitants of the ancient mansion were proportionately aged, he assumed a deferential expression as steps approached, and prepared to prefer with all due respect the request which he had come many miles to make. The door opened with unexpected rapidity, but the neatly arranged speech did not glide glibly off the young man's tongue, and the change which came over him was comically sudden; for, instead of an old woman, a blooming girl stood upon the threshold, with a petulant expression on her charming face, which only made it more charming still.

"What did you wish, sir?" asked the rosy mouth, involuntarily relaxing from a vain attempt to look severe, while the hazel eyes softened with a mirthful gleam as they rested on the comely, but embarrassed countenance before her.

"Beg pardon for making such a noise. I merely wished to inquire if the famous chair in which Washington sat when he visited the town is here," replied the stranger, clutching off his hat with a very different sort of respect from that which he had intended to show, and feeling as if he had received a shock of some new and delightful sort of electricity.

"Yes;" and the girl began to close the door, as if she knew what question was coming next.

"Could I be allowed to sketch it for 'The Weekly Portfolio'? All such relics are so valuable this year that we venture to ask many favors, and this is such a famous affair I 've no doubt you are often troubled by requests of this sort," continued the artist, with the persuasive tone of one accustomed to make his way everywhere.

"This is the fifth time this week," replied the damsel, demurely; though her lips still struggled not to smile.

"It 's very good of you, I 'm sure, to let us fellows in, but the public demand is immense just now, and we only obey orders, you know," began the fifth intruder, fervently hoping the other four had been refused.

"But Mrs. Hill never does let artists or reporters in," was the gentle quencher which arrested him, as he was industriously wiping his feet on the door-mat.

"Never?" he asked, stopping short, while an expression of alarm changed suddenly to one of satisfaction.

"Never," answered the damsel, like a sweet-voiced echo.

"Then the other fellows lost their chance, and that makes the old thing doubly valuable. If I could see Mrs. Hill for a moment, I 've no doubt she will allow *me* to sketch the chair."

"She is not at home."

"So much the better; for, when I tell you that I 've come fifty miles to pick up antiquities in this town, I know you *won't* have the heart to send me away without the gem of the collection," replied the artist, nothing daunted; for his quick eye read the artless face before him, and saw a defiant expression come over it, which made him suspect that there had been a falling out between mistress and maid, if such they were. He was sure of it when the girl threw open the door with a decisive gesture, saying briefly, —

"Walk in, if you please; she won't be home for an hour."

"What a little beauty!" thought the young man, admiring her spirit, and feeling that the "stupid old place" contained unexpected treasures, as he followed her into the room where the ubiquitous Father of his Country was reported to have dried his august boots, and drunk a mug of cider some hundred years ago.

It seemed as if the ghosts of many of the homely household articles used then had come back to celebrate the anniversary of that thrilling event; for there was nothing modern in the little room but the girl and her guest, who stared at the tall andirons on the hearth, the bright, brass candlesticks above it, the spinning-wheel on one side, a dresser on the other strewn with pewter platters, porringers, and old china, while antique garments hung over the settle by the fire.

"Bless my soul, what a capital old place!" he ejaculated, taking it all in with an artist's keen appreciation. "I feel as if I'd gone back a century, and the General might come in at any minute."

"*That* is the chair he used, and *this* the tankard he drank from," answered the girl, pointing out the sacred objects with a reverential air which warned her visitor that he must treat the ancient and honorable relics with due respect.

Then feeling that this was an unusual stroke of luck, he hastened to make the most of it, by falling to work at once, saying, as he took a seat, and pointed his pencils, —

"There is such a lot of treasures here that I don't know where to begin. I hope I shall not be very much in your way."

"Oh, no! if you don't mind my going on with my work; for I can't leave it very well. All these things are to be sent away to-morrow, that's why the place is in such confusion," replied the girl, as she fell to polishing up a brass snuffer-tray.

"Here 's richness!" thought the artist, with a sigh of satisfaction, as he dashed at his work, feeling inspired by his picturesque surroundings.

The dull winter sky gloomed without, and a chilly wind sighed through the leafless elms; but within the little room fairly glowed with the ruddy firelight that shone in the bright brasses, glimmered over the tarnished silver of the quaint vests on the settle, and warmed the artist's busy hand, as if it liked to help him in his task. But the jolly flames seemed to dance most lovingly about their little mistress; bathing the sweet face with a softer bloom, touching the waves of brown hair with gold, peeping under the long lashes at the downcast eyes that peeped back again half arch, half shy; glorifying the blue apron that seemed to clasp the trim waist as if conscious of its advantages, and showing up the dimples in the bare arms working so briskly that even the verdigris of ages yielded to their persuasive touch.

"Who can this pretty Priscilla be? I must make her talk and find out. Never shall get the eyes right, if she does n't look up," thought the artist, who, instead of devoting himself to the historical chair, was basely sketching the girl whose youth and beauty were wonderfully enhanced by the antiquity around her.

"Mrs. Hill is a rich woman, if all these treasures have a history. Even if they have n't, they would bring a good price; for things of this sort are all the rage now, and the older the better," he said aloud in a sociable tone, as he affected to study the left arm of the famous chair.

"They are not hers to sell, for they belonged to the first Mrs. Hill, who was a Quincy, and had a right to be proud of them. The present Mrs. Hill does n't value them a bit; but *she* was a Smith, so *her* family relics are nothing to boast of," answered the girl, using her bit of wash-leather as if the entire race of Smith ought to be rubbed out of existence.

"And she is going to sell all these fine old things, is she?" asked the artist, with an eye to bargains.

"No, indeed! they belong to — to the first Mrs. Hill's daughter, named after her, Dorothy Quincy," the girl began impetuously, but checked herself, and ended very quietly with a suddenly averted head.

"A fine name, and I should n't think she would be in haste to change it," said the artist, wondering if Miss Dorothy Quincy was before him.

"Not much hope of that, poor thing," with a shake of the head that made several brown curls tumble out of the net which tried to confine a riotous mass of them.

"Ah, I see, a spinster?" and the young man returned to his work with greatly abated interest in the subject.

The bright eyes glanced quickly up, and when they fell the snuffer-tray reflected a merry twinkle in them, as their owner answered gravely, —

"Yes, a spinster."

"Is she one of the amiable sort?"

"Oh, dear, no! very quick in her temper and sharp with her tongue. But then she has a good deal to try her, as I happen to know."

"Sorry for that. Spinsterhood *is* trying, I fancy, so we should be patient with the poor old ladies. Why I asked was because I thought I might induce Miss Dolly to let me have some of her relics. Do you think she would?" he asked, holding his sketch at arm's length, and studying it with his head on one side.

"I 'm very sure she won't, for these old things are all she has in the world, and she loves them dearly. People used to laugh at her for it, but now they are glad to own her and her 'duds,' as they called them. The Smiths are looking up every thing they can find of that sort, even poor relations. All these things are going down to a fair to-morrow, and Miss Dolly with them."

"As one of the relics?" suggested the artist, glancing at a green calash and a plum-colored quilted petticoat lying on the settle.

"Exactly," laughed the girl, adding with a touch of bitterness in her voice, "Poor Miss Dolly never got an invitation before, and I'm afraid it's foolish of her to go now, since she is only wanted to show off the old-fashioned things, and give the Smiths something to boast of."

"You are fond of the old lady in spite of her temper, I see."

"She is the only friend I've got;" and the speaker bent over the tray as if to hide emotion of some sort.

"I shall probably have to 'do' that fair for our paper; if so, I'll certainly pay my respects to Miss Dolly. Why not? Is she so very awful?" he asked quickly, as the girl looked up with a curious mixture of mirth and malice in her face.

"Very!" with a lifting of the brows and a pursing up of the lips delightful to behold.

"You think I won't dare address the peppery virgin? I never saw the woman yet whom I was afraid of, or the man either for that matter, so I give you my word I'll not only speak to Miss Dolly, but win her old heart by my admiration for her and her ancestral treasures," said the artist, accepting the challenge he read in the laughing eyes.

"We shall see, for I 'm going with her. I do the spinning, and it 's great fun," said the girl, prudently changing the conversation, though she evidently enjoyed it.

"I never saw it done. Could you give me an idea of the thing, if it is not asking too much?" proposed the artist in his most persuasive tone, for somehow play of this sort was much more interesting than the study of old furniture.

With amiable alacrity the girl set the big wheel buzzing, and deftly drew out the yarn from the spindle, stepping briskly to and fro, twirling and twisting with an ease and grace which convinced the admiring observer that the best thing ever invented to show off a round arm, a pretty foot, a fine figure, and a charming face, was a spinning-wheel.

This opinion was so plainly expressed upon his own countenance that the color deepened in the girl's cheeks as she looked over her shoulder to see how he liked it, and dropping the thread she left the wheel still whirling, and went back to her work without a word.

"Thank you very much; it 's beautiful! Don't see how in the world you do it," murmured the young man, affecting to examine the wheel, while his own head seemed to whirl in sympathy, for that backward glance had unconsciously done great execution.

A moon-faced clock behind the door striking eleven recalled the idler to his task, and resuming his seat he drew silently till the chair was done; then he turned a page, and looked about for the next good bit.

"Rather warm work," he said, smiling, as he shook the hair off his forehead, and pushed his chair back from the hearth.

"This is what makes the place so hot. I 've been learning to make old-fashioned dishes for the fair, and this batch is going down to show what I can do."

As she spoke, the girl threw open the door of a cavernous oven, and with an air of housewifely pride displayed a goodly array of brown loaves round as cannon-balls, earthen crocks suggestive of baked beans and Indian pudding, and near the door a pan of spicy cakes delectable to smell and see. These she drew forth and set upon the table, turning from the oven after a careful inspection of its contents with the complexion of a damask rose.

"Delicious spectacle!" exclaimed the artist, with his eyes upon the pretty cook, while hers were on her handiwork.

"You shall taste them, for they are made from a very old receipt and are called sweethearts," said the innocent creature, setting them forth on a large platter, while a smile went dimpling round her lips.

"Capital name! they 'll sell faster than you

can make them. But it seems to me you are to have all the work, and Miss Dolly all the credit," added this highly appreciative guest, subduing with difficulty the rash impulse to embrace Miss Dolly's rosy handmaid on the spot.

She seemed to feel the impending danger, and saying hastily, "You must have some cider to go with your cake: that 's the correct thing, you know," she tripped away with hospitable zeal.

"Upon my soul, I begin to feel like the Prince of the fairy tale in this quiet place where every thing seems to have been asleep for a hundred years. The little beauty ought to have been asleep too, and given me a chance to wake her. More of a Cinderella than a princess, I fancy, and leads a hard life of it between Miss Dolly and the second Mrs. Hill. Wonder what happy fellow will break the spell and set her free?" and the young man paced the kitchen, humming softly, —

> "And on her lover's arm she leant,
> And round her waist she felt it fold;
> And far across the hills they went,
> In that new world which is the old,"

till the sound of a light step made him dart into a chair, saying to himself with a sudden descent from poetry to prose, "Bless her little heart, I 'll drink her cider if it 's as sour as vinegar."

In came the maid, bearing a tankard on a salver; and, adding several sweethearts, she offered the homely lunch with a curtsey and a smile that would have glorified even pork and beans.

"You are sitting in the General's chair, and here is the tankard he used; you can drink his health, if you like."

"I 'd rather drink that of the maker of sweethearts;" and, rising, the artist did so, gallantly regardless of consequences.

But the cider was excellent, and subsiding into the immortal chair he enjoyed his lunch with the hearty appetite of a boy, while the damsel began to fold up the garments airing on the settle, and lay them into a chest standing near; the one quite unconscious that he was drinking draughts of a far more potent liquor than apple-juice, the other that she had begun to spin a golden thread instead of yarn when she turned the great wheel that day.

An eloquent sort of silence filled the room for a moment, and a ray of sunshine glanced from the silver tankard to the bright head bent over the chest, as if to gild the first page of the romance which is as fresh and sweet to-day as when the stately George wooed his beloved Martha. A shrill voice suddenly broke that delicious pause, exclaiming, as a door opened with a bang, —

"Not packed yet! I won't have this rubbish cluttering round another minute — " There the voice abruptly fell, and the stranger had time to see a withered, yellow face in a pumpkin hood stare sharply at him before it vanished with an exclamation of unmistakable disapproval.

"Miss Dolly seems more afraid of me than I of her, you see," began the young man, much amused at the retreat of the enemy; for such he regarded any one who disturbed this delightful *tête-à-tête*.

"She has only gone to put her cap on, and when she comes back you can pay your respects to — Mrs. Hill;" and the girl looked over the lid of the chest with dancing eyes.

"Then I 'd better be off, since reporters and artists are not allowed on the premises," exclaimed the visitor, rising with more haste than dignity.

"Don't hurry; she is only a woman, and you are not afraid, you know."

"I 'm afraid *you* will get a scolding," began the artist, pocketing his sketch-book, and grasping his hat.

"I 'm used to that," said the girl, evidently enjoying the rout with naughty satisfaction.

But the sharp, black eyes and the shrill voice had effectually broken the pleasant day-dream; and Mrs. Hill in a pumpkin hood was quite enough for his nerves, without a second appearance in one of the awe-inspiring caps such ladies affect.

"I could n't think of repaying your kindness by intruding any longer, now that I 've got my sketch. A thousand thanks; good-morning;" and, opening the first door he came to, the dismayed man was about to plunge into the buttery, when the girl arrested his flight and led him through the long hall.

On the steps he took breath, returned thanks again with grateful warmth, and pulling out a card presented it, as if anxious to leave some token behind which should prevent being forgotten by one person at least.

"John Hancock Harris" read the card, and glancing up from it, with sudden interest in her eyes, the girl exclaimed impulsively, —

"Why, then you must be a relation of —"

"No, I regret to say I 'm not related to the famous Governor, only named for him to please my father. I 've always been contented with a modest initial until now; but this year every one does their best to hang on to the past, so I 've got proud of my middle name, and find it useful as well as ornamental," hastily explained the honest young fellow, though just then he would have liked to claim kinship with every member of the Continental Congress.

"I hope you will be worthy of it," answered the damsel with a little bow, as if saluting the man for his name's sake.

"I try to be," he said soberly, adding with that engaging smile of his, "May I ask to whom I am indebted for this very profitable and agreeable call?"

Instantly the sweet sobriety vanished, and every feature of the pretty face shone with mirthful malice as the girl answered sweetly, —

"Miss Dolly. Good-morning," and closed the door, leaving him to stare blankly at the griffin on the knocker, which appeared to stare back again with a derisive grin.

CHAPTER II

A CINDER AND A SPARK

ONE of the few snow-storms of the memorably mild winter of 1876 was coming quietly down, watched with lazy interest by the passengers in a certain train that rumbled leisurely toward the city. Without it was cold and wintry enough, but within as hot as an oven, for, with the usual American disregard for health, there was a roaring fire in the stove, every ventilator shut, and only one man in the crowded car had his window open.

Toward this reckless being many a warning or reproachful glance was cast by rheumatic old gentlemen or delicate women who led the lives of hot-house flowers. But the hearty young fellow sat buried in his newspapers, regardless alike of these expressive glances and the fresh wind that blew in an occasional snow-flake to melt upon his shoulder, hair, or beard.

If his face had not been obscured by the great sheet held before it, an observer might have watched with interest the varying expressions of amusement, contempt, indignation, and disgust which passed over it as he read; for it was a very expressive face, and too young yet to have put on the mask men so soon learn to wear. He was evidently one of the strong, cheery, sympathetic sort of fellows who make their way everywhere, finding friends as they go from the simple fact that they are so full of courage and good-will it is impossible to resist them. This had been proved already; for during that short journey three old ladies had claimed his services in one way or another, a shy little girl had sat upon his knee for half an hour and left him with a kiss, and an obstreperous Irish baby had been bribed to hold its tongue by the various allurements he devised, to the great amusement, as well as gratitude, of his neighbors.

Just now, however, he looked rather grim, knit his brows as he read, and finally kicked his paper under the seat with an expression which proved that he had as much energy as kindliness in his composition, and no taste for the sorrowful record of scandal, dishonesty, and folly daily offered the American public.

"Upon my word, if this sort of thing goes on much longer, the country won't be fit for a decent man to live in," he said to himself, taking a mouthful of fresh air, and letting his eyes wander over the faces of his fellow-travellers as if wondering which of the eminently respectable gentlemen about him would next startle the world by some explosion of iniquity. Even the women did not escape the scrutiny of the keen blue eyes, which softened, however, as they went from one possible Delilah to another; for John Harris had not yet lost his reverence for womankind.

Suddenly his wandering glance was arrested, a look of recognition brightened his whole countenance, and an involuntary "Hullo!" rose to his lips, instead of the romantic "Ha, 'tis she!" with which novel heroes are supposed to greet the advent of the charmer.

The object which wrought so swift and pleasant a change in the young man's mood and manner was a girl's face seen in profile some seats in front of him. A modest little hat with a sweeping feather rested easily on a mass of wavy hair, which was not spoilt by any fashionable device, but looped up in a loose sort of braid from which rebellious tendrils here and there escaped to touch her white throat or shade her temples. One particularly captivating little curl twined round her ear and seemed to be whispering some pleasant secret, for the blooming cheek dimpled now and then, the soft lips smiled, and the eyes were full of a dreamy thoughtfulness. A book lay in her lap, but her own fancies seemed more interesting, and she sat watching the snow-flakes flutter down, lost in one of the delightful reveries girls love, quite unconscious of the admiration of her neighbors, or the fixed stare of the young man behind her.

"Miss Dolly, by all that 's good!" he said to himself, suddenly forgetting the sins of his native land, and finding it quite possible to stop a little longer in it. "She said she was going to town with the old things, and there she is, prettier than ever. If it had n't been for those provoking papers, I should have seen her when she got in, and might have secured a seat by her. That stout party evidently does n't appreciate his advantages. I can't order him out, but I 'll watch my chance, for I really ought to apologize for my stupidity yesterday. Wonder if she has forgotten all about it?"

And John fell into a reverie likewise, for he was in just the mood to enjoy any thing so innocent and fresh and sweet as the memory of little Dolly at her spinning-wheel. It all came back to him with a redoubled charm, for there was a home-like warmth and simplicity about it that made the recollection very pleasant to a solitary fellow knocking about the world with no ties of any sort to keep him safe and steady. He felt the need of them, and was all ready to give away his honest heart, if he could find any amiable creature who could be satisfied with that alone, for he had nothing else to offer. He was rather fastidious, however, having an artist's refined taste in the matter of beauty, and a manly man's love of the womanliness which shows itself in character, not clothes. But he had few opportunities to discover his ideal woman, and no desire to worship a fashion plate, so here was an excellent heart to let, and no one knew it, unless they had the skill to read the notice in the window.

The reveries of both young people were rudely disturbed by the " stout party," who having finished his paper, and taken a comprehensive survey of his thoughtful little neighbor, suddenly began to talk as if he did " appreciate his advantages," and meant to make the most of them.

John watched this performance with deep interest, and it soon became rather exciting; for Miss Dolly's face was a tell-tale, and plainly betrayed the rapid transitions of feeling through which she passed. The respectful attention she at first gave in deference to the age of the speaker changed to surprise, then to annoyance, lastly to girlish confusion and distress; for the old gentleman was evidently of the Pecksniffian order, and took advantage of his gray hairs to harass the pretty damsel with his heavy gallantry.

Poor Miss Dolly looked vainly about her for any means of escape, but every seat was full, and she was quite unconscious that an irate young man behind her was burning to rush to the rescue if he had only known how. As no way appeared, John was forced to content himself with directing such fiery glances at the broad back of the ancient beau it was a wonder they did not act like burning-glasses and set that expanse of broadcloth in a blaze.

A crisis soon arrived, and woman's wit turned the tables capitally; for when the old gentleman confiscated her book under pretence of looking at it, and then, laying his arm over the back of the seat, went on talking with a fat smile that exasperated her beyond endurance, Dolly gave him one indignant glance and opened her window, letting in a blast of cold air that made her tormentor start and shiver as if she had boxed his ears.

"Good! if that does not rout the enemy, I 'm much mistaken," said John to himself, enjoying it all with the relish of a young man who sees an old one usurping his privileges.

The enemy was not routed, but his guns were silenced; for, having expostulated with paternal solicitude, he turned up his coat-collar and retired behind his paper, evidently much disgusted at finding that two could play at the game of annoyance, though the girl had to call the elements to her aid.

"If I dared, I 'd offer to change seats with him; not because he is suffering agonies at the idea of getting tic-douloureux or a stiff neck, that would only serve him right, but because *she* will get the worst of it. There, she has already! Confound that cinder! why did n't it get into his eye instead of hers?" added John, as he saw the girl shrink suddenly, and begin to wink and rub her eye with distressful haste, while the "stout party" took advantage of the mishap to close the window with an expression of vengeful satisfaction on his rubicund visage. He offered no help, for his first rebuff still rankled in his memory, but placidly twirled his thumbs, with a sidelong glance now and then at his companion, who, finding all her winking and rubbing in vain, shrouded her face in a veil, and sat a pathetic picture of beauty in distress, with an occasional tear rolling over her cheek and her dear little nose reddening rapidly with the general inflammation caused by that fatal cinder.

This affecting spectacle was too much for John, who not only felt the chivalrous desire of a man to help the gentle sex, but remembered that he owed the girl a good turn for her hospitality the day before, not to mention the apology he quite burned to make. Knowing that the train would soon stop a few minutes for the passengers to lunch, he resolved then and there to cast himself into the breach and deliver the doubly afflicted damsel at all costs.

Happily the station was reached before any great damage was done to the girl's features, or the young man's impatience became uncontrollable. The instant the stout gentleman rose to seek refreshment John dived for his valise, and, cleaving his way through the crowded aisle, presented himself beside the empty place, asking, with an attempt to look and speak like a stranger, which would not have deceived Dolly a bit, had she not been half-blind, "Is this seat engaged, madam?"

"No, sir," she answered, unveiling to discover what new affliction fate had sent her.

It was delightful to see the one wistful eye light up with a look of recognition, the one visible cheek flush with pleasure, and the lips smile as they added, with the impulsive frankness of a tormented girl, "Oh, please take it quickly, or that dreadful man will come back!"

Quite satisfied with his welcome, John slipped into the coveted place, resolving to keep it in spite of a dozen stout gentlemen.

"Thanks, now what else can I do for you?" he asked, with such an evident desire to lend a hand somewhere that it was impossible to decline his services.

"*Could* you take this thing out of my eye? It hurts dreadfully, and I shall be a spectacle by the time I get to Aunt Maria's," answered Dolly, with a little moan that rent the hearer's susceptible heart.

"That is just what I want to do, and you may trust me; for I've been a great traveller, and have had much experience in the extraction of cinders," said John, adding, as he produced a pencil in a capable sort of way, "now open your eye wide, and we'll have it out in a jiffy."

Dolly obeyed with a courage and confidence most flattering, and John peered into the suffering eye with an intensity which it was impossible for the most artful cinder to escape.

"I see it!" he cried, and turning back the lid over his pencil he delicately removed the black atom with a corner of Dolly's veil.

It was all over in an instant, and both displayed great nerve and coolness during the operation; but, as soon as it was done, Dolly retired into her handkerchief, and John found himself as flushed and breathless as if he had faced some great danger, instead of merely looking into a girl's eye. Ah! but it was a very eloquent eye in spite of the cinder, — large and soft, tearful and imploring, and the instant during which he had bent to examine it had been a most exciting one; for the half-open lips were so near his own their hurried breath fanned his cheek, the inquisitive little curl tumbled over her ear to touch his wrist as he held up the eyelid, and a small hand had unconsciously clutched softly at his arm during the inspection. Bless you! the famous scene between Uncle Toby and the Widow Wadman was entirely surpassed on this occasion, because the actors were both young and neither artful.

"Such relief!" sighed Dolly, emerging from a brief retirement, with a face so full of gratitude that it was like a burst of sunshine after an eclipse.

"Let me see if it is all right;" and John could not resist another look into the clear depths through which he seemed to catch delicious glimpses of an innocent young heart before maiden modesty drew the curtain and shut him out. As the long lashes fell, a sudden color in her cheeks seemed to be reflected upon his, and with a hasty, —

"It is a good deal inflamed, so I'm going to prescribe a wet bandage for a few minutes, if you can spare your handkerchief," — he hurried away to the water tank near by.

"That's very comforting. Thank you *so* much!" and Dolly patted her invalid eye assiduously; while John, feeling that he had earned his place, planted his valise on the seat with a defiant glance over his shoulder, then turned to Dolly, saying, "You must have some lunch," and waiting for no denial dashed out of the car as if on an errand of life and death.

He was gone but a moment or two; but in that time Dolly had smoothed her hair, retied her hat, whisked a nicer pair of gloves out of her pocket, and taken a rapid survey of herself in a tiny glass concealed from other eyes in the recesses of her bag. She had just time to close and cast the aforesaid bag recklessly upon the floor as her knight came up, bearing a cup of tea and a block of cake, saying in the pleasantly protecting way all women like, —

"Dr. Harris prescribes refreshment after the operation, and this is the best he can find. Your aged admirer was at the counter, eating against time and defying apoplexy," he added with a laugh, as Dolly gratefully sipped the tea, which, by the way, was as weak as that made at the famous Boston tea-party, when, as every one knows, water was liberally used.

"You saw him, then, when he was plaguing me?"

"I did, and longed to throw him out of the window."

"Thanks. Did you recognize me before you spoke?"

"Of course I did, and wanted to approach, but did n't dare till the cinder gave me an excuse."

"The idea of being afraid of *me!*"

"How could I help being afraid, when you told me Miss Dolly was 'awful'?" asked John, twinkling with fun, as he sat on the arm of a seat sociably eating a sandwich, which under other circumstances would have struck him as being a remarkable combination of sawdust and sole-leather.

Before Dolly could reply except by a guilty blush, a bell rang, and John hurried away with the empty cup.

A moment or two later the stout gentleman appeared, wiping his mouth, evidently feeling in a better humor, and ready to make up with his pretty neighbor. Smiling blandly, he was about to remove the valise, when Miss Dolly laid her hand upon it, saying with great dignity,

"This seat is engaged, sir. There are plenty of others now, and I wish this for my friend."

Here John, who was just behind, seeing his prize in danger, gave a gentle shove to several intervening fellow-beings, who in turn propelled the "stout party" past the disputed place, which the young man took with an air of entire satisfaction, and a hearty "Thank you!" which told Dolly he had overheard her little speech.

She colored beautifully, but said with grateful frankness, —

"It was n't a fib: a friend in need is a friend indeed, and in return for the cinder I 'm glad to give you a seat."

"Blessed be the cinder, then!" murmured John, feeling at peace with all mankind. Then taking advantage of the propitious moment, he added in a penitential tone, —

"I want to apologize for my stupidity and unintentional rudeness yesterday."

"About what?" asked Dolly, innocently, though her eyes began to sparkle with amusement.

"Why, taking it into my head that Miss Hill must be oldish, and going on in that absurd way about spinsters."

"Well, I *am* a spinster, and not so young as I have been. *I* ought to apologize for not telling you who I was; but it was so very funny to hear you go on in that sober way to my face, I could n't spoil it," said the girl, with a look that upset John's repentant gravity; and they laughed together as only the young and happy can.

"It is very good of you to take it so kindly, but I assure you it weighed upon my conscience, and it is a great relief to beg pardon," he said, feeling as if they had been friends for years.

"Have you been sketching old things ever since?" asked Dolly, changing the conversation with womanly tact.

"Yes: I went to several places further on, but did n't find anything half so good as your chair and tankard. I suppose you are taking the relics to town now?"

"All but one."

"Which is that?"

"The pumpkin hood. It is the only thing my stepmother admires among my treasures, and she would not give it up. You rather admired it, did n't you?" asked Dolly, with her demurest air.

"I deserve to be laughed at for my panic," answered John, owning up manfully; then pulled out his sketch-book, with an eye to business even in the middle of a joke.

"See here! I tried to get that venerable hood into my sketch, but could n't quite hit it. Perhaps you can help me."

"Let me see them all," said Dolly, taking possession of the book with a most flattering air of interest.

"Nothing there but queer or famous things,

all a hundred years old at least," began John, quite forgetting his stolen sketch of a pretty girl cleaning a snuffer-tray, which he had worked up with great care the night before. Perhaps this made the book open at that particular page, for, as the words left his lips, Dolly's eyes fell on her own figure, too well done to be mistaken, even if the artist's face had not betrayed him.

"What 'queer' or 'famous' *old* person of the last century is that, please?" she asked, holding it off, and looking at it through her hand, while her lips broke into a smile in spite of her efforts to look unconscious.

Knowing that a pretty woman will easily forgive a liberty of that sort, John got out of the scrape handsomely by answering with mock gravity, —

"Oh, that 's Madam Hancock, when a girl. Did you never see the famous portrait at Portsmouth?"

"No. The dress is rather modern, and not quite in keeping with the antique chair she is sitting in," observed the girl, critically.

"That 's to be added later. I have to work up things, you know, — a face here, a costume there, and so on: all artists do."

"So I see. There 's the hood; but it wants a cape," and Dolly turned the leaf, as much amused at his quickness as flattered by his compliment.

There were not many sketches as yet, but she

admired them all, and, when the book was shut, chatted on about antiquities, feeling quite friendly and comfortable; for there was respect, as well as admiration, in the honest blue eyes, and the young man did not offend as the old one had done.

"As you are interested in curiosities, perhaps you may like to see some that I have here in my bag. I am very fond and proud of them, because they are genuine, and have histories of old times attached to them," she said presently.

"I shall feel much honored by being allowed to look at them," replied the artist, remembering that "people used to laugh at poor Miss Dolly and her 'duds.'"

"This little pin, made of two hearts in diamonds and rubies, with a crown above, used to be worn by my mother's great aunt, Madam Hancock. She was a Quincy, you know. And this long garnet buckle fastened the Governor's stock," began Dolly, displaying her store with a gentle pride pleasant to see.

"Most interesting! but I can't help feeling grateful that this J. H. does n't have to wear a stock requiring a foot-long buckle like that," answered John, picturing himself in the costume of the past century, and wondering if it would suit his manly face and figure.

"Now don't laugh at this relic, for it is very curious, though *you* won't appreciate it as a woman would;" and Dolly unfolded an old-fashioned housewife of red velvet, lined with faded yellow damask. "That was made by my dear mother out of a bit of the velvet lining of the Governor's state-coach, and the coverlet that a French Comte tore with his spurs."

"Come, that sounds well! I appreciate coaches and spurs, if I 'm not up to brooches and needle-books. Tell the story, please," besought John, who found it the most delightful thing in the world to sit there, following the pretty motions of the small hands, the changeful expression of the winsome face, and enjoying the companionship of the confiding creature beside him.

"Well, you see, when Madam married Captain Scott many of the Governor's things were taken from her, among them the state-coach. By the way, it is said to be in existence now, stored away in somebody's barn down in Portland. You had better go and sketch it," began Dolly, smoothing out the old housewife, and evidently glad to tell the little story of the ancestress whom she was said to resemble, though she modestly refrained from mentioning a fact of which she was immensely proud.

"I will!" and John soberly made a memorandum to visit the ancient coach.

"When my great-great aunt was told she must give up the carriage, she ripped out the new velvet lining, which had been put in at her expense, and gave the bits to her various nieces. Mother made a spencer of hers, and when it was worn out kept enough for this needle-book. The lining is a scrap of the yellow damask counterpane that was on the bed in which the Frenchman should have slept when he came with Lafayette to visit Madam, only he was so tipsy he laid on the outside, and tore the fine cover with his spurs. There's a nice Comte for you!"

"I'd like to see the spurs, nevertheless. Any more treasures?" and John peered into the bag, as if he thirsted for more antiquarian knowledge.

"Only one, and this is the most valuable of all. Stoop down and look: I'm afraid I may be robbed, if I display my things carelessly."

John obediently bent till the sweeping feather of her hat touched his cheek, to the great annoyance of the banished peri, who viewed these pleasant passages from afar with much disfavor.

"This is said to be Madam's wedding ring. I like to think so, and am very proud to be named for her, because she was a good woman as well as a" —

"Beauty," put in John, as the speaker paused to open a faded case in which lay a little ring of reddish gold.

"I was going to say — as well as a brave one; for I need courage," added the girl, surveying the old-fashioned trinket with such a sober face that the young man refrained from alluding to the remarkable coincidence of another John and Dolly looking at the wedding ring together.

She seemed to have forgotten all about her

companion for a moment, and be busy with her own thoughts, as she put away her treasures with a care which made it a pleasure to watch her tie knots, adjust covers, repack her little bag, and finally fold her hands over it, saying gravely, —

"I love to think about those times; for it seems as if people were better then, — the men more honest, the women more womanly, and everything simpler and truer than now. Does it ever seem so to you?"

"Indeed it does; for this very day, as I read the papers, I got quite low-spirited, thinking what a shameful state things have got into. Money seems to be the one idea, and men are ready to sell their souls for it," answered John, as soberly as she.

"Money is a good thing to have, though;" and Dolly gave a little sigh, as she drew her scarf over the worn edges of her jacket.

"So it is!" echoed John, with the hearty acquiescence of a man who had felt the need of it.

"My name and these old treasures are all my fortune, and I used to be contented with it; but I 'm not now, dependence is so hateful!" added the girl, impulsively; then bit her lip, as if the words had escaped in spite of her.

"And this is all mine," said John, twirling the pencil which he still held; giving confidence for confidence, and glad to do it, if it made them better friends, for he pitied little Miss Dolly, suspecting what was true, that her home was not a happy one.

She thanked him mutely for the kind look he gave her, and said prettily, —

"Skill is money; and it must be a very pleasant life to go about drawing beautiful or curious things."

"So it is sometimes, — yesterday, for instance," he answered, laughing.

"*I* have no modern accomplishments to earn a living by. Mine are all old-fashioned; and no one cares for such nowadays, except in servants. I may be very glad of them, though; for playing lady does n't seem half so honest as going out to service, when one has nothing but an empty pair of hands," she said with a wistful yet courageous look at the wintry world outside, which made her companion feel a strong desire to counsel and protect this confiding young Columbus, who knew so little of the perils which would beset her voyage in search of a woman's El Dorado.

"Come to me for a recommendation before you try it. I can vouch for your cooking, you know. But I 'd advise you to play lady till you discover a good safe place. I don't believe you 'll find it hard, for the world is likely to be very kind to such as you," he answered, so cheerily that she brightened like a flower to which a stray sunbeam is very welcome.

A shrill whistle announced that the journey

was over, and everybody began at once to fuss and fumble. John got up to take his valise from the rack, and Dolly began to struggle into her rubbers. She was still bending down to do this, with as little damage as possible to her best gloves, when she heard a sounding slap and a hearty voice cry out, —

"Hullo, John!" then add in a lower tone, "So there *is* a Mrs. Harris, you sly dog, you?"

"Hush! there is n't. How are you, George?" returned another voice, beginning in a hurried whisper and ending in an unnecessarily loud salutation.

What happened for a minute or two after that Dolly did not know; for the rubbers proved so refractory that she only rose from the encounter flushed and hurried, as the train entered the station.

"Let me make myself useful in looking after your baggage," said her self-constituted escort, handing her out with great respect and care.

"Thank you: all my things come by express, so I 've nothing to do but get into a carriage.

"Then allow me to see you safely there, for the sake of the treasures, if nothing else;" and John led her away, utterly ignoring the presence of "George," who stood looking after them, with a face full of good-humored interest and amusement.

"I 'm very much obliged. Good-by," said Dolly, from the coach window.

"Not good-by: I 'm coming to the fair, you know," answered John, lingering at the door as if loath to lose sight of his little friend.

"I forgot all about it!"

"I did n't; for I depend on the cakes and ale and all the other good things promised me."

"You will find them there," with a smile, and then a sudden blush as she remembered that he had not only agreed to speak to "Miss Dolly," but to "win her old heart."

He remembered also, and laughed as he bowed with the same audacious look he had worn when he made that rash vow.

"I wonder if he *will* come?" thought the girl, as she drove away.

"As if *I* should forget!" said John to himself, as he trudged through the snow, quite regardless of his waiting friend; for from the little cinder had been kindled a spark of the divine fire that moves one of the great engines which transport mankind all the world over.

CHAPTER III

CONFIDENTIAL

JOHN HARRIS promised to "do" the fair, and kept his word handsomely; for he was there every day for a week, lunching in the old-fashioned kitchen, and then, in his official capacity, sketching every relic he could lay his eyes on. Such punctuality caused the pretty waiters to smile affably upon this faithful devourer of primitive viands, and the matrons to predict great things from the young artist's application to his work.

Little guessed the girls and the gossips that love was ravaging their generous patron's heart more persistently than he did their tables, and that nature not art caused his devotion to modern beauty rather than ancient ugliness. For all John saw in the crowd that filled the place was Dolly, tripping to and fro tray in hand, spinning at her wheel, or resting beside Aunt Maria, twin sister of Mrs. Hill, in an imposing cap instead of the pumpkin hood. Pretty Dolly was the belle of the kitchen; for she alone of all the dozen damsels on duty looked her part, and was in truth a country girl, rich in the old-fashioned gifts and graces of health, modesty, housewifely skill, and the sweet maidenliness which girls who come out at sixteen soon lose forever. Her dress, too, was wonderfully complete and becoming, though only a pink and white chintz, a mob-cap, and an uncompromising apron, with the pin-ball, scissors, keys, and linen pocket hanging at the side. The others looked like stage soubrettes, and acted like coquettish young ladies who knew nothing about their work. But Dolly was genuine throughout, so she proved a great success; and Aunt Maria took all the credit of it to herself, felt that she had done a good thing in bringing so much youth, energy, and loveliness to market, and expressed her satisfaction by talking a great deal about "our family," which, as she was a Smith, was certainly large enough to furnish endless gossip.

Another person watched, admired, and hovered about the girl like a blue-bottle fly about a rose; and that was Mr. Aaron Parker, a dapper little man of fifty, who, having made a snug fortune, was now anxious to marry and settle. Aunt Maria was evidently his confidant and friend; and it was soon apparent that Aunt Maria intended to make a match between her niece and this amiable gentleman, who set about his wooing with old-fashioned formality and deliberation.

All this John saw, heard, or divined with the keenness of a lover, while he watched the events of that week; for he very soon made up his mind that he adored "Miss Dolly," as he always called her to himself. The short time which had elapsed between the car episode and the opening of the fair seemed endless to him; and, when he came beaming into the kitchen the very first day, his heart sang for joy at sight of that bonny face once more. She welcomed him so kindly, served him so prettily, and showed such frank and friendly pleasure at meeting him again, that the lonely fellow felt as if he had suddenly found a large and attached family, and yielded to the charm without a struggle. She seemed to belong to him somehow, as if he had discovered her, and had the first right to admire, help, and love her; for he alone of all the men there had seen her at home, had looked deepest into the shy, bright eyes, and heard her call him "friend."

This delightful state of things lasted for a few days, during which he felt as if quaffing nectar and tasting ambrosia, while he drank the promised cider and ate the spicy "sweethearts" which Dolly always brought him with a smile that went directly to his head, and produced a delicious sort of intoxication. He never could have but a word or two, she was so busy; but, as he sat apart, pretending to sketch, he was living over those brief, blissful moments, and concocting wonderfully witty, wise, or tender speeches for the morrow.

Well for him that no one looked over his shoulder at such times, for his portfolio would have betrayed him, since it was a wild jumble of andirons and mob-caps, antique pepper-pots and pretty profiles, spinning-wheels, and large eyes with a profusion of lash; while a dainty pair of feet in high-heeled slippers seemed to dance from page after page, as if the artist vainly sought to exorcise some persistent fancy by booking it over and over again.

Suddenly a change appeared both in the man and in his work; for Parker had arrived, and clouds began to gather on the horizon which was rosy with the dawn of love. Now John discovered that the cider was sour and the cake stale, for the calls of a voracious rival cruelly abbreviated his moments of bliss. Now he glared and brooded in corners where once he had revelled in dreams of a dim but delightful future. Now the pages of his sketch-book bore grotesque likenesses of a round, snub-nosed countenance in all sorts of queer places, such as a clock-face, under a famous cocked hat, or peeping out of a memorable warming-pan; while a dapper figure was seen in various trying attitudes, the most frequent being prone before the dancing feet, one of which was usually spurning a fat money-bag, with contempt in every line of the pretty slipper.

At this stage, the fair ended, and Aunt Maria bore the charmer away, leaving John to comfort himself with the memory of a parting look of regret from behind Governor Hancock's punch-bowl, which Dolly embraced with one arm, while the other guarded Madam's best china tea-pot.

Maddening was it to haunt the street before Aunt Maria's door, and hear a gay voice singing inside fit to melt a paving stone, to say nothing of a young man's heart. More maddening still to catch occasional glimpses of the girl shut up in a carriage with the dragon, or at concerts and theatres under the escort of Mr. Parker. But most maddening of all was the frequent spectacle of this enamoured gentleman trotting up the street, simpering to himself as he went, and freely entering at the door which shut the younger lover out of Paradise.

At such trying periods, John (now very far gone indeed, for love feeds on air) would feel a wild desire to knock the little man down, storm Aunt Maria's mansion, and carry his Dolly away from what he felt assured was an irksome bondage to the girl. But, alas! where could he carry the dear creature when he had got her? For all the home he possessed was one room in a dull boarding-house, and his only fortune the salary his pencil earned him. Then, as he groaned over these sad facts, a great temptation would assail him; for he remembered that with a word he could work the miracle which would give him half a million, and make all things possible but the keeping of his own self-respect.

Hard times just then for John Harris; and

for some weeks he went about his daily duties with such a divided mind and troubled spirit that the stoniest heart might have pitied him. But comfort came when least expected, and in helping another he got help himself and hope beside.

One gusty March morning he arrayed himself in his best, put a posy in his buttonhole, and went gallantly away to Aunt Maria's door, bound to make a call in spite of her frowns at the fair, and evident desire to ignore his existence since. Boldly ringing the forbidden bell, he inquired for the ladies. Both were engaged; and, as if nothing should be wanting to his chagrin, as he went down the steps Mr. Parker, bearing a suggestive bouquet, went up and was instantly admitted.

It was too much for poor John, who rushed away into the park, and pulling his hat over his eyes tramped wrathfully down the mall, muttering to himself, —

"It 's no use; I *must* give in; for with a fortune in my pocket I could carry all before me, — bribe Aunt Maria, outbid Aaron, and win my Dolly, if I 'm not much mistaken."

Just then a sharp yelp roused him from his excited reverie, and looking up he found that he had kicked a fat poodle, who was waddling slowly along, while some way before him went a little figure in a gray hat, at sight of which John's heart gave a leap. Here was bliss! Dolly alone at last, and he could defy the dragon and all her machinations. Parker and his fine bouquet were nowhere; Harris and his buttonhole posy had the best of it now; and, leaving the fat poodle to whine and waddle at its own sweet will, the happy man hurried forward to make the most of this propitious moment.

As he drew near, he observed that a handkerchief went more than once to the face which drooped in a thoughtful way as the feet paced slowly on.

"Bless her heart! she is catching cold, and dreaming dreams, here all alone," thought John, as, stepping to her side, he said gently, that he might not startle her, "Good-morning, Miss Dolly."

He did startle her, nevertheless, and himself as well; for, as she turned quickly, he saw that her face was bathed in tears. Instantly all his own troubles took wing; and, with no thought but how to comfort her, he said impetuously, —

"I beg pardon, but do tell me what is the matter?" He came upon her so suddenly that there was no time to hide the tell-tale tears. He looked so eager, kind, and helpful, she could not be offended at his words; and just then she needed a friend so much, it was hard to resist confiding in him. Yet, womanlike, she tried to hide her little worries, to make light of her girlish grief, and turn a brave face to the world. So she brushed the drops from her eyes, put on a smile, and answered stoutly, —

"It was very foolish of me to cry, but it is so dull and lonely here I think I was a little homesick."

"Then perhaps you won't mind if I walk on a bit with you and apologize for kicking your little dog?" said John, artfully availing himself of this excuse.

"No, indeed. He is Aunt Maria's dog; but how came you to do it?" asked the girl, plainly showing that a human companion was very welcome.

"I was in a brown study, and did it by accident. He 's so fat it did n't hurt him much," answered the young man, assuming his gayest manner for her sake. Then he added, with an excuse which did not deceive her a bit, —

"The fact is, I 'd ventured to call on you to see if I could get a sketch of the punch-bowl; but you were engaged, the girl said, and I was rather disappointed."

"What a fib! I 'm sorry I was out; but the house was gloomy and Aunt rather cross, so I ran away under pretence of giving old Tip an airing."

"Ah, you don't know what you lost! Mr. Parker went in as I came out, with such a nosegay! — for Aunt Maria, I suppose?" and John tried to look quite easy and gay as he spoke.

Dolly's face darkened ominously, and a worried look came into her eyes as she glanced behind her, then quickened her steps, saying, with a little groan that was both comic and pathetic, —

"It does seem as if it was my doom to be tormented by old gentlemen! I wish you 'd get rid of this one as you did of the other."

"Nothing would give me greater pleasure," answered John, with such heartiness that a sudden color dried Dolly's wet cheeks, as she remembered that he had got rid of tormentor number one by taking his place.

Cheered by the knowledge that a champion was ready to defend her, she ventured to show him a safer way in which to serve her, saying very soberly, —

"I think I may be glad of the recommendation you once promised me. Should you mind giving it?"

"Are you tired of 'playing lady' so soon?" he asked anxiously.

"So tired that I felt to-day as if I 'd like to run away and take service with the first person who would engage me."

"Don't!" exclaimed John, with such energy that the fat poodle barked shrilly and made a feeble charge at his boots, feeling that something was wrong somewhere. "Run away home, if you must run, but pray don't get discouraged and do anything rash," he went on with great earnestness; for he saw by her face that she was in some real trouble.

"I have n't even a home to run to; for Mrs. Hill agrees with Aunt that it 's time I ceased to be a burden. It 's very hard, when I only ask a safe corner in the world, and am willing to work for it," cried the girl, with an irrepressible sob; for the trials of many weeks had grown unbearable, and a kind word made the full heart overflow.

Neither spoke for a minute, then John said with a respectful earnestness which touched her very much, —

" Miss Dolly, you once called me a friend, and I was very proud to be so honored. Forget that I am anything else, and, if you have no one wiser and older to consult, trust me, and let me help you. I 've knocked about the world enough to know how hard it is for a man to get an honest living, doubly hard for a woman, especially one as young and beautiful as you are. There are safe corners, I am sure; but it takes time to find them, so pray be patient and do nothing without care."

" I called you a friend in need, and so you are; for, strange as it may seem, there *is* no one to whom I can go for disinterested advice. I know so little of the world that I 'm afraid to trust my own judgment, yet I am driven to decide between dependence of a sort I despise, or to stand alone and take care of myself. *Will* you advise me? " and she looked up with an appealing glance, which read such a reassuring answer in the honest eyes full of sincerest sympathy that she was comforted before he spoke.

"Indeed I will! for what are we all here for, if not to help one another? Do you know I think there is a sort of fate about these things, and it's no use to struggle against it. We seem to be two 'lone, lorn' creatures thrown together in queer ways, so let's agree to be old friends and stand by each other. Come, is it a bargain?"

He seemed so firmly convinced of the inevitability of this fate that the girl felt relieved from farther scruples, and agreed in all good faith.

"Now about the troubles?" began John, trying to look old, reliable, and wise; for he guessed the one she was most reluctant to tell.

"I suppose marrying for an establishment or earning their bread is a question most poor girls have to settle sooner or later," observed Dolly, in a general sort of way, as an opening; for, in spite of his praiseworthy efforts, her young counsellor did not succeed in looking like a sage.

"If pretty, yes; if plain, no. We need n't discuss the latter class, but go on to the question," returned John, keeping to the subject in hand with masculine pertinacity.

"I'd rather be an old man's housekeeper than his wife; but people won't believe it, and laugh at me for being what they call so foolish," said the girl, petulantly; for she did not seem to be getting on well with her confidences.

"I thought from what I saw at the fair that

Parker seemed ready to offer both situations for your acceptance."

John could not help saying that, for a jealous pang assailed him at the mere idea. He feared that he had spoilt the *rôle* he was trying to play; but it happened to be the best thing he could have done, for the introduction of that name made things much easier for Dolly, as she proved by kindling up as suddenly as if the word had been a match to fire a long train of grievances.

"He did; and Aunt scolds me from morning till night, because I won't accept the fine establishment he offers me. That 's what I was sent here for! My stepmother wants me out of the way, Aunt Maria hands me over to Mr. Parker, and he takes me because I know how to cook and nurse. I might as well be put up at auction and sold to the highest bidder!" she cried, with eyes flashing through indignant tears.

"It 's abominable!" echoed John, with equal indignation, though the words "highest bidder" rung in his ears, as he thought of the fortune waiting for him, and the youth which would tell so strongly in the race against "old Parker," as he irreverently called the little man; for fifty seems a patriarchal age to four-and-twenty.

"I know that sort of thing is done every day, and thought quite right; but I am so old-fashioned it seems terrible to marry merely for a home. Yet I 'm very tired of being poor, and I *should* like a taste of ease and pleasure while I can enjoy them," added Dolly, with a very natural longing for the bright and happy side of life.

"And I could give her all she wants," thought John, with the temptation getting stronger every minute. But he only said a little bitterly, "You 'd better give in, if you want ease and pleasure, for money can buy anything."

"No, it can't buy love, and that is better than all the splendor in the world," answered the girl, in a tone that thrilled her hearer to the heart. "What *I* call love seems to have gone out of fashion; and that is what troubles me; because, if there *is n't* any such thing, I may as well take the next best, and try to be contented. No one seems to value love for itself alone, to feel the need of it as much as light and air, to miss it when it goes, or try to earn and keep it as the most precious thing in the world. Money and position are every thing, and men work and women marry for these, as if they had no other hope or end; and I 'm frightened at the things I see and hear in what is called society."

"Poor child, I don't wonder; but I assure you there *is* an ocean of love in the world, only it gets put out of sight in the rush, wasted on those who don't deserve it, or damned up by adverse circumstances. It exists though, the real genuine article, waiting for a market. *Do* believe it, and wait for it, and I 'm sure it will come."

John was so divided between a rash impulse to prove his point by a declaration then and there, and the conviction that it would be altogether premature, his metaphors got rather mixed, and he had to pull himself up abruptly. But Dolly thought it a beautiful speech, was glad to believe every word of it, and accepted this piece of advice with admirable docility.

"I 'll wait, and meantime be looking about for the safe corner to run to when Aunt Maria gets tired of me, because I don't mean to go home again to be a burden." Then, as if anxious to slip away from a too interesting topic, she asked with a very winning expression of interest and good-will, —

"Now what can I do for you? I 'm sure you have worries as well as I, and, though not very wise, perhaps I might advise in my turn."

"You are very good, but I could n't think of troubling you;" and the young man looked both pleased and flurried by the girl's offer.

"We agreed to help one another, you remember; and I must do my part, or the bargain won't be a fair one. Tell me what the brown study was about, and I 'll forgive the kick poor Tip got," persisted Dolly; for her feminine instinct told her that a heavy cloud of some sort had been lifted to let sunshine through for her.

John did long to know her opinion on a certain matter, but a man's pride would not let him speak as freely as the girl had done, so he took refuge in a mild subterfuge, and got advice on false pretences.

"It was only a quandary I was in about a friend of mine. He wants my judgment in a case something like yours, and perhaps you *could* help me with an opinion; for women are very wise in such matters sometimes."

"Please tell me, if you may. I should so love to pay my debts by being of some use;" and Dolly was all attention, as she pushed back her veil as if to get a clear and impartial view of the case about to be submitted.

Fixing his eyes on the sparrows who were disporting themselves among the budding elm-boughs, John plunged abruptly into his story, never once looking at his hearer and speaking so rapidly that he was rather red and breathless when he got through.

"You see, Jack was plodding along after a fashion all by himself, his people being dead, when an old friend of his father's took it into his head to say, 'Come and be a son to me, and I'll leave you a handsome fortune when I die.' A capital thing it seemed, and Jack accepted, of course. But he soon found that he had given up his liberty, and was a slave to a very tyrannical master, who claimed him soul and body, heart and mind. That did n't suit Jack, and he would have broken away; but, as you say, he was 'tired of being poor, and wanted a little ease and pleasure in his life.' The old man was failing, and the money would soon be his, so he held on, till he suddenly discovered that this fortune for which he was waiting was not honest money, but, like many another great fortune, had been ground out of the poor, swindled out of honest men, or stolen from trusting friends, and hoarded up for a long lifetime, to be left to Jack with the curse of dishonesty upon it. Would you advise him to take it?"

"No," answered the girl, without a moment's hesitation.

"Well, he did n't, but turned his back on the ill-gotten money, and went to work again with clean but empty hands," added John, still looking away, though his face wore a curiously excited expression under its enforced composure.

"I 'm glad, very glad he did! Was n't it noble of him?" asked Dolly, full of admiring interest in this unknown Jack.

"It was very hard; for you see he loved somebody, and stood a poor chance of winning her without a penny in his pocket."

"All the nobler in him then; and, if she was worth winning, she 'd love him the more for the sacrifice," said Dolly, warmly; for the romance of the story took her fancy, though it was poorly told.

"Think so? I 'll mention that to Jack: it will cheer him up immensely, for he 's afraid to try his fate with nothing to offer but his earnings."

"What 's his business?" asked Dolly suddenly.

"Connected with newspapers, — fair salary, good prospects, — not ashamed to work," answered John, staring hard at the sparrows, and wiping his forehead, as if he found the bleak day getting too warm for him.

"Is the girl pretty?"

"The most captivating little creature I ever beheld!" cried John, rapturously.

"Oh, indeed," and Dolly glanced at him sharply, while a shadow passed over her face, as she asked with redoubled interest, "Is she rich?"

"Has nothing but her sweet face and good name I believe."

"Is n't that enough?"

"Indeed it is! but Jack wants to make life beautiful and easy for her, and he can by saying a word. He is awfully tempted to say it; for the old man is dying, has sent for him to come back, and there is yet time to secure a part of the fortune. He won't take it all, but has a fancy that, if he leaves half to charity, it would be a sort of purification to the other half; and he might enjoy it with his love. Don't you think so?"

"No, it would spoil the whole thing. Why cannot they be contented to begin with nothing but love, and work up together, earning every clean and honest penny they spend. It would be a comfort to see such a pair in this mercenary world, and I do hope they will do it," said the girl, heartily, though a slightly pensive tone had come into her voice, and she stifled a small sigh, as she put down her veil as if there was nothing worth seeing in the landscape.

"I think they *will* try it!" answered John, with decision, as he smiled sympathetically at a pair of sparrows chirping together at the door of one of the desirable family mansions provided for their use.

Here Tip ended the dangerous dialogue by sitting down before Dolly with a howl of despair, which recalled her to her duty.

"The poor old thing is tired, and must go in. Good-morning, and many thanks," she said, turning toward the steps, which they would have passed unseen but for the prudent poodle's hint.

"Good-by, and a thousand pardons for boring you with my affairs," began John, with a penitent, yet very grateful glance.

"By the way, I 've been so interested in Jack's affairs that I 've forgotten exactly what your advice was to me," she added, pausing on the upper step for a last word.

With his hat in his hand and his heart in his eyes, John looked up and answered in a tone that made few words necessary, —

"Don't sell yourself for a home."

And Dolly answered back with a sweet, shrewd smile that made him flush guiltily, —

"Don't smother your conscience with a fortune."

CHAPTER IV

APRIL FOOLS

TIP'S constitutionals were taken with praiseworthy regularity about that time, and the poor asthmatic animal was nearly walked off his legs by the vigor with which his little mistress paraded the park at unfashionable hours. A robust young man, who did not look as if he needed early walks, was continually meeting Dolly by accident as it were, till on the fourth *rencontre* they both burst out laughing, gave up all further subterfuge, and felt that it was vain to struggle against fate. The next time they met, both looked very sober; and John said, watching her face as he spoke, —

"It is all over with me, Miss Dolly. The old man is dead, and my chance is lost forever."

"You look so solemn, I'm afraid he left you something, after all."

"Not a penny. All went to various charities, and I have only my salary and these two hands."

"I'm glad of that! I'd like to shake those

honest hands, and wish them all success. May I?" she said, putting out her own with such cordial approval in voice and eyes that John lost his head, and, holding both the small hands fast in his, answered all in one fervently incoherent burst, —

"May you? Let me keep them, and then I *shall* succeed! Dearest Dolly, you said you did n't want anything but love; and here 's a whole heart full, aching to be poured out. You said you 'd like to see Jack and his wife working their way up together, contented to be poor. Here 's Jack and the wife he wants, if she cares enough for him to try that beautiful experiment. You said you had n't any home to run to when those cruel women called you a burden. Run to me, my darling, and be the pride and joy and comfort of my life!"

No one saw what Dolly did but Tip, who sat lolling out his tongue in an imbecile manner; and no one heard what she said but some bright-faced crocuses blooming early in that lonely corner of the park. But from what took place afterward, it was evident that her reply had not been entirely unpropitious; for her hand lay on John's arm, her face was in an April state between smiles and tears, and to her eyes midsummer warmth and radiance seemed to have fallen suddenly upon the earth. It is hardly necessary to mention that the other party in this little transaction looked as if *he* owned the entire world, was yearning to embrace all mankind, and had nothing more to ask of Heaven in the way of happiness.

"You don't regret saying yes, like an angel," asked this unreasonable lover, five minutes after he had surprised her into uttering that momentous monosyllable.

"Not yet."

"You know that it is very selfish of me to ask you, when I 've nothing to give; and very unwise in you to take me, because you have much to lose."

"Why, what?"

"The devoted Parker and his plump pocket-book."

It was good to hear Dolly laugh at that, and to see John glance defiantly at an elderly gentleman in the distance, as if all that harmless portion of the race ought to be exterminated, to leave room for happy young fellows like himself.

"He will believe now that, when I say 'No,' I mean it," answered Dolly, with an assumption of dignity, which changed with comic suddenness to one of dismay, as she added, "Oh, my heart, what *will* Aunt Maria say!"

"Don't tell her just yet, or she will shut you up, whisk you away, or do some awful thing to part us. Keep this delicious secret for a little while, and we can enjoy many happy minutes in peace."

"Yes, John," with a docility that was altogether captivating to the new commander-in-chief.

"I must look about me, and be getting ready to take you into my home as well as my heart, when the storm breaks. There is sure to be one, I fancy; and, for my part, I rather relish the idea. The air will be clearer and things more settled after it."

"I don't know what they will say and do to me, but I shall not mind, now I have you to take care of me;" and Dolly's other hand went to join the one on John's arm, with a confiding gesture which glorified the old coat-sleeve, in his eyes, more than any badge it could have worn.

"I suppose we *must* live somewhere, and eat occasionally, since we are mortal. Love certainly *is* the best capital to start on, but a trifle of cash is necessary likewise; so we must take a little thought for the morrow. Wish the city would provide us with a house rent free, and board thrown in, as it does our feathery confidants here," observed the husband elect, eying the plump sparrows with a vague sense of domestic cares already stealing over his masculine mind.

"Don't think of all those worries yet. Just love and be happy for a time, and things will settle themselves somehow," cried Dolly, whose womanly nature would not be so soon defrauded of the sweet romance which comes but once in a lifetime.

"Very well. We'll give a month to clear bliss, and then talk about the honeymoon."

But, with the charming inconsistency of her sex, no sooner had she forbidden a subject than she felt an intense desire to talk about it; and after a moment's pause, during which her lover had been looking down at her thoughtful face in silent rapture, Dolly emerged from a brief reverie, clapping her hands and exclaiming, —

"John, I've got the most delicious idea that ever was. Now don't laugh and say, 'It is n't practical,' for I know it is; and it would be so new and appropriate and economical, and altogether nice, that I hope you'll approve. We shall want a home by and by, shall we not?"

"I want it now, if you've no objection."

"Be serious. Well, a room or two must content us at first, and we want them to be decent, not to say pretty and comfortable, don't we?"

"They can't help being all three, if you are there, my Dolly."

"No, John, not in public! Now answer me this: won't you have to save up a long time, to get enough to buy furniture and things, no matter how simple?"

"I'm afraid I should; for at present my housekeeping stock is about as large and varied as that of Tommy Traddles. His consisted of a bird-cage and a toasting-fork, I believe; mine, of an easel and a boot-jack. Would n't they do to begin with?"

"Please don't joke, but listen; for *this* is the new idea. Take my dear old relics and furnish our nest with them! What *could* be more economical, picturesque, and appropriate for this centennial year?"

Dolly stopped short to see how this amazing proposal struck her lord and master. It seemed to take him off his legs; for he sat suddenly down upon a seat that fortunately was behind him, and looked up at the beaming little woman with an expression of admiration and contentment, which answered her question so emphatically that she nestled down beside him with all her doubts laid at rest.

"I thought you'd like it! Now let's plan it all out, and see what we've got. Every thing is as old as the hills, you know; but still so good and strong we can get years of wear out of it. We don't have such well-made furniture nowadays," she went on, happily blind to the deficiencies of the time-worn chairs, clumsy tables, and cracked china, which were all her store.

"My blessing on every stick of it! I was n't thinking about the furniture, though. I was rejoicing over the fact that, if I need n't save up for that sort of thing, we could be married all the sooner. That's the beauty of the idea, don't you see?" and John regarded the originator thereof with unmitigated satisfaction.

"So we can; but *do* think about the furniture, because you ought to be interested in helping me make an artistic home," said Dolly, knowing that the word "artistic" would arrest his attention, and keep him to the subject in hand; for as yet the other idea was too new to bear much discussion.

"I will. In fact, I see it now, all complete. Two or three rooms in an old house, if possible, — they are always the cheapest, my love; so don't look as if you saw cobwebs and blue mould, and felt black beetles running over your feet. In one room we 'll have that spider-legged table on which you cleaned the snuffer tray, and the claw-footed chairs: there were three, I think, — one for each of us, and the third for a friend. Then on the dresser we 'll put all the porringers out of which we are to eat mush and milk, and the pewter platters for an occasional 'biled dish,' — that 's the proper name for the mess, is n't it? Likewise the dear fat tea-pots, the red china cups, all cracked, the green-handled knives and forks, the wooden spoons, funny pepper-pots, and all the rest of the droll rattletraps."

"Don't forget *the* tankard," cried Dolly, as John paused for breath in the middle of his rhapsody.

"That will be in our parlor, set forth in state on the little stand I used to have my lunch at during the fair. I 'm afraid I scratched your initials all over it, that being a trick of mine about that time."

"I thought you did it! Never mind, but go on, please."

"We shall put flowers in the immortal mug, and I shall paint them, earn sums, and grow famous, such will be the inspiration of my surroundings. For, while I sit in the General's chair at my delightful work, you in the pretty chintz gown and the fly-away cap, — promise me to wear it, or I won't go on?"

"I 'll wear anything you like, in the house, and can have a water-proof and a linen duster for the street. Artists' wives usually do have to make guys of themselves, I believe."

"Thank you, dear. Well, you will always be doing one of three things, making sweethearts, spinning, or looking over my shoulder. I prefer the latter occupation on the whole, and when I 'm at home that will be your mission. During my absence, you can attend to the housework you love so well, and do so prettily. Never did I see such brilliant candlesticks in my life; and as for the copper tea-kettle, it was like a mirror. I saw you steal peeps at it more than once, Little Vanity, that day as I sat stealing a sketch of you."

"Then you think it can be done, John?" ignoring the accusation.

"It not only *can,* but it *shall* be done, and I should n't wonder if we set the fashion of furnishing bridal bowers with relics of all sorts, throwing in a glue-pot gratis, to mend up the old things when they tumble to pieces. I 'm great at that, and can get my living as a cabinet-maker when art fails."

"I do believe you can do everything, John!"

"No, I could n't cure pneumonia, if you should get it by sitting in this chilly wind. Now I 've got you, I intend to take great care of you, my little treasure."

It was so sweet to Dolly to be cared for, and so delightful to John to do it, that they forgot all about poor Tip till he tumbled into the pond, and was with difficulty fished out by his ears and tail, being too fat to do anything but float. This catastrophe shortened an interview which might otherwise have been prolonged till nightfall, for

> "Lightly falls the foot of time
> That only treads on flowers."

"Why, John, do you know that this is the first of April?" asked Dolly, as they went homeward, with Tip forlornly dripping in the rear. "A very fitting day for such an imprudent couple as we are to begin their journey," she added, enjoying the idea immensely.

"So it is! Never mind! we 'll prove that we are no fools, though a mercenary world may call us so," returned John, as blithe as she.

Alas, poor things! they thought their troubles were all over, now they had found each other; whereas a cruel fate was laughing at them round the corner.

CHAPTER V

THE DECLARATION OF INDEPENDENCE

UNFORTUNATELY for these deluded young persons, their month of bliss turned out to be the most tempestuous one they had ever passed; for, before the first week was over, some malignant imp inspired Aunt Maria to spy, from a certain end window which commanded a corner of the park, the lingering adieux of the lovers, and then it was all up with them.

A single stormy debate, during which John manfully claimed his Dolly, she stoutly defended her right to love whom she chose, and Aunt Maria thundered and lightened unavailingly, resulted in the banishment of the claimant, the strict seclusion of the damsel, and the redoubled devotion of the decorous but determined Parker, who, cheered on by his ally, still besieged the rebellious heart, undaunted by the reinforcements lately received.

The prospect was certainly not a hopeful one; but the young people never lost courage, rather enjoyed it on the whole, and revolved endless schemes in their busy brains, which they confided to one another by means of notes slipped under Tip's collar when he took his solitary airings on the steps. For a time persecution lent its zest to their love; but presently separation grew unbearable, and they were ready for revolt.

"I *must* see you," wrote John, in note number 37.

"You *shall,*" answered Dolly, and bade him meet her at one of the many Centennial Balls which afflicted the world in 1875-76.

To hear was to obey; and though said ball was to be eminently select, thanks to a skilful use of his middle name, John was able to keep the appointed tryst, well knowing that there is no solitude like that to be found in a crowd. Costumes were in order; and there was a general resurrection of ancient finery, which made the handsome hall look as if time had rolled back a hundred years. Every one who had a hair powdered it, and those who had not made up the deficiency by imposing wigs. Spindle-legged gentlemen affected top-boots and spurs; those blessed with a manly development of calf pranced in silk stockings and buckled shoes. British and Continental uniforms amicably marched shoulder to shoulder; dimity and brocade mingled prettily together; and patriotic ardor animated the hearts under the lace stomachers and embroidered waistcoats as warmly as of old, for the spirit of '76 was all alive again.

Aunt Maria looked like a parrot of the most brilliant plumage; for the good lady burned to distinguish herself, and had vainly tried to wear a suit of Madam Hancock's belonging to Dolly. Fortunately, Madam was a small woman, and Aunt Maria quite the reverse; so she was forced to give it up, and content herself with being one of many Martha Washingtons who filled the dowagers' corner.

So Dolly bloomed into the sweetest little old-time lady ever seen, and was in truth by nature as by name a Dorothy Quincy. Not as the matron, but as the maid, with all her curly locks turned over a roller before they fell on her white neck, where shone the jewelled hearts she prized so much. Lilies of the valley embroidered her white gown, and nestled among the lace that rose and fell upon her bosom. From under her quilted satin petticoat "her little feet stole in and out," wearing Madam's wedding-shoes, so high in the heels and so pointed at the toes that Dolly suffered martyrdom with a smiling face, and danced at the risk of her life. Long gloves, with Lafayette's likeness stamped on the back, kept splitting at the time-worn seams, so plump were the arms inside. A quaint scent-bottle hung at her waist; and she hid her blushes behind a great fan, whose dim mirror had reflected faces history has made immortal.

"You are simply perfect, Miss Hill, and nothing could be added," whispered the still hopeful Parker, who was on duty and much elated by the fact; for the girl was unusually friendly that evening for reasons of her own.

"Except the Governor," she answered, peeping over her fan with eyes full of anxiety as well as merriment; for John had not yet appeared, and the little man beside her was very funny in a voluminous white neck-cloth, furred coat-collar, and square-toed shoes, carefully kept in the "first position." He had longed to personate the character she suggested. Stature forbade, however; and he had contented himself with personating Benjamin Franklin, flattering himself that his placid countenance and neat legs would be remarkably effective, also the fact that he had been connected with the printing interest in early life.

"If you had only told me, I would have attempted it for your sake: you have but to express a wish, and I am charmed to gratify it," murmured the enamoured Benjamin, with a tenderly reproachful sigh, which stirred his rampant shirt-frill like a passing breeze.

At that moment, as if a wish *had* brought him, a veritable John Hancock stood before them, looking comelier than ever, in a velvet suit, as he laid his cocked hat upon his heart and asked, with a bow so deep that it afforded a fine view of the garnet buckle in his stock, —

"May I have the honor, Madam?"

Glad to hide a traitorously happy face, Dolly made him a splendid curtsey, and took his arm with a hasty —

"Excuse me, Mr. Parker. Please tell Aunt I 'm going to dance."

"But — but — but — my dear Miss, I promised not to lose sight of you," stammered the defrauded Franklin, turning red with helpless rage, as the full audacity of the lovers burst upon him.

"Well, you need n't. Wait for me here till my dance is over, then Aunt won't know any thing about it," laughed wilful Dolly over her shoulder, as she was swept away into the many-colored whirlpool that circled round the hall to the entrancing music of a waltz.

While it lasted, words were needless; for eyes did the talking, smiles proud or tender telegraphed volumes of poetry, the big hand held the little one so close that it burst quite out of the old glove rosy with the pressure, and the tall head was often so near the short one that the light locks powdered the dark ones.

"A heavenly waltz!" panted Dolly, when it ended, feeling that she could go on forever, blind to the droll despair of poor Parker, as, heroically faithful to his trust, he struggled frantically to keep the happy pair in sight.

"Now we 'll have a still more heavenly promenade in the corridor. Ben is busy apologizing to half a dozen ladies whose trains he has walked up in his mad career after us, so we are safe for a time," answered John, ready to brave the wrath of many Aunt Marias; for the revolutionary spirit was high within him, and he had quite made up his mind that resistance to tyrants *was* obedience to the little god he served just then.

"Oh, John, how glad I am to see you after all this worry, and how nice it was of you to come in such grand style to-night! I was so afraid you could n't manage it," said Dolly, hanging on his arm and surveying her gallant Governor with pardonable pride.

"My blessed girl, there was nothing I could n't manage with the prospect of meeting you before me. Has n't it been hard times for both of us? You 've had the hardest, I 'm afraid, shut up with the dragon and no refuge from daily nagging and Parker's persecution. If you had n't the bravest little heart in the world, you 'd have given up by this;" and, taking advantage of a shadowy corner, John embraced his idol, under pretence of drawing her cloak about her.

"I 'll never give up the ship!" cried the girl, quoting Lawrence of the "Chesapeake," with a flash of the eye good to see.

"Stand to your guns, and we 'll yet say, 'We 've met the enemy, and they are ours,'" answered John, in the words of brave Perry, and with a ring to his voice which caused a passing waiter to pause, fancying he was called.

Beckoning to him, John gave Dolly a glass of lemonade, and, taking one himself, said with a look that made the toast a very eloquent one to both of them, —

"The love of liberty — and — the liberty of love."

They drank it silently, then paced on again, so intent upon their own emotions that neither saw a flushed and agitated countenance regard them from a doorway, and then vanish, smiling darkly.

"Governor!"

"Dearest Madam!"

"Things have come to a crisis, and I 've taken a resolution," began Dolly, remembering that time was short.

"So have I."

"This is mine, — I 'm going to Philadelphia."

"No!"

"Yes."

"How? when? why?"

"Be calm and listen. Aunt has given me just three days to choose between accepting P. and being sent home in disgrace. I don't intend to do either, but take matters into my own hands, and cease to be a burden."

"Hear! hear! but how?"

"At the fair the kitchen was a success, and there is to be a grand one at the Exposition. Girls are wanted to wait there as here; they are taken care of, and all expenses paid while they serve. I know some nice people who are going for fun, and I 'm to join them for a month at least. That gives me a start, and afterward I certainly can find something to do in the city of Brotherly Love."

"The knowledge that *I 'm* to be there on duty had nothing to do with this fine plan of yours, hey, my Dolly?" and John beamed at her with such a rapturous expression she had to turn him round, lest an advancing couple should fancy he had been imbibing something stronger than lemonade and love.

"Why, of course it had," she answered with adorable candor. "Don't you see how lovely it will be to meet every day and talk over our prospects in peace, while we are working away together till we have earned enough to try the experiment we planned in the park?"

Stopping short, John grasped the hand that lay on his arm, looking as if suddenly inspired, and exclaimed in a solemn yet excited tone, —

"*I 've* got a plan, a superb plan, only it may startle you a bit at first. Why not marry and go together?"

Before Dolly could find breath to answer this momentous question, a bomb-shell, in the shape of Aunt Maria, exploded before them, and put an end to the privy conspiracy and rebellion.

"You will *not* go anywhere together, for my niece is in the care of this gentleman. I did think we should be free from annoyance here, but I see I was mistaken. Mr. Parker, will you oblige me by taking Dolly home at once?"

Every feather in the old lady's gray wig trembled with ire, as she plucked the girl from one lover and gave her to the charge of the other, in whom the conflicting emotions of triumph and trepidation were so visible that the contrast between his countenance and costume was more comical than ever.

"But, Aunt, it isn't time to go yet," protested Dolly, finding submission very hard after her taste of freedom.

"It is quite time for persons who don't know how to behave with propriety in public. Not a word! Take my wrap, and go at once. Mr. Parker, please leave her in Mrs. Cobb's care, and return to enjoy yourself. There is no reason why *your* evening should be spoilt;" and Aunt Maria bundled poor Dolly into an ugly shawl, which made her look like a lovely tea-rose done up in brown paper.

This sudden fall from the height of happiness to the depths of helpless indignation left John speechless for an instant, during which he with difficulty resisted a strong desire to shake Aunt Maria, and spit Benjamin Franklin on the sword that hung at his side. The sight of his Dolly reft from him, and ruthlessly led away from the gayety she loved, reminded him that discretion was the better part of valor, and for her sake he tried to soften the dragon by taking all the blame upon himself, and promising to go away at once. But, while he was expostulating, the wary Parker carried off the prize; and, when John turned to say good-night, she had vanished, and Aunt Maria stalked away, with a grim laugh at his defeat.

That laugh made him desperate; and, rushing down-stairs, he was about to walk away in the rain, regardless of the damage to his costly suit, when the sound of a voice checked his reckless flight, and, looking back, he saw Dolly pausing on the stairs to say, with a glance from the ancestral shoes to the wet pavement outside, "I don't mind wetting my feet, but I cannot spoil these precious slippers. Please get my overshoes from the dressing-room: I'll wait for you here."

"Certainly, certainly; and my coat also: we must be prudent after such heat and excitement," replied Mr. Parker, glad to guard himself against the rheumatism twinges which began to afflict his lightly clad extremities.

As he hurried back, a voice whispered, "Dolly!" and, regardless of the perilously high heels, she ran down to join a black velvet gentleman below, who said in her ear, as he led her toward the door, —

"I *must* have a word more. Let me take you home; any carriage will do, and it's our last chance."

"Yes, John, yes; but oh, my shoes!" and for one instant Dolly lingered, as reverence for her relics contended with love for her Governor.

But he was equal to the occasion, and, having no cloak to lay under his queen's feet, just took her in his arms, and before she knew it both were in the coach, an order given, and they were off.

"Oh, John, how could you?" was all she said, casting away the big shawl, to put both hands on the powdery shoulders before her; for her escort was on his knees, quite in the style of the days when Sir Charles Willoughby carried Evelina off in his chariot.

How he did it John never knew; but there he was, as unconscious of his long limbs as if he had been a cherub, so intent was he on improving this precious moment.

"I 'd like to do a great deal more than that, but not to-night, though I 'm sorely tempted to run away with you, Dolly," he answered, feeling as if it would be impossible to relinquish the little bundle of silk and swan's down his arm enclosed.

"Oh, John, please don't! How could I in this dress, and no place to go to, or anything?"

"Don't be frightened, dear: I won't be rash. But, seriously, it must come to that, and the sooner the better; so make up your mind to it, and I 'll manage all the rest. This is my plan, and yours will make it all the easier. We *will* go to Philadelphia; but we 'll be married first, and that shall be our wedding journey."

"But I 'm not ready; we have n't any money; and only three days! I could n't, John, I could n't!" and Dolly hid her face, glad, yet half-frightened, at this prospect of such a release from all her woes.

"I knew it would startle you at first; but getting married is the easiest thing in life when you set about it. You don't want any wedding finery, I 've got money enough, and can borrow more if I need it; and three days is plenty of time to pack your trunk, have a farewell fight with Aunt Maria, and run away to be the happiest little wife that ever was. Say yes, darling; trust everything to me, and, please God, you never shall regret it."

Dolly had doubted the existence of genuine love nowadays, and John had assured her that there were oceans of it. There certainly seemed to be that night; and it was impossible to doubt the truth of his assertion while listening to the tender prayers and plans and protestations he poured into her ear, as they rolled on, regardless of the avenging furies behind, and the untried fate before them. Storms raged without, but peace reigned within; for Dolly showed signs of yielding, though she had not consented when the run-away ride ended.

As John set her down in the hall, he added as a last appeal, —

"Remember, there were 'Daughters of Liberty,' as well as sons, in the old times you love so well. Be one, and prove yourself worthy of your name, as you bid me be of mine. Come, sweetheart, resist tyranny, face poverty, love liberty, and declare your independence as bravely as they did."

"I will!" and Dolly signed the declaration her Hancock headed, by giving him her hand and sealing the oath with a kiss.

"One word more," he said hurriedly, as the clatter of an approaching carriage sounded through the street: "I may not be able to see you again, but we can each be getting ready, and meet on Monday morning, when you leave for '*home*' in good truth. Put a lamp in the end window the last thing Sunday night as the bells ring nine, then I shall be sure that all is right, and have no delay in the morning."

"Yes, John."

"Good-night, and God bless you!"

There was no time for more; and as distracted Parker burst out of one carriage, and Aunt Maria "came tumbling after," happy John Harris stepped into the other, with a wave of the cocked hat, and drove away in triumph.

CHAPTER VI

PEACE IS DECLARED

THE age of miracles is not over yet, and our young people wrought several during those three days; for in love's vocabulary there is no such word as fail.

Dolly "stood to her guns" womanfully, and not only chose to go "home," but prepared for her banishment with an outward meekness and an inward joy which made each hour memorable. Aunt Maria had her suspicions and kept a vigilant watch, she and her maid Cobb mounting guard by turns. Parker, finding that "no surrender" was the countersign, raised the siege and retreated in good order, though a trifle demoralized in dignity when he looked back during the evacuation and saw Tip bolt upright in the end window, with the rebel flag proudly displayed.

John meanwhile was circulating briskly through the city, and showing such ardent interest in the approaching Exposition that his mates christened him "Centennial Harris;" while the higher powers felt that they had done a good thing in giving him the job, and increased his salary to make sure of so excellent a servant. Other arrangements of a private but infinitely more interesting nature were successfully made; and he went about smiling to himself, as if the little parcel done up in silver paper, which he was constantly feeling for in his vest pocket, had been a talisman conferring all good gifts upon its happy owner.

When the third night came, he was at his post long before the time, so great was his impatience; for the four-footed traitor had been discovered and ordered into close confinement, where he suffered, not the fate of André, but the pangs of indigestion for lack of exercise after the feast of tidbits surreptitiously administered by one who never forgot all she owed to her "fat friend."

It seemed as if nine o'clock would never come; and, if a policeman ever was where he should be, the guardian of that beat would have considered John a suspicious character as he paced to and fro in the April starlight. At last the bells began to chime, promptly the light appeared, and, remembering how the bell of the old State House rang out the glad tidings a hundred years ago, John waved his cherished parcel, joyfully exclaiming, "Independence is declared!

ring! ring! ring!" then raced across the park like another Paul Revere when the signal light shone in the steeple of the old North Church.

Next morning at an early hour a carriage drove to Aunt Maria's door, and with a stern farewell from her nightcapped relative Dolly was sent forth to banishment, still guarded by the faithful Cobb. The mutinous damsel looked pale and anxious, but departed with a friendly adieu and waved her handkerchief to Tip, disconsolate upon the door-mat. The instant they turned the corner, however, a singular transformation took place in both the occupants of that carriage; for Dolly caught Cobb round the neck and kissed her, while smiles broke loose on either face, as she said gleefully, —

"You dear old thing, what *should* I have done without you? Am I all right? I do hope it's becoming. I had to give up everything else, so I was resolved not to be married without a new bonnet."

"It's as sweet as sweet can be, and not a bit the worse for being smuggled home in a market-basket," returned the perjured Cobb, surveying with feminine pride and satisfaction the delicate little bonnet which emerged from the thick veil by which its glories had been prudently obscured.

"Here's a glass to see it in. Such a nice carriage, with white horses, and a tidy driver; so appropriate you know. It's a happy accident, and I 'm so pleased," prattled the girl, looking about her with the delight of an escaped prisoner.

"Bless your heart, Miss, it 's all Mr. Harris's doings: he 's been dodging round the corner ever since daylight; and there he is now, I do declare. I may as well go for a walk till your train is off, so good-by, and the best of lucks, my dear."

There was barely time for this brief but very hearty congratulation, when a remarkably well-dressed highwayman stopped the carriage, without a sign of resistance from the grinning driver. Cobb got out, the ruffian, armed not with a pistol, but a great bouquet of white roses, got in, and the coach went on its way through the quiet streets.

"May day, and here are your flowers, my little queen."

"Oh, John!"

A short answer, but a very eloquent one, when accompanied with full eyes, trembling lips, and a face as sweet and lovely as the roses.

It was quite satisfactory to John; and, having slightly damaged the bridal bonnet without reproof, he, manlike, mingled bliss and business, by saying, in a tone that made poetry of his somewhat confused remarks, —

"Heaven bless my wife! We ought to have had the Governor's coach to-day. Is n't Cobb a trump to get us off so nicely? Never saw a woman yet who could resist the chance of her helping on a wedding. Remembered every thing I told her. That reminds me. Was n't it lucky that your relics were boxed up in dear Aunt Maria's shed, so all Cobb had to do was to alter the directions and send them off to Philadelphia instead of home?"

"I 've been in a tremble for three days, because it seemed as if it could n't be possible that so much happiness was coming to me. Are you quite sure you want me, John?" asked Dolly, careless for once of her cherished treasures; for she had been busy with hopes and fears, while he was attending to more material affairs.

"So sure, that I 've got something here to bind you with. Do you mind trying it on to see if it fits, for I had to guess at the size," answered John, producing his talisman with all a bridegroom's pride and eagerness.

"Please let me wear that as a guard, and use this one to be married with. I 've a superstition about it, for it suits us and the year better than any other;" and Dolly laid the little ring of reddish gold beside the heavier one in John's palm.

"So it does, and you shall have it as you like. Do you know, when you showed it to me three months ago, I had a fancy that it would be the proper thing for me to put it on your finger; but I did n't dream I ever should. Are you very certain that you don't regret the advice you gave my friend Jack?" asked the young man, thinking with fond solicitude of the great experiment that lay before them; for he knew by experience how hard this world's ways sometimes are, and longed to smooth the rough places for the confiding little creature at his side.

"Do I look as if I did?" she answered simply, but with a face so full of a true woman's instinctive faith in the power of love to lighten labor, sweeten poverty, and make a heaven of the plainest home, that it was impossible to doubt her courage or fear her disloyalty.

Quite satisfied, John pocketed the rings and buttoned Dolly's gloves, saying, while she buttoned his, both marvellously enjoying this first service for each other, "Almost there now, and in less than half an hour we shall be so safe that all the Aunt Marias in Christendom can't part us any more. George has stood by me like a man and a brother, and promised that everything should be all right. The church will look a trifle empty, I dare say, with only five of us to fill it; but I shall like it better than being made a spectacle of; so will you, I fancy."

"The church? I thought runaways were married in an office, by a justice, and without much ceremony to make it solemn. I'm very glad it is n't so, for I shall never have but one wedding, and I'd love to have it in a sacred place," faltered Dolly, as a sudden sense of all it meant came over her, filling her girlish heart with tender awe.

"I knew that, dear, and so I did my best to make you feel no lack of love, as I could not give you any splendor. I wish I had a mother to be with you to-day; but George has lent me his, so there will be a woman's arms to cry in, if you want to drop a tear; and fatherly old Dr. King will give you to the happiest man alive. Well, well, my Dolly, if you 'd rather, cry here, and then let me dry your tears, as, please Heaven, I will do all your life."

"So kind, John, so very kind! I can't thank you in words, but I 'll show by deeds how much I honor, trust, and love my husband;" and nobly Dolly kept her word.

No one saw them as they went in, but the early sunshine made a golden path for them to tread, and the May wind touched them with its balmy kiss. No congratulatory clamor greeted them as they came out; but the friendly sparrows twittered a wedding march, and the jovial George sent them merrily away, by saying, as he gave John's hand a parting grasp, —

"I was right, you see, and there *is* a Mrs. Harris!"

If any one doubts it, let him look well about him, and he may discover the best thing America could send to her Exposition: an old-fashioned home, and in it an ambitious man who could not be bought, a beautiful woman who would not be sold; a young couple happy in their love and labor, consecrating this centennial year, by practising the old-fashioned virtues, honesty and thrift, independence and content.

THE END.